THE ASEY MAYO TRIO

PHOEBE ATWOOD TAYLOR

THE
ASEY MAYO
TRIO

Three Asey Mayo Cape Cod Mysteries

A Foul Play Press Book

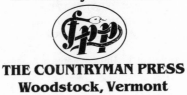

THE COUNTRYMAN PRESS
Woodstock, Vermont

Copyright © 1943 by Phoebe Atwood Taylor

This edition first published in 1990 by Foul Play Press,
an imprint of The Countryman Press, Inc.,
Woodstock, Vermont 05091.

ISBN 0-88150-171-9

Printed in the United States of America

10   9   8   7   6   5   4   3   2   1

CONTENTS

THE THIRD MURDERER

CAST OF CHARACTERS

ASEY MAYO—*the super detective*

JENNIE MAYO—*his talkative cousin*

PAGE KENDALL—*owner of the Snow house*

NICHOLAS FOX—*a newspaperman*

ELIZABETH TYLER—*Page's best friend*

BOB PRATT—*owner of the inn*

KATHARINE PRATT—*his stepmother*

CALVERT HAMILTON—*senatorial candidate*

JULIE HAMILTON—*his sultry daughter*

PETE PULSTER—*who moved the house*

EDDIE PULSTER—*known as Little Arsenic*

ENOCH SNOW—*ancient of the family*

JOHN PARSONS—*a selectman*

DOC CUMMINGS—*medical examiner*

THE THIRD MURDERER

As THE AMPLE FIGURE of his housekeeper-cousin Jennie at last loomed in sight on the opposite shore of Weesit's Gull Pond, Asey Mayo jumped to his feet and shouted at her a digest of his mounting impatience.

"Jennie, I wasted enough time while you hunted for Mayflowers! Hustle *back* here! Hurry—" He broke off as a gust of east wind drove in from the oceanside, flinging his own words back in his face but convoying Jennie's to him clearly.

"The hollow's so full I could pick all day! See?" Brandishing a sample of her gleanings, she turned and disappeared again into the tangle of scrub oaks and scrub pines.

With a shrug, Asey walked back to the rock where he'd been sitting for the past hour and where he'd presumably continue to sit until Jennie chose to return.

While he'd ferreted out so many motives that the newspapers had given him the label of Hayseed Sleuth and Codfish Sherlock, he would be completely stumped if asked to figure out Jennie's lifelong passion for "firsts," like spotting the first robin or plucking the first corn. Her annual hunt for the first Mayflowers, he thought, as he struck a match, amounted to a holy crusade. . . . He raised his head suddenly as he became aware of something large and white among the trees near where Jennie had disappeared.

"What in time!" He stared unbelievingly across the pond. No sane man, he told himself sharply, could see what he was seeing!

It wasn't just that, in the twinkling of an eye, a white Cape Cod house with blue blinds had popped into view as if a genie had uncorked it from a magic bottle! It was that the house wasn't even standing there quietly, like a respectable mirage.

It was moving through the pines with cumbersome dignity, as if an invisible giant were drawing it along by a string!

"Asey, such lovely Mayflowers!" Jennie's return was prefaced by the crackling of leaves and the snapping of twigs. "So pink, and fragrant—"

"D'you see what I see over there?" Asey demanded.

"The house moving? Sure. I saw that fifteen minutes ago."

"Just what," Asey felt taken aback by her casual acceptance of the phenomenon, "is goin' on?"

"Why, it's only the old Snow place being moved. Of course, it *does* look funny from here," she added. "I guess it's because the bushes hide the truck. It's perched on Pete Pulster's big flat truck thing—what're you mutterin' about?"

"Columbus and the egg," Asey told her with a chuckle. "Now you point out that a truck's involved, I can even hear the motor. But for a minute I thought it was a Walt Disney house flyin' on its own wings."

Jennie pointed. "Look, they're stoppin'! Bet they're stuck in a rut. The lane that runs round the pond is awful boggy.

Seems such a *pity* to shove that little old house around after it's been sitting by the inlet all these years. *I*," she spoke with more than her usual firmness, "don't hold with moving houses. It's bad luck. Particularly *that* house."

"Why so?"

"The *last* time they moved it—Asey, don't you ever *peek* at the clippings I send you when you're off at the Porter Plant?"

"I read every word," Asey assured her. "Last batch had a recipe for orange cake, an' a blueprint for a crocheted tidy."

"Hm. I guess," Jennie said, "I sent you the wrong items. Anyway, you must've heard about the old Snow house. It stood on Main Street till they moved it here sixty-odd years ago. Look, they're startin' up again! Yes, I think it's a pity to move it any more. But I s'pose it's better than having the Kendall girl and the Fox boy and the Hamiltons all blacking each other's eyes about it. . . . Now," she inquired with asperity, "what's so awful funny?"

"You," Asey said. "Here you are in the woods, miles from home. You see a house seemingly roamin' through space, and you not only don't blink, you even know as much about it as if it was your own hen coop. How do you *do* it?"

"Why, the Snow place's been in the papers for months!" Jennie said. "It belonged to that Mrs. Hamilton who died. It's her brother-in-law who's running for senator. She left the house itself to Page Kendall, and the land to the Fox boy. . . . Hold this while I wrap wax paper around the flowers, will you?"

Asey whistled as she nonchalantly held out to him an ebony-handled Commando knife with a curving blade. "Where'd you get this lethal thing?"

"I bought it for Lizzie's boy in the Marines, only it was so handy, I kept it. It's fine for cutting things outdoors, and I can't imagine how I ever got on without it in the kitchen. See how clean it cut the Mayflower stems? I didn't yank up a root!"

"It's nice to think," Asey grinned as he touched the razor-sharp blade, "that when the boys come home with their old Commando knives, you women'll pick flowers with 'em!"

Jennie retrieved the knife and thrust it into the center of her large bouquet. "I can't understand why you don't know all about that house, even with your being away so much. Mrs. Hamilton left the house to Page and the land to Nick Fox because she was godmother to both of 'em, see, and she hoped it might bring 'em together again. They'd been engaged, and broke up. But it didn't work. They just fought like tigers about rights of way and such. And, to make matters worse, Calvert Hamilton tried to break the will and get the house and land for himself. But Page Kendall got it, and she's having it moved. . . . Oh, look, it's going lickety-split around the pond!"

"Sprintin' like a colt—oho!" Asey said as the house came to an abrupt halt, and a truck horn blared out. "That's for us. My car's in the way. Come along!"

Jennie followed him up the path that led from the water's edge to the rut lane.

At first glance, Asey's rakish open Porter roadster appeared to have become an integral part of the underpinning of the Snow place. The two small-paned front windows and the blue front door of the old half-house, which extended beyond the truck carriage, literally hung over the rumble seat and the canvas boot of the lowered top. The corner of the house had come within inches of slicing off the windshield.

"Hi, Asey!" The fat, red-faced driver leaned across the cab of the truck. "Guess I miscalculated. Thought I could clear your windshield. I can't go ahead!"

"Neither can I," Asey returned, "without mowin' through two trees." He surveyed the mud under the truck's rear wheels. "An' if you sideslip an inch backin' up, you'll smash me. Stay put, Pete. I'll pull forward a couple feet an' angle back down the path out of your way."

"Thanks . . . Aw, Eddie, come here!" Pete Pulster made a futile grab at the fat child in dungarees and a striped shirt, a miniature edition of himself, who hopped out of the truck and slid into the roadster.

"Scram!" Asey lifted him out. "With all that house spillin' over, there isn't room for a third of me, let alone the two of us!"

Before he finally succeeded in angling the roadster down the path, he had twice plucked Eddie from under the car and twice prevented him from removing the fishing tackle in the rumble seat.

"Put back that rod! Oh, scram, you!" Asey chased the child up the path. "Scram!"

He waited until the house went past, then drove the roadster up to the lane just in time to see Eddie making a near-suicidal jump onto the truck's running board.

"That Eddie," Jennie picked her flowers up from the ground, "is the worst boy I ever— Did you take my knife?"

Asey shook his head. "You stuck it in your bouquet."

"Then Eddie stole it!" Jennie said promptly. "I *saw* him bend over and smell the flowers, but I was too busy lookin' at the house to watch him close. You follow 'em, Asey, and get that back! I won't let that Eddie steal my good knife!"

"Maybe you dropped it comin' up the path, or—"

"I never! It was in the flowers when I laid 'em down," she pointed to the foot of a pine tree, "right there! That Eddie swiped it while I was walking around the house. Now, you go *after* him!"

"First, let's hunt around," Asey suggested.

Jennie beamed in triumph when he returned empty-handed from his search of the path. "I said he took it! Now, get it!"

"Okay," Asey said resignedly. "Where's the house goin'?"

"I don't know exactly. What're you a detective for, if you can't find a moving house? After all, it isn't any old needle in a haystack! Even *I* could follow muddy truck-tire tracks!"

"Smart woman," Asey said. "I can't even *say* muddy truck-tire tracks without taxin' my tongue!"

Ten minutes later, just over the Pochet town line, they spotted the house bowling merrily along ahead on the main road.

"Go past!" Jennie said. "Make Pete stop!"

"The side of the house sticks out so far," Asey protested, "I can't see what's comin' at the—"

"*That* driver did!" Before the words were out of her

mouth, a maroon coupé had flashed past both them and the truck.

"Nope. That driver took a chance and got away with it, an' I'm not—"

"Asey!" Jennie's scream was so blood-curdling that Asey stopped the car and looked anxiously at her face, from which the color had suddenly drained. "Oh, don't *stop!*" She paused and wet her lips. "Go *on,* go *see* about it, quick!"

"Jennie, what's the matter with you?"

"That hand! There was a hand at the side window of that house. Get going, quick! There was a hand at the window!"

"If any hand," Asey said, as he drove on, "appeared at any window of that house, you can be sure it wasn't anything more scarey than Dead-end Eddie Pulster! Don't ever yell like that again. You took ten years off my life!"

"You'll take twenty off mine," Jennie retorted, "if you don't get ahead of that house and stop it! I know a hand when I see one, and that wasn't any grubby little boy's paw! It was white and clawlike, and—" She shivered. "Oh, hurry *up!*"

Asey shot the roadster to within a few feet of the house. "There, you can almost stick your own hand—" He braked quickly as the truck first slowed down and then sped forward again.

"*Now* what are you stoppin' for?" Jennie asked impatiently. "Oh, dear!" She sat on the edge of the seat and glared angrily at the engine of a freight train that was rumbling across the tracks in front of them. "Where'd *that* come from? I never heard the bell!"

"That's why I didn't want to cut past the house," Asey told her gently. "The truck was makin' too much noise to hear a bell or a whistle, and I knew it was near freight time."

"Isn't there any *end* to it?" Jennie drummed her fingers on the door. "I never *saw* so many flat cars! And that house gettin' away from us all the time—I knew in my bones it shouldn't be moved! I knew—well, I s'pose we'll just have to wait and see what happens, that's all. We'll just have to wait and *see!*"

Asey grinned. "You sound as ominous an' full of doom," he remarked, "as a soap-opera announcer. '*Did* Eddie steal Jennie's knife? *Was* a clawlike hand wagglin' in the window of the movin' house? Wait and *see*, tomorrow mornin'! Of course, it's fun to get dramatic-like, but I think you're kind of overdoin' this."

"Oh, you do, do you? Just you wait till we catch up with that house!"

When they caught up with it a quarter of an hour later, parked in a small open field off the main road, Asey chuckled. "Seems like it reached its destination without any doom overtakin' it," he observed.

"In the first place, this can't be its destination!" Jennie said crisply as they got out of the roadster. "This's part of the new Pochet school grounds, and town property. Moreover," she pointed inside the truck, "there's Pete Pulster's jacket and his lunch box, but where's Pete? Where's Eddie? And furthermore, what's the front door of the house open for? Boost me up! I'm going in and see what's going on!"

But the interior of the old Snow place, which reminded

Asey of a small and overstocked antique shop, was in apple-pie order and quite bare of Pulsters or anyone else.

While Jennie, still burning with grim curiosity, opened every available door, Asey lingered in the minute living room and stared at the collection of fish spears and old whale harpoons hanging over the old-fashioned fireplace.

"I must say," Jennie announced plaintively from the next room, "*I* don't understand what's *happened*, or why this's parked *here*, or where Pete is. What're you doing by that old Dutch oven? What're you looking at? What's *in* there?"

Her scream as she bent over and peered inside made her previous vocal effort sound like a refined whisper.

"Asey! Asey Mayo, it's a girl in there! She's dead! She's been murdered!" Jennie's voice achieved a crescendo. Then she turned to Asey. "That," she added in perfectly normal tones, "that's *my* Commando knife that stabbed her!"

It certainly resembled the ebony handle of the curved knife whose blade he'd tested with his forefinger over by Gull Pond, Asey thought. But after glancing at Jennie's white face, he shook his head.

"Nonsense!" He tried to sound reassuring. "There's any number of knives with handles like that. Who is she? Do you know her?"

"It looks like the Kendall girl to me. She has brown hair. And that blue jacket and blue scarf—I forgot to tell you it was her who went roarin' past us, Asey."

"Roarin' past? You mean she was in that maroon coupé over by the railroad crossin'?"

Jennie nodded. "I recognized her car. She's an actress in the Summer Barn Theater, you know. Looks sort of actressy, with all that make-up. Well, I guess this one's as plain as A-B-C to you already, Asey!"

Looking at her sharply, Asey found to his amazement that she was quite serious.

"Yes," a slight note of disappointment crept into Jennie's tones as she continued, "I guess this's goin' to be an easy one. Most as plain as the nose on your face. That Eddie, he stole my knife out of the Mayflowers, and then Page Kendall rushed past us to stop Pete, and she did, while he was waiting for the freight to pass, and she and Pete had a row, and Pete killed her with my knife, and now he's run away. I *knew* it all the time. But I certainly must say, I never expected anyone'd use *my* knife!"

"You," Asey said, "*knew* what all the time?"

"Why, that there'd be a murder, of course! That's why I told you it was such a pity to move that house again, and just invite trouble. If only you'd bothered to read those clippings I sent you," Jennie wound up, "you'd know that every single time the Snow place gets moved, *some*body gets murdered!"

Asey tilted his yachting cap back on his head and stared at her. "*What?*"

"Sure! Old Addie Snow killed her husband when it was moved onto Main Street—she didn't want it moved, you see," Jennie explained. "Then—"

"Wait up! Was *this* the place they used to call 'Murder House'?"

"Goodness me, yes, didn't you realize that? Sometimes I think you stay away from the Cape too long! Then," Jennie went on, "a Snow daughter-in-law killed her husband because *she* didn't want the place moved from Main Street way off to the fag end of nowhere up by the inlet. And now this poor girl here! Funny how things run in threes, isn't it? One move, one murder. Another move, another murder. A third move—"

"Jennie," Asey interrupted her philosophic résumé, "s'pose you go over to the school—I guess that's the nearest place—an' phone Doc Cummings to hustle here, will you? We need a medical examiner. An' don't go blurting this news around to everyone you meet, please."

After helping her down to the ground, he returned to the living room and sat down gingerly on a fragile-looking Hitchcock chair.

He found it difficult to bear in mind that he was inside a house which was in transit, so to speak, and not solidly planted on the ground. Considering that the building had been lifted from its foundation, then raised up on the truck carriage and moved a good six miles, the interior was in a miraculous state of tidiness. Perhaps the harpoons and spears over the fireplace were canting a bit to one side, perhaps the Currier and Ives prints of dour-faced kittens hanging over the gaily painted quilt chest in the corner were slightly askew.

But nothing seemed to have been upset by the process of moving.

Or by any action within the tiny room, either.

The full ash tray had skated almost to the edge of the center piecrust table, where the least bit of violence would have knocked both it and the table over. Even the briefest of struggles, Asey thought as he mentally measured distances, would have created a shambles among the crowded antiques.

And yet, apparently, the girl whose body lay in the Dutch oven had been stabbed here in this room. She must have been killed in here, he decided. Not even Superman could have managed to carry a body through the clutter of Early Americana in the old Snow place without knocking over a few pewter porringers or a couple of spinning wheels. She must have been killed very near the fireplace, probably in front of it, and then have been lifted up to the wide Dutch-oven door, and thrust into the oven, out of sight.

Asey leaned back against the faded gold-leaf stenciling of the Hitchcock chair. Why, he wondered, had someone carefully left one of her blue rope-soled sandals on the floor by the hearth when everything else was so neat, so undisturbed, so innocent of what the papers always referred to as foul play? Had the sandal been deliberately left there to call attention to the oven and to the oven door, which had been ajar a few inches?

He felt very sure of one thing, anyway. Fat, easygoing Pete Pulster, henpecked by his wife and bullied by his children, was probably the last person on Cape Cod capable, in Asey's estimation, of committing a brutal murder like this!

A sudden gust of cool east wind poured in through the open side window, which faced the rear of the truck, and for a moment the starched ruffled curtains blew straight out into the room.

With a muttered exclamation, Asey got up and strode over to the window. Then he smiled. The flapping things which had caught his attention were two white cotton gloves, pinned up to dry on the outside hem of the curtain.

That took care of Jennie's vision of the white, clawlike hand, he decided with relief as he walked back to the Dutch oven and peered inside.

"Now why," he murmured aloud, "does all this seem so screwball? Why'n time did Pete park here, an' then beat it? Why'd someone put her in here so careful, an' then leave that blue shoe outside like a marker?"

Reaching over to the mantel, he twisted a candle out of its pewter holder, lighted it, and again examined the oven.

His forehead was furrowed when he blew out the candle two minutes later.

If this girl was Page Kendall, as Jennie thought, why was her scarf initialed E.T.? Why was her gold bracelet engraved E.T.? Why did the handkerchief in her pocket bear the monogram E.T.?

Acting on sudden impulse, Asey pushed open the front door, swung down off the house, entered the cab of the truck, and picked up the newspaper he remembered seeing beside Pete Pulster's lunch box. If there'd been even half as much public fuss and interest about this house as Jennie's chatter indicated, the *Pochet Weekly News* certainly would take notice of the moving in its weekly summary of local affairs.

A brief glance at the front page showed that the house-moving was clearly the event of the week. Returning to the Hitchcock chair in the living room, he skipped through the *Pochet News's* version of the Snow homestead's comings and goings throughout the years, and its commentary on the individuals involved, particularly with this last moving.

Page Kendall, "a current guest at the now-open Shell Inn," got by far the longest and most sympathetic write-up.

Her roles in the Barn Theater's productions were listed and favorably remarked on, and the editor noted that, as a former summer resident, she had won permanent possession of the Yacht Club's sailing trophy. Nicholas Fox, who'd been willed the land on which the Snow house stood over by the inlet, was succinctly summed up as returned from service in the South Pacific. "Previous to the war, he had his own business in Boston," the editor commented, "which failed." The brother-in-law of Mrs. Hamilton, whose will had caused all the present to-do, was even more perfunctorily mentioned. "Calvert Hamilton, who stopped public access to the inlet through his property last year," the paper said curtly, "is running for a public office. His daughter Julie is a debutante."

Asey turned the page. Under the heading "Snow Place—continued" suddenly appeared the puzzling statement that the rumor of an airport had again set the town buzzing. "But, as usual, the *News* has been unable to track down one single concrete fact. We insert this item here instead of in the Editor's Comment so everyone will see it. Snow Pictures on Page Four."

With a grin, Asey turned to them.

Two seconds later, a long low whistle of amazement issued from his lips, and he almost jumped across the hooked rugs to the oven, with the paper in his hand.

Pretty, dark-haired Page Kendall, pictured in several poses on Page Four, and the pretty, dark-haired girl who had been killed were not the same person! To both of them, he thought critically, you could apply many of the same adjectives. Both were slim, young, good-looking, and dark.

Both wore their hair so that the general effect was a cluster of short curls. But this girl was very definitely not Page Kendall!

He wheeled around as he heard the noise of someone starting to climb up to the front door.

"Jennie, I begun to think you was lost! Where have you—" He broke off.

Not Jennie, but a tall, hatless young man in gray flannels and a zippered tan poplin windbreaker pulled himself up to the threshold, and then stepped briskly into the tiny living room.

"Page, why have you stopped—" He paused. "Oh! Oh, hello! You're Asey Mayo, aren't you? I'm Bob Pratt. Er— to be perfectly frank," he added with a smile, "you're probably the last person I ever expected to find in here. Hadn't heard you were home, even. Usually the *Pochet News* waves a paragraph of flags whenever the Codfish Sherlock returns."

"I only dropped in last night for a few days," Asey said. "You huntin' for Page Kendall?"

Bob Pratt nodded. "When I saw the house here, I assumed she'd be here too. I'm after a picture of Murder House in its third transit. For the *Pochet News*," he explained. "What in the world is this parked *here* for, anyway?"

"Are you," Asey countered with another question, "an editor of the *News*, maybe?"

"Not me. I worked on a paper before I went into the army," Pratt said, "but I'm an innkeeper, now. Mother and I are running the Shell Inn—that Victorian job over by the inlet. You probably know it. All stucco and sea shells, and porches and rocking chairs. The *News* is currently Nick Fox's baby." He made a gesture toward the cab of the truck. "Where's Pete Pulster? Where's Page? Have you seen her? And what's this house parked *here* for?"

"I was sort of hopin'," Asey said, "that you could maybe tell me those answers. Say, when did this Nick Fox take over the *News*?"

"About four months ago," Pratt answered. "I promised to get a picture of this place for him, because he's—er—he's rather avoiding Page. She—" He stopped short. "Look, nothing's wrong, is it? I mean, I keep associating you in my mind with murder and sudden death and assorted catastrophes. Look, everything's all *right*, isn't it?"

Asey pointed to the Dutch oven. "P'raps you'll take a look in there."

"In the *oven*?" Bob Pratt stared at Asey, as if he weren't sure Asey wasn't joking. Then he slowly crossed the room. "In here? In this—oh!" He stepped back. "Page! No—no, it's not Page!"

"Who is it?" Asey inquired. "You know her?"

"It's Elizabeth Tyler. Liz Tyler. Page's best friend!"

Pratt turned around so that Asey wouldn't see his face. "That is, she—" Again, he broke off. "Mayo, this is ghastly! When did it happen? When did you find her? Who did it?"

Asey walked over and stood beside him. Never, he decided objectively, had he ever seen a more abrupt and shattering change than that which had taken place in this young man. When Pratt had swung up into the doorway, he'd been smiling, gay, and voluble. Now he looked gray and haggard and, while his voice was grimly under control, it had an edge like a sharp blade.

"So she's Page Kendall's best friend, huh?" he said aloud.

"They've both been staying at the Inn with mother and me." Pratt didn't, Asey noted, answer his question. "Until the house dispute got ironed out, Page refused to live in it."

"I see. This Liz Tyler," Asey persisted, "was Page's best friend, you say?"

"Mayo, I'm not going to let you extract from me any false impression about Liz and Page!" Pratt said earnestly. "Page came to town to try and settle this house mess, and Liz came along to help her kill time between lawyers' bickerings. Yes, they were good friends! Yes, they also had an occasional falling out. It's simply sheer fate that they had one this morning, rather publicly. But it bears no relation to this ghastly business here, and I frankly resent your insinuating a lot of best-friend-quarrel motivation at this early stage of the game!"

"I get your point." Nothing in Asey's expression indicated that he had been told just exactly what he wanted to find out.

"Now, d'you know all the details about this place, I wonder? Alice Hamilton left—"

"She left this house to Page, and the land to Nick Fox. The Bring-'Em-Back-Together Department. Uh-huh, I been told all about that angle," Asey said.

"It sounds silly enough when you put it that way," Pratt remarked, "but Alice Hamilton was a shrewd woman, and she knew Page and Nick pretty well. I think her plan nearly worked. That is, this house-and-land business might have brought 'em together if—well, Nick had a rough time in the South Pacific. He was invalided home, you know, and he's been a bit touchy. Then Calvert Hamilton's daughter's been pursuing him madly, which complicated the issue. You know Julie Hamilton?"

Asey shook his head. "The *Pochet News* just summed her up as a debutante."

"That," Pratt said, "was sheer editorial restraint on Nick's part. He's good and sick of being Julie's prey. She looks like a deb in the movies, if you know what I mean. Long blond hair and a sulky mouth. And she's almost never off the back of a horse. And because Calvert'd get Julie the moon if she expressed any slight yen for it, he tried to wangle this house away from Page so Julie—and presumably Nick, too—could have it. Honestly, Mayo, when this damn building set off this morning, I drew a breath of relief! Mother and I both suspected that Calvert'd pull a fast one at the last minute. You see, Julie still wants this house!"

"So you were at the inlet when the house started off? I wonder," Asey sat down and motioned toward a Boston rocker, "if you'd maybe tell me about that."

Pratt swung the rocker around so that its back was to the oven and said somewhat reluctantly that there wasn't much to tell.

"This was loaded on the truck carriage late yesterday afternoon, and it could've been moved then, but Pete balked. Said he wasn't going to take the chance of getting a flat or getting stuck in the mud as he came around the pond lane, and having to leave the truck and the house there all night. And he refused point-blank to drive out the short way, straight from the inlet to the main road, because he mistrusted the little bridge over the Herring Brook. Pete can be pretty prima donna-ish about his trucking. Personally," he concluded as he fumbled at the pockets of his wind-breaker and finally located a package of cigarettes, "I think Pete wanted the audience he knew he'd have today, when the move was officially scheduled. Nobody would have seen him last evening."

"Page Kendall was over at the inlet this mornin', I s'pose," Asey said. "And Liz Tyler, was she there, too?"

"Oh, all the interested parties were there. Nick kept in the background. He didn't want to come at all, but Page insisted. Said he must make sure she didn't trespass on his damned land—I quote—more than she ought. Hamilton and Julie were on the other side of their stone wall, coldly watching. On horseback. Mother said they made her feel like a peasant being surveyed by landed gentry. Then there were curious bystanders—perhaps fifteen or twenty. Local people. This had been considerably publicized, you know. Nick's played it up in the *Pochet News* because it's about all the news he's had. No one's been born lately, or gone to Boston, or even shingled a roof."

"Now, I wonder!" Asey said thoughtfully, and then grinned. He was beginning to understand Jennie's insistence on coming way over to Gull Pond for Mayflowers when a hundred other localities would have done as well. Of course, she'd come to see Murder House being moved, and the May-flowers were a subterfuge. "I wonder, now," he said aloud, "where in time Jennie's gone to!"

"I'm certain of one thing," Bob Pratt said as Asey walked over to the window. "Whoever killed Liz actually meant to kill Page. Page was the focal point of all this house fuss.

Liz had nothing to do with it. She was just here, just an innocent bystander. She's shorter than Page, and the two aren't at all alike, but they're both dark, and they have a couple of costumes that are the same. Page is wearing a blue-jacket-and-red-skirt outfit today, just like Liz's. It's a case of mistaken identity, without any doubt. Don't you agree?" He paused, and then repeated the question.

"No," Asey said. "I don't know as I do."

"What?" Pratt looked dumfounded. "Why, of course it is, Mayo! I'm sure of it!"

"I'm sure," Asey returned, "that the murderer very much hoped you'd feel sure of it. It's a very smart job. This house movin' was well advertised, an' then there was the murder build-up from the other movin's an' all this squabblin' about the house. Uh-huh, someone was real bright to take advantage of the setup and do away with Liz Tyler."

"Mayo, what're you talking about? A lot of people were sore with Page, but people practically didn't know Liz! Of course it's mistaken identity, pure and simple!"

"Whoever killed Liz Tyler," Asey said gently, "wasn't firin' a gun from a distance or heavin' a weighted flower pot from a second-story window in the general direction of a dark-haired girl who was wearin' a red skirt and a blue wool coat. This was a short-range job. An' remember that she wasn't stabbed in the back!"

"But Liz wasn't involved with anyone or anything!" Pratt protested. "Page *was*!"

"When you stab someone head-on," Asey said, as he raised the window shade, "you're near enough to 'em to know if you're stabbin' the specific victim you had in mind or not. I don't see how the murderer could've missed recognizin' the girl. Furthermore, an expert thrust like this wasn't the work of any nearsighted person!"

Neither, he mentally added, as he peered out for some sign of Jennie, was it the work of someone unknown to the girl. The murderer hadn't been any sinister stranger from whom she'd made any effort to escape, or from whom she'd felt any need to defend herself. The undisturbed condition of the room proved it was someone she knew and trusted, who'd struck before she could guess what was coming.

"I hadn't figured all that out," Pratt said slowly. "I was thinking more in terms of who was involved with people. But when was she killed? And where? This couldn't possibly have happened up at the inlet! It must have happened after Pete parked the house here!"

"We got to find Pete," Asey said, "an' see if he stopped anywheres else. Jennie and I followed along behind him some of the way, till we got held up at the railroad crossin'." Idly, he reached out and fingered the white cotton gloves pinned on the curtain. "Who do these belong to, I wonder?"

"What? Oh, those gloves?" Pratt shrugged. "Page or Liz, I suppose. They're always draping gloves and stockings around to dry, over at the Inn. Drives mother crazy."

"D'you happen to remember who Liz left the inlet with?" Asey inquired casually.

"No!" Pratt's denial came so rapidly that Asey suspected he'd been waiting for the question and had the answer perched on the tip of his tongue. He shook his head a little truculently, too, Asey noticed, as if he rather expected to be cross-examined on the point.

"Well, with all the crowd that was there, I guess we can most likely find out." Asey glanced down out of the window, and then strolled back to the Hitchcock chair. "I wonder if you can recall who left the inlet first, Pratt." He didn't exactly raise his voice, but he spoke with great distinctness. "Can you maybe give me a little picture of the scene? After all, Liz Tyler was there an' alive, an' now she's here an' murdered. We got a lot of piecin' up an' fittin' in an' tyin' together ahead of us. I s'pose Page Kendall was in that maroon car of hers?"

"She drove off in it just as the house was starting, and the Hamiltons cantered away about then, too," Pratt said. "Then—let's see. Nick walked over to his beach wagon after reminding me to get the picture for him. Said he was going back to the office to write a 'For Sale' ad for the land. He'd always said if the house was moved, he'd snap up the first offer anyone made him, and never look in that direction again. And mother gave me the mortgage check to mail and tied a string on my pocket button," he pointed to his jacket, "so I'd remember to mail it after I got to the post office. I occasionally get there and forget. Then mother started to walk back to the Inn, and I drove to town and mailed the check and glanced at the morning paper. Then I came to take Nick's picture. He told me to wait till the house was well inside Pochet. He likes his news pictures strictly local."

"An' you haven't any idea who Liz left with?"

"No."

"You should have!" Page Kendall, in a red skirt and short blue coat, with a blue scarf tied over her dark curls, spoke as she swung herself up over the threshold of the front door.

One glance at the anger written all over her face was enough to convince Asey, who had seen her pass beneath the window, that he'd made no error in deciding to let her learn of the murder by eavesdropping. "You should know, Bob Pratt! Liz left the inlet with you!"

"Page, where'd you come from?" Pratt jumped up from the rocker. "I didn't hear you!"

"Obviously you didn't, or you wouldn't be lying about Liz! She left with you!"

"But she didn't, Page! I drove to town alone! Liz didn't leave with me!"

Page walked over to him, drew back her hand, and a second later blood was gushing from Bob Pratt's nose.

"That's what you've had coming to you for the last month!" Page's cheeks were flushed, but her voice was low and controlled. "I've taken your interference—and your mother's, too—because I didn't want any more trouble than I already had. Now—"

"Page, you don't know what's happened!"

"Yes, I do! I heard!" She turned to Asey. "I know who you are, of course. I heard what you said about Liz. I'm glad you're here. If I'd known you were home, I'd have hired you to come and sit in this damned house today, just to thwart tradition! What—" Her voice broke. "What happened to Liz?"

As Asey told her, he watched the tears well from her eyes, and for a moment he thought she was going to break down completely. Then she bit her lip until it seemed as if it would bleed.

"I think maybe you don't want to see her now," he concluded, and put out a restraining hand as she started to cross the room. "That Commando knife wasn't a pretty weapon."

"Commando knife? You mean one of those awful things with a curved blade?" Page whirled around and faced Bob Pratt. "One like yours?"

"See here, Page," Bob paused long enough to accept Asey's proffered handkerchief and substitute it for his own, which he'd been holding to his nose, "don't go flying off half-cocked! I know you feel badly—"

"Badly! One of my best friends lying there, and you know I feel badly! You'll find out how badly I feel! *You*'ve got a Commando knife! I've seen it with your other war trophies!"

"Page, this isn't any time for dramatics!"

"You've got a Commando knife!" Page said. "And Liz left the inlet with you! I know she did!"

Asey stepped between them. "Take it easy, Miss Kendall! You—"

"But don't you see?" Page took his arm and shook it. "Don't you understand? *He* did it! He's got a knife, and he left with Liz! She *told* me she was going with him!"

"Did you see her leave with him?" Asey inquired.

"No, but she said she was going with Bob! She told me so!"

"Page," Bob said, "I'm not going to let you stand there and implicate me in your best low, thrilling, melodramatic tones! You're playing it beautifully, you're turning your best profile toward Mayo, but I'm not going to let you get away with it, not after I've done my best to keep *you* out of it! Liz was in *your* coupé when you left the inlet, and you know she was!"

"Really?" Page's laugh was a masterpiece of irony. "Really, now! And I suppose I'm also the man she refused to marry, last night? Or could that possibly—just *poss*ibly be you, too?"

Bob stopped mopping at his nose long enough to manage a wry smile. "There you are, Mayo. Pratt drove Liz from the inlet, Pratt was a rejected suitor, Pratt had a Commando knife—which he hasn't seen or thought of in months. And to sew it all up, Pratt was even a Commando once, himself. Our Miss Kendall was so busy emoting, with accusatory gestures, she forgot that. Put them all together, they spell Murderer . . . Where are you going, Mayo?"

"I'm goin'," Asey said, "to see what's become of my cousin Jennie, who set off more'n half an hour ago to call Doc Cummings. The two of you stay put here till I come back, please, an'—"

"You're leaving us?" Page interrupted. "Here? Alone?"

"Somebody ought to be here," Asey said, "an' you two are all that's handy. Besides," he added, "there's safety in numbers. I'll be back in five minutes. Try not to mutilate each other any more'n you can help!"

He heard Bob Pratt's amused comment to Page, as he swung down to the ground. "Just the audience point of view, of course, but I'd say that the Codfish Sherlock didn't take your act too seriously."

"Act? You think I was putting on an act? Let me tell you, Bob Pratt, if you had another nose, I'd take a crack at that, too! I meant every word—"

Asey grinned as he set off toward the Pochet school, whose gilt cupola he could see shining through the pines ahead. Probably the cops wouldn't approve of his leaving at the scene of the crime two people who'd just been doing their level best to thrust each other into the suspect category, but he honestly doubted if the pair would stop squabbling long enough to think of tampering with any evidence.

At any rate, Page's dramatics had disclosed some reason for Bob's reaction to the sight of Liz Tyler. Even making allowance for theatrical exaggeration, their relationship had evidently been something more than merely that of inn-keeper and guest.

As for Page Kendall—Asey shook his head. He was going to reserve judgment on her until she'd calmed down. Her acting was probably less a matter of deliberately trying to implicate Bob Pratt than of expressing her own feelings about Liz in the only way she knew. . . .

Before starting up a well-worn footpath which led directly to the school building, Asey paused a moment and frowned. The school was nearer than he thought; it obviously had a phone; he knew that the local operators kept as close track of Doc Cummings as they did of the clock; and Jennie was too interested in Murder House's newest tragedy not to have rushed through her little chore and bustled back at once. Had she reached the doctor, he would have driven to the scene as fast as his car could carry him.

What, on a journey so short, safe, and generally devoid of pitfalls, could have happened to her?

Then there was fat Pete Pulster, too.

"What become of *him*?" Asey muttered aloud. "An' Dead-end Eddie? The three of 'em couldn't hardly have dissolved into thin air!"

He turned and looked back at the prim little white house, sitting so sedately on the truck in the field.

Then he felt his mouth open and his lower jaw begin to sag.

Clearly visible in the kitchen window was a white, claw-like hand!

His return trip to the house was a matter of seconds.

In one jump, he swung himself up onto the back-door step, jammed his thumb down on the old-fashioned iron latch, and shoved.

The door was locked.

Swinging down, he raced around to the front door and clambered up into the living room, where Bob and Page were still noisily arguing with each other.

He shoved past them into the dining room, wriggled around two antique spinning wheels, and pushed open the kitchen door.

The little room was empty.

In rapid succession, he jerked open a closet door, the pantry door, and a door that let down an ironing board which hit Page, following after him, on the head.

"Sorry," Asey said perfunctorily. "By golly, I can't understand it! I was watching this place all the while I was sprintin' back here, an' he couldn't've gone out any way but that back door! Did either of you see him?"

"See who?" Bob asked.

"Anyone! Didn't you hear anyone in here? No, I can see you was too busy yellin' at each other . . . Look out, please. I'm goin' to hunt!"

For the next five minutes, he ransacked the house from

the eaves and the upstairs bedrooms to the last corner cupboard in the dining room.

Then he jumped down to the ground and minutely examined the outside of the building.

"Look," Bob joined him, "I hate to interrupt what's clearly a definite train of thought, but what's the matter? What're you hunting?"

"The owner," Asey said, "of a white an' clawlike hand."

"Er—anybody we know?"

"If you know anyone answerin' that description," Asey returned, "speak up!"

"Not me." Bob glanced up at Page, standing in the doorway. "What about you? Does a white, clawlike hand ring any bells within you?"

"I was one once," Page said. "In my first play, when I was twelve. A noise was heard without, and a white, clawlike hand appeared through the curtains left center. I was both, and got hives from the whitewash I painted my arm with. What became of this hand you saw, Asey?"

He shrugged. "Like everybody else except you two, it's vanished," he said. "For all I know, it flew up the chimney. Now, I'm goin' to call Cummings an' the cops. Pratt, you two stay here, an' keep quiet enough so's you'll know if you got visitors. I opened the back door. Lock it."

Bob stopped him as he turned away. "You know, Mayo, I really thought Liz went with Page, and she thought Liz went with me, but apparently she left with two other people entirely. We can't figure it out!"

"Don't brood over it," Asey said. "Someone of the onlookers'll be sure to have noticed. Now, keep your eyes peeled! An' if you catch sight of any white, clawlike hands, grab 'em, with or without an attached body!'"

In the Pochet school, the teacher who left her classroom to show him the telephone looked surprised when he asked about Jennie.

"Oh, I know Jennie Mayo—no, she hasn't been here. No one's been here this morning. I'm quite sure, because I can see the door from my desk."

"Thanks," Asey said. "I'd gathered she hadn't got here."

Under the fascinated surveillance of the third grade down the hall, he spoke with Cummings and asked him to call the state police.

Then he walked slowly down the steps and around the gymnasium ell back toward Murder House.

A workman in white overalls was bending over a bulkhead, and Asey toyed with the thought of asking him if he'd seen Jennie. But he dismissed the notion almost as soon as it entered his head. If anything noticeably untoward had taken place, Jennie would have attracted not only the attention of a stray workman; she'd have roused every grade in the school.

"Located your cousin?" Bob asked when he returned to the house.

"No," Asey said, "an' because Jennie isn't someone you can pick up an' tuck away in your pocket, I'm goin' to take a look around the woods. Doc an' the cops are comin' in a few minutes. You stay here till they come."

"I think Bob needs Cummings professionally," Page said. "His nose started bleeding again, and he won't let me wash off his jacket with water from the pail. Look at him. Doesn't he look awful?"

"I intend to leave that stain as a reminder of your brutality," Bob said. "Mayo, shall we tell the cops to follow you, or—"

But Asey had already departed.

Halfway to the pine woods, he swung around suddenly on his heel, ran back to the house, and made a beeline for the kitchen.

He was standing in the middle of the spattered wooden floor, staring down at a trap door which he'd opened, when Page and Bob caught up with him.

"Now why," he said a little plaintively, "why make me beat my brains to a frazzle figurin' this out? Why in time didn't one of you think to tell me about this?"

"The trap door? Why should we have?" Page asked blankly. "I mean, it just used to lead to a little hole in the cellar, but there isn't any cellar at the moment. Only truck. Whatever would you want to know about it for?"

"Because," Asey said, "this's where old White-claw went! That little linoleum mat's stuck to the floor, an' it overlaps the door entirely, see? An' I never noticed! Never thought to notice. Never even considered a cellar till the notion just hit me like a bolt out of the blue. Yessir, that's where he dissolved to. He ducked down here. There's enough room for someone to squeeze in between the floor an' the truck carriage."

"But when'd he get out?" Page demanded. "Why didn't we hear him or see him? We were right here!"

"Probably when he heard us go pilin' upstairs to comb

the eaves closets for him," Asey said, "he just lifted up the trap door an' slipped out quiet. He had time enough to leave a dozen times, by the front door or the back."

"But where is he now? Where'd he go?"

"Your guess is as good as mi—" Asey stopped short, and then he smiled. "I'm the biggest dum fool in the county! Why would a workman huddle over a bulkhead an' never look up to see who was goin' by? An' that teacher told me nobody'd been around at all! Oh, to think I went an' let him slide through my fingers, an' he's probably gone with the wind by now!"

"Wait!" Page grabbed his arm as he strode into the living room. "D'you really think you know who the person was? Wait! Where are you going?"

"Back to the school," Asey said, "to see if the bird's generous enough to give me a second shot—"

"But who *is* he?"

"A man in white overalls." Asey jumped out through the front door. "Tell doc when he comes!"

Perhaps, he thought as he raced back toward the school, perhaps this wasn't quite such a lost cause as it might seem. The white, clawlike hand he'd seen in the kitchen window must be the same one Jennie had seen earlier in the side window. It must belong to the same person. After all, even Murder House couldn't mass-produce white, clawlike hands in quantity! That meant that the owner of the hand must have been in the house all the time. At least from a mile beyond the railroad crossing until a few minutes ago. He had, so to speak, come with the house.

But whatever his ultimate destination might be now,

he'd have to get to it on foot. He had no vehicle in which to whisk himself away.

After scanning the school grounds, Asey leaned against the wire backstop of the softball field and tilted his yachting cap back on his head.

"Now, let's figger!" he murmured. "Let's see! Maybe you come from Timbuktu, but my guess is that you're a local product. If you lived in Pochet, you'd have set off in the other direction, away from the school. Not toward it. So you probably come from Weesit. If you think you've been spotted, you won't be walkin' home in plain sight on the main road. You'll go by the old wood lanes. An' if you know the locality well enough to dare tackle that network of lanes, you'll also know the shortest route. So—yup, I guess maybe I'll take a chance an' do a little circlin' in the roadster, an' get ahead of you!"

He was secretly rather pleased with the spot he picked in which to ambush his quarry. From his vantage point on a hillock, he could cover two overgrown wood lanes and a path, any one of which should be the choice of a Weesit-bound walker who knew his way around. But as the minutes lengthened into half an hour, he began to entertain grave doubts as to the success of his maneuver. At the end of three-quarters of an hour, he slowly started back to where he had parked the roadster in a clump of scrub oaks.

"Codfish Sherlock, huh?" he mimicked Jennie's most acid tones. "Old Smarty Hayseed Sleuth! First you walk smack past him. N'en you take to the woods an' bash up your finders so's to give him every opportunity of by-passin' you! What made you so all-fired sure he was a local boy, because he was wearin' overalls? Didn't Bob Pratt tell you that Liz Tyler didn't know people hereabouts? Didn't—"

The roadster's horn blared out suddenly, shattering the stillness and sending a flock of crows cawing away over the treetops.

"No, you don't!" Asey muttered. "If you think I'm goin' to dash for the car, you're sadly mistaken! I'm goin' to creep up on you like a red Indian after a rabbit!"

He was so entirely successful that when he appeared by the side of the roadster, fat Pete Pulster jumped two feet into the air and yelled.

"Gee! Gee, Asey, you scared the pants off me!"

"What," Asey demanded, "are you doin' here?"

"Asey, I never had such a time! Look!" He pointed to his right ankle, which was swollen to nearly twice its normal size. "Sprained, see? Honest, I didn't know how I was ever goin' to get home. Then I seen your car an' it was like a miracle. Say, you're some Sherlock, all right! How'd you ever come to guess this was where to find me?"

"I didn't," Asey said. "I just—"

"Aw, you're too modest!" Pete interrupted. "All I can say is, it's white of you. Help me get in, will you? I got to sit down or I'll fall down. That young one!"

"Meanin' Eddie?" Asey eased Pete into the roadster. "Did he hang a bear trap on you, or just trip you?"

"I caught my foot in a root. What a day!" Pete sighed wearily. "It can't hardly be more than noon, but it seems like I been up a million years since breakfast. I tell you, Asey, this ain't the way I planned today!"

Asey chuckled as he started the car. "Me, I was goin'

fishin'," he said. "Instead I got shanghaied into a Mayflower crusade, an' then— Pete, tell me. After you started from the inlet with the Snow place, where'd you stop first?"

"For Eddie."

"Was he under the wheels," Asey inquired, "or did you pick him out of the carburetor?"

"I had to get him out of a tree," Pete said. "I didn't know he was there, see?"

"Where? In the tree?"

"No, no! He was hiding behind the truck seat, see, in the cab. I didn't suspect he was there till I got to the crest of the hill just the other side of Gull Pond. He'd been teasin' to come today, an' I said no, an' so when I found him, I said I'd learn him good! So he jumped out an' climbed a tree. Wouldn't come down till I promised not to spank him."

"In a nutshell," Asey said, "you stopped on the hill before you came to the pond—for how long?"

"Oh," Pete hesitated, "maybe ten minutes. I'd probably been there an hour if that Hamilton girl hadn't come by on her horse. That brought Eddie down quick. He likes horses —did you say somethin'?"

"I said, 'Well, well'!" Asey informed him. "So Miss Julie Hamilton was there! She didn't go inside the house, did she, Pete?"

"Oh, no! I never would've let anybody go in!" Pete said quickly. "No, sir! Not into that house!"

"I see. N'en," Asey said, "you stopped at the far end of the pond, because Jennie an' I seen you. What was your problem there?"

"Log of wood in the way," Pete said. "I only stopped to

move it out of the rut. What're you so curious about my stoppin' for, Asey? Nothin's missin' from the house, is it? Nothin's wrong? Page Kendall ain't mad at me again, is she? Honest, Asey, I *had* to get Eddie down out of that tree, an' I *had* to move that log, an' you can tell yourself that I *couldn't* get past your car! And I wouldn't never have stopped by the Pochet school, but I *had* to leave Eddie off there!"

Asey slowed down. "An' that—" he couldn't keep some of his amazement from creeping into his voice—"*that's* the reason why you parked the house in that field?"

"Why, sure! Because if Eddie skips school just once more, see, they're goin' to expel him!" Pete explained simply. "I *had* to stop there an' drop him off!"

"So you don't—" Asey paused.

Obviously, he thought, as he looked reflectively at his passenger, Pete knew nothing whatever about Liz Tyler, lying there in the Dutch oven of the house he'd been moving!

"Hey, that tree ahead!" Pete said suddenly. "It's in your way. You'll hit it."

"I went over it comin'," Asey said, "an' I think we can go over it now. What happened to Eddie, Pete?"

"He give me the slip. Minute I parked, he beat it. I chased him an' chased him an' chased him, an' this," he pointed to his ankle, "is what I got for my pains. *I* don't know where he went to. But I know what he's goin' to get when I lay hands on him! Asey, is Page awful sore with me?" he added anxiously. "I guess she must be, if she sent *you* to hunt me! But I can take the house over to Bay Lane for her. I can manage that, in spite of my foot. You'll kind of head her off, won't you, if she starts spittin' fire at me? She's such a one for boilin' over!"

"I noticed that in her. Say, Pete," Asey tried to sound casual, "what about that friend of hers, that Liz Tyler?"

Pete sniffed. "Don't know why you call her a *friend*!" he said. "She was the one busted things up when Page was engaged to Nick Fox, you know, an' she's done nothin' but chase Bob Pratt ever since she's been in town. Bob's mother's fit to be tied, they say . . . Asey, I wish you'd stop starin' at me like you'd never seen me before, an' pay some attention to the road! You make me nervous!"

"Sorry," Asey said. "So you don't think much of Liz?"

"Never heard of anyone who did," Pete returned, "except Page, an' Bob Pratt. A trouble-maker, that's what that girl is, just a flibberty-gibbet trouble-maker. Why, just this mornin', she went an' raised all that hullabaloo at the inlet —I s'pose Page told you about that."

"I don't know as she mentioned it," Asey said.

"Well, Liz was crazy to ride over inside the house— honest, Asey, I wish you'd watch the road a *little* mite! I don't want a broken neck to go with my sprained ankle!"

Asey suppressed his desire to tell Pete that his assorted tidings were of considerably more interest than the road. "I'll take more care," he said. "What in time did Liz want to ride inside the house for?"

Pete shrugged elaborately. "What's any woman want to do crazy things for? Liz just got this whim into her head she wanted to move along with the house, an' that's all there was to it. Page said absolutely no, an' it wasn't safe. Course, it *was* safe, really, but with all that's happened to that house durin' its movin's, she didn't want to take no chances. So Liz said Page was a fuss, an' Page said far from bein' a fuss, she was a very patient girl, particularly about money. I gathered," he said in confidential tones, "that Liz'd been doin' considerable borrowin', see?"

"Uh-huh. And so they quarreled?"

"Quarreled? Why, they had a *real* fight! Just this side of kickin' an' scratchin', they was, when Bob Pratt calmed 'em down by remindin' 'em that a couple dozen people was drinkin' it all in. Page stalked away with her head up in the air, an' the next thing I knew, Liz was wavin' a ten-dollar bill under my nose an' whisperin' sweet in my ear that it was mine if I'd let her sneak into the house an' ride over to Bay Lane in it." Pete sighed. "She stuck it into my hand, see, an' I wasn't really goin' to take it, but Page saw the whole thing and thought I was, an' boy, did she boil over at me! Honest, this's been a day!"

"It does seem like you endured a lot." Asey decided that he was beginning to understand why no one seemed to know whom Liz Tyler left the inlet with. "Did you let her ride with you, finally?"

"Why, of course not!" Pete said righteously. "No! No indeed, Asey! Why, if I did, an' if Page found out, why, that girl would tear me apart!"

Asey looked at him sharply out of the corner of his eye. "If I'd been you," he remarked casually, "I think I'd have taken the money. You'd never make ten dollars any easier an', after all, it wasn't as if she wouldn't be safe enough, like you said."

"You really think so?" Pete asked eagerly. "Because—now, you won't tell Page, will you? Because that was just what I figgered, Asey, an' so I let her sneak in! To tell you the gospel truth, I was sort of sore with Page for blowin' me up in front of everybody just on account of holdin' that bill in my hand . . . Say, are you on the right lane?"

"I think so." Asey spoke with all the confidence he could muster, and hoped that Pete wouldn't realize that he was being driven about in virtual circles until the last ounce of information had been pumped out of him. "It looks right to me. Say, what was the trouble between Page and Nick Fox? How'd Liz bust that up?"

"She came to visit Page," Pete said. "I don't know what she did, but before she'd been here a week, they was all washed up. That was before Nick went into the navy."

"All this fuss about the house an' the land, now." Asey killed time by stopping and lighting his pipe. "I've known other cases over my way where people got left a house an' land separately, but they most usually always managed to solve it somehow."

"They'd probably have solved this," Pete didn't seem to notice that Asey had turned off the engine, "if Liz Tyler hadn't egged Page on to be so ornery! Page had the house; Nick had all the land. Page wanted to buy enough land from him so as she'd have a right of way to the place an' some land around it. But Nick wouldn't sell. Said to take what she wanted; he'd give it to her. An' she said she'd either buy it or he could keep it. That's what this whole ruckus was about—aside from Calvert Hamilton's buttin' in."

"Sort of ingrowin' pride, huh?"

"I don't know what you'd call it. Just plain stubbornness, I guess. Anyway, Nick finally got sore. You can't hardly blame him none! He told her to take her house off his property, an' so she did. I noticed this mornin' she was rubbin' it in to him, too. Offered to give him a check for squattin' illegal on his land, an' asked if he thought we'd damaged the grass much. I thought to myself while I watched Nick's face that if the house ever had another movin' murder, it would be him doin' Page in. She was askin' for it!"

"What you think about this Nick Fox?"

"Oh, I guess he's all right. He's doin' a good job on the *News*. But he was in a hospital a long time after he was wounded, an' he's sort of queer sometimes. Says queer things."

"This Pratt," Asey said, "he's another newcomer, ain't he?"

"My wife likes him an' his mother, but I think they're crazy, tryin' to make a go of that old Shell Inn," Pete said. " 'Course it's pretty up there, but who wants to stay in the old rattletrap? Why, everyone that ever got mixed up with it just failed an' lost their shirts. Bad business judgment, if you ask me. He's crazy over Liz Tyler. You bein' interested," Pete dropped his voice, "you might like to know—"

"Know what?" Asey inquired, as Pete paused and laughed.

"Well, one night I seen Liz at the movies with Pratt, an' she was lookin' up at him with those big brown eyes, an' you'd thought he was the only man in her world. An' later that same night—I got this hurry call to take a load of fish to Boston, see—well, there was Liz parked with Calvert Hamilton in that green roadster of his, down on the old wharf road! Old enough to be her father, he is, too. They didn't," Pete said, with what amounted to a leer, "even see me goin' by. I don't think they even smelled the fish!'"

"What a lot," Asey said with a chuckle, "you fellers in the truckin' business get to find out about!"

"You'd be surprised, some of the things I know," Pete said. "But the funny thing is, Asey, when I tell my wife, it always seems she knew all the time. Take Hamilton an' Liz. When I told her what I'd seen, she just said, so what? Seems everybody knew Liz was playin' around with him. They'd been seen before. That's why Bob Pratt's mother is so mad at Bob's fallin' for Liz. She—say, I don't like to hurry you none, but I think we should ought to hustle back to the house so's I can get along with it. Page'll be sizzlin'!"

Asey started the roadster. "I been so interested," he said with perfect truth, "in what you been sayin'. Tell me, what did Eddie do with the knife he swiped?"

"Eddie swiped a knife? When? Whose?"

Asey told him about Jennie's Commando knife that had been in with the Mayflowers over at the pond. "She had this idea," he concluded, "that Eddie might've taken it."

"Oh, he didn't, Asey! Jennie's mistaken!" Pete said earnestly. "Because I remember when Eddie jumped up on the truck there, I'd just hit some tree roots, and Eddie had to hang on with both hands to keep from fallin' off. He didn't have anything in his hands, an' that was enough of a bump so's he'd have cut himself if he'd stuck a knife in his belt. An' I know it's not in the truck. Honest, I know he didn't take it! He's not a bad kid, Asey. Not really. He's just sort of got a lot of energy."

"Uh-huh." There was one more thing, Asey thought, which he ought to try to extract from Pete before they got back to the main road and the house. "I wonder, d'you know anybody with a white, clawlike hand?"

"A *what*?" Pete stared at him. "You crazy?"

"S'pose," Asey said, "I put it another way. You get around. You see things. Like Calvert Hamilton an' Liz Tyler, for example."

Pete, glowing slightly under Asey's praise, allowed that he'd always thought of himself as a very noticing man.

"Well," Asey continued, "this mornin', when you drove your truck over to the inlet to pick up the house, did you happen to notice anybody whitewashin' anything, or paintin' anything white? Like trellises or fences or barns or boats? Somebody wearin' white overalls?"

Pete thought for a moment.

"Only Nick Fox," he said.

Asey braked the roadster to a quick stop. "Want to look at the rear tires," he said in response to Pete's question. "Seems's if they're draggin'."

He wondered, as he got out and pretended to examine the tires minutely, just what he could next conjure up to delay this expedition if Pete should contribute any more amazing little tidbits of information.

"I think," he said, when he returned and slid in behind the wheel, "we'd better take it awful easy, Pete. I know you're in a hurry, but these tires look bad. What would the editor of the *Pochet News* be paintin'?"

Pete laughed. "I asked him was the pen-pushin' business so bad he'd had to take to real work, an' he said he was whitewashin' that ell shed where the *News's* press is. He'd been hard at work when Page phoned an' ordered him to come over to the inlet an' watch the start of the movin'. Honest, he was white from head to foot! I don't think he'd ever tackled any whitewashin' before. Hey!" he protested, as Asey swung onto the main tarred road, "what you turnin' this way for?"

"Got to put air in them rear tires," Asey informed him blandly.

He did so with well-assumed concern at the gas station next to the *Pochet News* building, to which he paid far more attention than he did to the tires.

Perhaps a quarter of one wall of the shed at the rear was crudely whitewashed. The remainder was untouched. A pail and some long-handled brushes stood on a sawhorse from which whitewash-smeared rags fluttered in the breeze.

Clearly, Asey decided, Nick Fox had not hurriedly whipped back from the inlet and got on with his whitewashing in any frenzied rush!

"Goin' to drop over an' get me a *News*. Be back in two shakes," Asey told Pete, and ignored his plaintive comment about wanting to hustle on to the house.

The *News's* small front office was divided by a wooden counter into two definite areas. On one well-swept side were two scrubbed wooden settees on one of which hung an empty, curving leather case.

Asey reached up and took it down. His instant suspicion that it couldn't have contained anything but a Commando knife was proved by the stamping on the back: "Richardson's Commando Number Ten."

"So!" He returned it to its hook, and then sat down on the settee and leaned back against the hard rungs. "Now, let's see if I can remember. Bob Pratt said Nick reminded him to take that house picture, an' then he got into his beach wagon. But he didn't say that Nick actually drove away!"

Probably, he reflected, nobody had taken much notice of anyone's departure. Everyone's interest was centered in the old Snow place, not in the bystanders.

It occurred to him again how smart it was to commit a murder while everyone was violently interested in watching something. When you came right down to brass tacks, he thought, an ideally perfect murder could have taken place during the first flight of the Wright brothers, or during a partial eclipse of the sun.

Even supposing that some overly observant citizen had noticed all the departures and their actual sequence, what would it really matter?

"Not one whit!" he promptly answered his own question. "In those woods you could drive off, swerve into the bushes an' hide your car, an' then hop back an' catch up with the house before it got as far as the pond. Easier still, you could park your car sort of inconspicuous in the first place, jump into the house, an' be there all the time."

Asey sighed. He might as well face the fact that anyone could have hidden away inside that house from the moment it left the inlet, just as Liz Tyler had!

He heard his roadster's horn blaring out under Pete's impatient thumb, and reluctantly got up from the settee. He hated to have to tell Pete about the murder. Probably Pete's was the last casual and unbiased information he'd ever be given on the situation. Everyone else would know, by now, and react accordingly. Doubtless Nick Fox was over at Murder House this minute, getting data for what would unquestionably be an extra edition of the *News*.

As he started out the door, someone bounded in, and the ensuing head-on collision left Asey with the feeling that he'd been tackled just short of the goal line by an infuriated fullback.

He looked up at the young man, who was at least six inches taller than himself, and then let his gaze travel down from the well-tanned face and snapping black eyes to the faded khaki pants and shirt and the worn tweed jacket.

"Asey Mayo, isn't it? I'm Nick Fox." He sounded a little embarrassed. "Hurt?"

"I think I'll survive." Asey wondered how he'd picked up the impression that Nick Fox was a smallish, sickly fellow, slightly on the neurotic side. He wondered, too, if someone with all that bulk could possibly squeeze into the space under the trap door of Murder House, and decided that if Fox held his breath, he could just about manage to fit in.

"Looks as if the *Pochet News* missed another scoop," Nick Fox said. "The grapevine never whispered a word about your coming home. Anything I can do for you?"

Asey glanced at him curiously and came to the conclusion that it was perhaps just editorial inexperience that brought forth such a deferent question. Most editors he knew would at once have demanded a description of the murderer and a play-by-play report of the crime.

"Perhaps," Nick went on politely, "you're another Snow relation? Another cousin?"

"Snow relation? Meanin' one of the Murder House Snow family?" Asey found himself recalling Pete's remark that Nick Fox sometimes said queer things. "What in the world ever give you that idea?"

"Thirty-four people," Nick said, "have either phoned or written and requested copies of those old photographs of the Snow place I printed in the paper this week. All of 'em were Snow relations. I just thought you might be another fifth cousin. Won't you sit down?" He pointed to a settee, and perched himself up on the wooden counter. "Hope you haven't been waiting long. I had to rush off to see a man who thinks he can repair my press. It's currently held together with bits of string. Er—have you any juicy news items on your person, maybe? I'm going to be sunk with the Snow house finally out of the way. I'd be grateful to the gills for a good rousing murder."

Asey deliberately let his yaching cap drop from his hand to the floor and took his time bending over to retrieve it. He didn't want Fox to see the look of blank bewilderment that he knew was glued on his face. So this wasn't the beating about the bush of an inexperienced editor at all. Fox didn't know about the murder! He didn't know what had happened to Liz Tyler!

"I understand," Asey put the cap back on his head, "that there was a little fight there at the inlet before the house movin' this mornin'."

"One last gesture, like the final sizzle of a rocket before it burns out," Nick said. "Well, now the house is gone, I haven't any interest in the land. I'm going to wash my hands of the whole mess and sell out. Like to buy it? Wonderful place for raising mosquitoes." He lighted a cigarette and then laughed shortly. "I knew there'd never be a solution as long as Liz Tyler was around lousing things up. Great old louser-upper, Liz is. Happen to know her?"

"She looks a bit like Page Kendall, doesn't she?" Asey asked.

"Like Page? Never! No two people in the world were ever less alike. It was Liz"— a touch of bitterness entered Nick's voice—"who pointed out to Page that I'd failed in the advertising business, and that you shouldn't ever marry anyone with such a taint. Of course, Page knew I'd lost my little shoestring—I honestly pulled some awful boners!— but she hadn't thought of it as a taint till Liz sold her the thought."

"Oh." Asey began to understand the caustic comment Nick had written about himself in the *News*. Something about having his own business, which failed.

"I've never known why Page is so swayed by Liz." Nick looked at Asey, and grinned suddenly. "I recognize that expression on your face. Everyone looks at me in the same pitying way every time I mention Page's name. Sure, I still love her. Never pretended otherwise."

"An' you're not doin' anything about it?"

"If from the depths of your vast experience with homicide," Nick said lightly, "you can tell me of a foolproof and preferably legal method of doing away with Liz Tyler, I'd not only listen intently; I'd also take careful notes. She's too good a swimmer to drown, and she never walks in the middle of the road when I'm driving, and she must be immune to arsenic—some girl whose guy she's swiped would surely have tried arsenic on her long before this!"

Asey pointed to the leather case hanging on the wall behind him. "Ever toyed with the idea of a Commando knife? Or is that just an empty case?"

"Trophy department." Nick held up his left hand, and for the first time Asey realized that two fingers were missing. "I took the knife that belongs in that case off a Jap—he'd got it off one of our boys—but he sliced a bit off me in the process. Julie Hamilton has it at the moment."

"Who," Asey inquired, "is she plannin' to slice up?"

"She isn't. She borrowed it for some do or other," Nick said. "A display at the Ladies' Aid or something. She's mingling with the natives to help elect father . . . Was it a subscription, perhaps?"

Asey stared at him.

"Or did the boy toss your cousin Jennie's copy into her best hydrangeas again?" Nick went on. "She complained bitterly once before."

"Will you tell me," Asey said, "just what you're talkin' about?"

"I'm only trying to find out why you're here, that's all. I mean," Nick said, "I'm honored and all that sort of thing, but I strongly suspect you didn't drop in without some good reason."

"Wa-el," Asey drawled, "I stopped by to see where you went after you left the inlet this mornin' in your white overalls an' all covered with whitewash. In short, were you the white, clawlike hand?"

"Now it's my turn," Nick said promptly. "*What?* Will you tell me what you're talking about?"

Asey's eyes never left Nick's face as he briefly summed up the latest tragedy in Murder House.

"Well?" he said at last, as Nick continued to stare across

at the empty leather case on the wall. "Any editorial comment?"

Nick ground his cigarette out on the wooden counter. "Residents of this town," he said, "confessed themselves appalled on being informed that the editor of the *Pochet News* was taken this afternoon to Barnstable jail, where he is being held as principal suspect in the murder of Miss Elizabeth Tyler, whom he had openly and cordially detested for a number of years."

"Aren't you kind of jumpin' to conclusions?" Asey asked.

"Missing from the wall of Editor Fox's office was a Commando knife with which the girl presumably was killed. An interesting sidelight was Fox's reiterated and categorical denial that he was or ever had been a white, clawlike hand dangling in any window. 'All the time people were seeing hands,' Fox stated, '*I* was seeing a man about a press.' Officials, however, were quick to point out that Fox could remember neither the name of this man nor the name of the company he represented, although he loudly proclaimed that if everyone would just wait quietly until next Thursday, the man would surely return with the part for the press."

"Honest," Asey said, "*don't* you remember his name?"

"I don't. It was something like Wingcroft, or Ashmont. I never have remembered names," Nick said. "That's one of the reasons why I was such a flop in advertising. I couldn't even remember *first* names. To continue, 'Editor Fox stated that until arrangements have been made to edit the *News* from his cell, subscribers are urged to bear patiently with the discontinuation of his paper. Rebates will be made in due time. Fox repeated that while he was not a white, clawlike hand, he easily understands how he's going to be one officially, or at least until a better white claw comes along.' " He paused. "Had I better tell you all, and get it over with? Because I *was* in the house when it started."

"So?"

Nick nodded. "I thought I saw Page go in at the last moment—red skirt, blue jacket. So I hopped in the back door and hid in a closet."

"An' what," Asey said, "was your underlyin' purpose?"

"I suppose," Nick lighted another cigarette, "you could sum it up as hope springing eternal in the human heart. I've kept telling myself that Page would change her mind, that the house really wouldn't be moved. As long as it was there, we at least had something in common to fight about. And Liz wouldn't be staying here forever. I guess I learned the line wrong as a child."

"Line?" Asey was catching on to Nick's habit of making mental leaps, but this one leaped too far.

"The fairy-story one. You know. 'So everything turned out fine and dandy in the nick of time.' My problem has always been in reading it, 'Everything turned out fine and dandy for Nick in time.' Well, to get on, I was peering through a crack in the closet door, and the kitchen door opened, and I saw it was Liz I'd followed, and not Page. So I slipped out quietly as Pete was stopping for something at the crest of the hill the other side of Gull Pond, and I got the hell away as fast as my legs—" Nick stopped short.

"What's the matter, remembered somethin'?"

"Is it fair to tell—yes, it is! In a mess like this, people have got to make their own explanations! I heard the sound of horses' hoofs. The Hamiltons. Mayo, just for the fun of it, leave us go call social on the Hamiltons, what do you say? Maybe they can cast some light."

"You figure they might have some reason for bein' involved with Liz Tyler?"

"I do like that purry voice of yours," Nick said, "when you're on the trap, so to speak. It lulls. Lulled me into telling you my feelings about Liz and about the nice Commando knife and all. You must lull the Hamiltons with it when you ask *them* why they might be involved with Liz. Only I rather guess you already know. Come on, let's go see 'em. A couple more fellow suspects, and I could while away the long prison days with gin rummy."

As Asey followed him down the front steps of the *News* building Nick stopped and turned around.

"I've been flippant about this," he said, "because I didn't know how else to be. I'm sorry Liz was killed, but I can't pretend I'm sorry that she'll be out of Page's life. And mine. I've told you the truth. I didn't stay in the house. I didn't kill her. I hope you'll believe me."

"It's the cops," Asey said, "you've got to convince. An' when some of their experts start combin' around an' peekin' through microscopes an' findin' specks of whitewash off the soles of them shoes you didn't change—"

"It's about time!" Pete called out in a hurt voice as they approached the roadster at the gas station. "An' it's goin' to be *your* funeral, Asey—hi, Nick!—an' not mine! *You* can explain to Page that *you* kept me."

"First," Asey said as he got in and started the car, "I'll explain some things to you!"

Pete took the news in stunned silence. Not until they were nearly at the Pochet school did he offer any comment whatever.

"But Liz answered me!" he said plaintively. "I yelled at her when I jumped off to chase Eddie at the school. I said I'd be right back in a minute, or somethin' like that. An' she answered me!"

"You sure of that, or did you just sort of take it for granted she answered?" Asey asked.

"I'm sure! That is, I think I'm sure! She must've got killed there at the school, Asey!" Pete said. "Lookit here, I stopped to get Eddie out of that tree, an' for that log in the way, an' for your car. Nobody could've planned on my makin' those stops because I didn't even plan on makin' 'em myself! So nobody could've planned to get into the house while it was goin', see?"

"How about the possibility of someone's being in the house all the time, just as Liz was?" Nick suggested.

Pete shook his head. "What I think is, you should always tackle these things the simple way. Now, say someone sees the house sittin' there by the school an' decides to rob it. They go in, Liz tells 'em to get out, an' they fight, an' she gets killed. I bet you the answer's somethin' simple like that. Like some tramp passin' by."

Nick looked at Asey. "Didn't he hear the—"

He abruptly swallowed the words "Hamiltons' horses" as Asey's elbow dug into his ribs.

"There's something in what Pete says." Asey stopped the roadster by the field. "The simpler you figure a thing—the simpler—the simpler—"

Pete stood up in the car and started to yell.

"What's the matter with you two?" Nick demanded.

Pete pointed toward the field. "No *house!*" he said weakly. "No house! It's *gone!*"

Asey leaned his elbows on the wheel. "Wa-el," he said philosophically, "it didn't trundle off by itself, that's sure. Probably the cops decided to drive it over to Bay Lane. We'll find it there."

But there was no trace of Murder House anywhere near the freshly dug foundations of the lot to which Pete guided him on Bay Lane.

"Where is it? This's her land!" Pete said excitedly. "This's where I was to take it, right here! What's happened, Asey? Where *is* the damn house?"

"Where's Page?" Nick said. "And Bob Pratt? What could have become of them?"

"For that matter, where's my cousin Jennie?" Asey returned. "An' Doc Cummings? An' the cops?"

"An' Eddie!" Pete said. "Where's Eddie?"

Nick laughed. "Should the three of us that're left form a human chain in self-protection, maybe? Hold hands and never let go? Asey, d'you suppose—I almost don't dare hope that Page might have taken the house back over the inlet, but why not try there?"

"If that girl attempts drivin' my truck an' that house around Gull Pond," Pete said unhappily, "good-by, truck! Go see, Asey! Step on it!"

As the roadster whizzed over the Pochet town line into Weesit, Nick howled in Asey's ear.

"Stop! There it is! You went past it."

Asey stopped and backed up.

The old Snow place now stood in a clearing off the main road, just over the Weesit line. Page was sitting in the front doorway, dangling her legs over the side, and on a stump some twenty feet beyond the house sat a grim-faced man who held a double-barreled shotgun on his knees. Asey recognized John Parsons, one of the Pochet selectmen.

"Hi, John," he said. "Uh—how come? Who brought the house back here?"

"I did! Not in *my* town!"

"How's that?" Asey said.

"I said, not in my town! As long as I'm a constable and a selectman of Pochet, I'm not going to have any murders in my town that didn't happen there! You got a murder in a Weesit house—all right! Like I told Doc Cummings, that murder's going right back to Weesit where it belongs! I'm not letting *my* town get a bad name from someone else's murder, and spoil all the summer trade! That house," Parsons fingered the shotgun significantly, "isn't crossing my town line!"

Asey bit his lip to keep from smiling. "Where's the state cops?" he asked. "Didn't they come?"

"Whoever Cummings phoned," Page answered, as she joined the group, "told him they were busy up the Cape with a million bigwigs and the governor—laying cornerstones, I think—and he'd send men as soon as he could. Er —John moved the house himself. He insisted. John wants no murders in Pochet."

"John," Nick said under his breath, "wants to burn a witch or two, from the look on his face!"

Page giggled. "Cummings said he thought that, with John

on guard, things would be safe till the cops came. Did you find your cousin Jennie, Asey?"

"No. What became of Bob Pratt?"

"Cummings twisted his wrist jumping down from the house," Page said, "and so he asked Bob to drive for him. He left you a note."

Asey took the folded prescription blank she held out to him. "Nice clean job," Cummings had written in his tiny hand. "She never knew what hit her. Remember Calvert Hamilton plays polo and has steel wrists. So did your murderer. My wife says Liz Tyler was asking for trouble."

Asey smiled and thrust the note into his shirt pocket.

"If you don't have anything to do right away," Page put her hand on his arm, "I'd like to talk with you for a minute. Or are you too busy?"

"I got nothin' that won't wait." Asey followed her beyond the house to the edge of the clearing. "What's your problem?"

"Clues. Have you any?"

"Wa-el," Asey said, "that depends on your point of view. Most people are inclined to think of clues as bein' only left-behind buttons, or cigarettes marked up with purple lipstick, or shreds of Harris tweed. If that's what you mean, I haven't any."

Page looked up at him curiously. "You sound almost a little scornful about them."

"I'm not. Only things like that don't mean much till you can connect 'em up," Asey said. "An', on the other hand, there's always a lot of seemingly obvious things around that don't appear to be clues at all, but probably really are if only someone had the wit to hitch 'em together. You think you found a clue?"

"This." She dropped into his hand a small gold pin marked with the initial "K." "Cummings gave it to me. He found it in the oven and took it for granted that the "K" was for Kendall. But it isn't mine!"

Asey turned the pin over in his fingers. "Know whose it is?"

Page nodded. "Yes. I can't understand why it was in the oven near Liz! It belongs to Bob Pratt's mother. Her name's Katharine. It's an old earring that she sent away and had made into a pin."

"Mrs. Pratt," Asey said thoughtfully, "wasn't any too happy about Bob an' Liz, was she?"

"No. Neither was I." Page hesitated a moment. "I feel I ought to explain things to you about Liz, because I'm sure Nick's been saying awful things about her, as usual. He never has liked her. But I did. I had a lot of fun with her here. I hardly ever saw her in the city. We did entirely different things there with entirely different sets of people. But here on the Cape we had a splendid time together— oh, dear, I wonder if I'm making myself at all clear about this relationship!"

"Uh-huh, I think so. There's one man I like to go fishin' with," Asey said, "who drives my cousin Jennie an' everyone else stark mad. But he's a fine fishin' companion. I like him as such an' for no other reason."

"That's exactly the sort of thing I'm driving at, and something Nick never could understand! I liked Liz *here*. Of course, she had qualities I didn't like, but I just didn't

bother about them. Her going with Bob was her business—
and truly, I'm sure she never cared seriously for him, even
though he was so crazy about her!"

Asey glanced at her sideways and wondered if the girl
realized that such a casually revealing statement was just
what the cops waited for. It was his experience that they
asked for no better suspect than a double-crossed or jilted
lover, unless it was a jealous mother on the warpath. Or
was Page, in this letting-down-the-hair mood, merely trying to accent in a subtle way her original accusation against
Bob Pratt?"

Aloud, he said, "I understand Liz borrowed a lot of
money from you."

"Oh, so you've heard about that fight! Yes, she was careless with money; she borrowed from everyone, and she was
a wheedler, and she loved sticking her fingers into other
people's affairs. I know all the criticisms of her!" Page said.
"But who's perfect, anyway? I told Katharine Pratt that
Liz wasn't serious! I told her if she'd stop antagonizing Liz,
Liz would stop playing with Bob!"

"Playin' with Calvert Hamilton, too, wasn't she?"

"She was his secretary one summer, and she's worked for
him off and on. They were always good friends. She amused
him," Page said, "and he liked taking her places. Of course,
Katharine Pratt made a lot of that, but I told her if Bob
didn't know about Liz and Calvert, he was the only one
who didn't. Liz never made any secret of it. Asey, I wasn't
flying off the handle when I yelled at Bob. He's been in my
hair, and so has his mother. They're so infernally ready to
tell you what's best for you to do! And Bob *does* have a
Commando knife exactly like the one that killed Liz!"

"So did Nick," Asey said, "an' so did my missin' cousin, Jennie Mayo. You got any idea how that pin came to be inside the oven? Was Mrs. Pratt in your house much?"

Page's answer rather surprised him. "Katharine's never been in the place, to my knowledge. I never asked her. Of course, I left the keys around in my room at the inn—" She left the sentence dangling, and then she shrugged.

"I see." Asey mentally applauded the shrug as an expert piece of timing. "What did you do this mornin' after the house left the inlet?"

"Why, I—" She stopped, and the color mounted in her cheeks. "I didn't do much of anything. Drove up to the village for some cigarettes, and then went on after the house. You know when I caught up with it."

"Uh-huh. But you went flyin' past my roadster an' past the house," Asey said, "just before the railroad crossin'. What was your rush then?"

Page turned away from him.

"I wonder, now," the purring note on which Nick had commented entered Asey's voice, "I wonder if maybe you didn't have some intention of stoppin' Pete an' sendin' the house to the inlet? Sort of a momentary sentimental impulse, as you might say?"

"No!" Page still didn't look at him. "I went to Bay Lane and waited. When the house didn't come, I drove back to see what the matter was, and found it parked near the school. I never wanted it back at the inlet! I was glad to get it away from there!"

"An' this mornin', when Pete drove it off, you never once thought what a fool Nick was for lettin' you let it go? Especially," Asey said, "because you'd ordered him to come an' watch, an' all he had to do was to forbid your movin' the house over his land—"

But Page had stalked off toward the house.

Asey grinned. Nick had taken the fact of his being a suspect without much more than a perfunctory protest. Page had rather deftly turned the spotlight of suspicion on the Pratt family.

"I think," Asey murmured as he strolled back to the house, "Nick feels his bein' involved will protect her, on account of that public fight she had with Liz. An' I wonder if Page isn't gnawin' away on the Pratts with the hope of keepin' Nick out of trouble. Huh!"

"Asey!" Pete hobbled over to him. "I don't see as you need me here. I can't do no more movin' till the cops come, can I? So will you drive me home? I'll get my wife to come an' hunt Eddie. The swellin's gone down some in my ankle, but it still hurts to walk on it."

"Eddie," Asey said. "Eddie an' Jennie. If—okay, I'll take you home. Nick, stay here an' keep the Pochet vigilantes company, will you? If Page should ask you, she can go any time she wants."

"She won't. I just heard her tell John the Grim that she intends to stay. Going to see the Hamiltons? Have fun!"

As Asey drove off with Pete, he remarked casually that he'd been considering Pete's theory of simple solutions.

"For example," he went on, "you're so sure Liz was killed there by the school. I keep wonderin' why."

"I told you I was sure I heard her answer when I yelled," Pete said, "so she must've been alive then!"

"I think it's even simpler than that," Asey returned. "I

think you want like fury to believe she was killed by the school, an' not on the crest of the hill just before Gull Pond. Because you're really scared to death to let Page know you let the Hamiltons go into the house, aren't you?"

Pete sighed. "They always say in stories about you that you always find out lies, an' I guess they're right. But they only wanted somethin' that belonged to Calvert Hamilton by rights. A silver cigarette box he set a lot of store by because his sister gave it to him."

"Why'd you only mention Julie, at first?"

"Well," Pete said lamely, "well, Hamilton didn't exactly *ask* me not to, but I got the idea he'd rather I didn't. But it was his own box. He told me all about it, an' how it got into his sister's house by mistake. He said Page never give 'em a chance to mention it. That's all they took, too, Asey. They showed it to me. Said it was way down in the bottom drawer of a corner cupboard, an' they thought Page didn't know it was there."

"Did it ever occur to you, Pete, that it might not have been there?"

"Why, Asey Mayo, if it wasn't there, how could they have brought it out an' showed it to me?" Pete demanded.

"Because," Asey said gently, "they could've had it with them all the time."

"Then what'd they want to go into the house for?"

"How long," Asey countered, "were they there?"

"Six or eight minutes, maybe. Long enough to hunt up the box."

"An' how long does it take to stab someone?"

Pete blinked. "I never thought—but you must be all

wrong! They *showed* it to me—an' it was tarnished like it'd been stuck away a long time. An' they put it into their saddlebags along with the stuff they were takin' up to the war display. You ought to see it," he added parenthetically. "It's things the local boys sent back. Guns, an' helmets, an' knives—" he stopped.

"You get my point?" Asey asked.

"I ain't got nothin' to say, Asey!" Pete sounded as if he were going to break into tears. "I shouldn't have let 'em—but I was so sore with Page for blowin' me up in front of everybody! Oh, if I hadn't let Liz ride, or let them in! Will I be a—what d'you call it? A something after the fact?"

"An accessory? I don't know. But I know what I want you to do. I want you to go home, an' sit down, an' think—"

"But I got to find Eddie!"

"I'll find him. I want you to write down everything you did an' saw an' can remember from the time you left the inlet till you stopped at the school. Be specific. Don't just say you stopped to pick a log up out of your way. Say what *kind* of a log. Understand?"

"You mean, like a *maple* log, say?"

"Uh-huh. Now, will you do that right away?"

It was a very contrite Pete he deposited on the doorstep of the Pulster home.

"I'll get straight to work, Asey. An' if you're goin' to the Hamiltons' now, I'll tell you the short cut to use." Pete gave him minute directions. "An' you'll find Eddie for me? Sure?"

Asey promised.

As he followed Pete's instructions and drove around the inlet, the old Shell Inn suddenly loomed up on the road ahead of him.

"Ouch!" Asey said, and stopped to look at it.

It had been years since he'd seen the strange, rambling, fieldstone building, but the oyster-shell and clam-shell and quohaug-shell decorations were just as hideous as he remembered them. Even more hideous, he decided, because weather and old age had so worked on the shells that the decorative effect was largely missing. A stranger would probably assume that children had pelted the place at random with old shells, and that some had happened to stick.

How the Pratts expected to make a success of their ramshackle inn, he couldn't imagine. Not unless they trained their guests to look constantly at the broad fields on either side, and to enter the building with their eyes firmly closed!

"Well, Mayo," he said as he started the car up again, "why not go to see Mrs. Pratt first? After all, her gold pin's the only tangible clue."

As he started to turn up the inn's overgrown driveway, Jennie and Eddie rose from the bushes in front of the shell-studded stone driveway pillars.

"Codfish Sherlock!" Jennie said with infinite scorn. "Hayseed Sleuth! Where you been? I should think this would've been the *first* place you'd come to. Now, let's go get her an' settle things!"

"Get who, an' settle what?"

Jennie was too busy plumping herself down on the roadster's seat to bother answering his question. "Get in, Eddie! Why, Asey, we been waitin' an' waitin' an' waitin' for you, an' I don't know what I'd have done to keep from starvin' if Eddie hadn't had a pocketful of penny licorice jawbreakers! Where you been?"

"How'd you meet up with Little Arsenic?" Asey asked.

"Why, on my way over to the school to phone Doc Cummings," Jennie said casually. "I seen him in the woods an' chased him an' finally caught him. I thought gettin' hold of someone who was with the house durin' the movin' was a lot more important than a little old phone call!"

"I see. An' me havin' visions of your bein' strangled by a white, clawlike hand!" Asey said. "I been worryin' about you!"

"I can't think why! Asey, Eddie *saw* her!"

"Saw who?"

"Mrs. Pratt, of course! He was up in a tree. You see, he was runnin' from Pete, over by the pond—"

"I know all about that." Asey cut short her explanation. "Get on with Mrs. Pratt. What about her?"

"She was carryin' a big cloth knittin' bag," Jennie said, "an' she was cuttin' crosslots from where the house started over toward the pond. She—you tell him, Eddie!"

Between Jennie's promptings and Eddie's repetitions, Asey achieved a clear picture of Mrs. Pratt, bearing a bag large enough to hold a dozen Commando knives and purposefully darting through the woods, apparently with the intention of intercepting the moving house.

"Then what?" Asey asked, when Eddie finally paused.

"Well, then I heard the horses comin', an' the Hamiltons came," Eddie said. "Then I forgot all about Mrs. Pratt."

"Let's see now," Asey said. "Pete would've gone down that hill very slow—"

"Oh, he did!" Jennie interrupted. "That's where *I* saw her, you know. Almost walkin' along beside it!"

"*You* saw her? Jennie, why in time didn't you tell me that hours ago, when we found Liz?"

"Because until I pumped Eddie, I thought it was Page Kendall in the oven," Jennie said, "an' I thought Pete'd killed her there where the house was stopped. You see, it just so happened that from where I was pickin' my May-flowers I could see the house over at the inlet—what'd you say?"

"I said I thought the flowers was sort of second fiddle," Asey told her. "Go on."

"After the house started up, I couldn't see it again until it come down the hill. That's where Mrs. Pratt must've got in, after the Hamiltons rode away, an' when the house was goin' so slow."

"Did you see her get in?"

Jennie shook her head regretfully. "I knew your patience was runnin' short, an' you'd yelled at me to hurry, so I started back, sort of hopin' the house would be passin' the roadster about the time I got there. What *I* think is that she got in an' killed Liz. You know Liz was in the house all the time? Eddie told me that."

"An' Mrs. Pratt's got a Commando knife!" Eddie said eagerly.

"That's right, Asey. We watched her while she cleaned the blade, out on the back porch here. We seen quite a lot of what she's been doin'! Only I can't figure out any more. Eddie says he never swiped my knife at all, an' I've got to believin' he's tellin' the truth. That makes my knife dangle."

"Makes it what?" Asey demanded.

"Dangle. Don't you see, if Mrs. Pratt killed Liz with her own knife, then what about my knife? Who took it? What become of it? I tell you, Asey, I've figured every way I know, an' I can't understand about my knife! First I decided Mrs. Pratt killed Liz with her knife an' got off the house when you an' I saw it stop at the far end of the pond—"

"When Pop stopped for a log," Eddie broke in.

"But then I thought, *who* took *my* knife?" Jennie went on. "So I figured she could've got out when Pete stopped for your roadster. He blew his horn when he was on the shore, remember, an' Eddie didn't get out till we come up to the lane an' talked with Pete. They was both inside the truck cab. So she could have got out easy before we come. An' then while you backed the roadster out of the way an' kept Eddie out of mischief, Pete was still in the truck, an' I was all eyes for the house. I s'pose she could have taken my knife then. Only, how could she have got back in? I wasn't watchin' the knife, but I *was* watchin' the house! An' if she'd killed Liz with her knife, why take *mine?* It won't make sense!"

"On the contrariwise," Asey said, "it does, in a queer sort of way. You've made a nice point, that someone who'd just killed Liz with their own Commando knife might've taken the one from the Mayflowers, an' thus provided themselves with a spare. You might even call it a spare alibi. She couldn't have killed Liz with her knife because, see—she had it on the back porch!"

"Oh. Now that's something," Jennie said slowly, "I never considered—but no, Asey, that won't work out! Because she *must* have gone back into the house. She *had* to go back! Because *she* was the white, clawlike hand!"

"Mrs. Pratt was?"

Jennie nodded. "That's a little something else Eddie an' I seen," she said with quiet pride. "Her long white gloves. I must say I was dumb not to think of gloves right off! Of course, the murderer would've worn gloves to keep from leavin' fingerprints! I bet you thought that out first thing!"

"I been stuck in a lot of whitewash," Asey said. "What about these gloves of hers?"

"She *burned* 'em! Yes, sir, she did! She poured kerosene oil on 'em an' burned 'em up! I suppose I should have stopped her, only—"

"Only we didn't dare," Eddie interrupted. "She scared us. She kept lookin' around, an' she had a big pile of rocks she'd been heavin' at a woodchuck hole, right there. *Big* rocks, too!"

"He's right," Jennie said. "I'll admit I had Eddie show me the way here because I had some notion of talkin' with her an' maybe even marchin' her off to you as the guilty one. But after watchin' her a while, I decided it was safer if we waited for you to come. She's—well, you'll see what I'm drivin' at!"

"Before we drop in on Mrs. Pratt," Asey said, "tell me one thing. Did you happen to spot a pair of white overalls on a clothesline anywhere hereabouts? No? Wa-ell, I think you an' Eddie ferreted out enough!"

"I don't have to go in with you, do I?" Eddie demanded

anxiously, as Asey started the roadster up the drive toward the front door. "I can sit in the car, can't I? I won't touch a thing, not even the fishin' tackle. I don't *like* her!"

After ringing the ship's bell on the shell-crusted front porch, Asey glanced back at the car.

Eddie was sitting bolt upright, like a child in church.

And Jennie, standing by his elbow at the screen door, wore a drawn, tense expression, as if she were waiting for something to explode.

"Yes?" Just the tone of Mrs. Pratt's cold monosyllable made Asey understand Eddie's reaction. "What is it?"

One look at her white dress, white hair and cold, pale-blue eyes, and he sensed why the usually fearless Jennie had hesitated to tackle her alone. Personally, he felt as if he were staring an ice cube in the face.

"What is it?" she repeated.

Asey introduced himself and displayed the pin Page had given him. "I've been told this is yours?"

"Yes." Mrs. Pratt made no move to open the door.

"Perhaps your son," Asey said, "hasn't had the opportunity of tellin' you about Liz Tyler. She—"

"He phoned me about it. Where did you find my pin?"

"In the Dutch oven," Asey said, "where Liz Tyler's body was. D'you have any idea how it got there?"

"I never entered that house in my life. I haven't seen the pin for a week."

Mrs. Pratt, Asey thought, employed none of Page's devices, like dramatic pauses or elaborate shrugs. But she definitely managed to convey the impression that if her pin had been in the oven, someone else had placed it there.

"You have a Commando knife?" Asey inquired. "I think your son said so."

"Yes. I've just cleaned it for the war-trophy display."

"I see. An' perhaps you could tell me what you did after you left the inlet this mornin', after the house had been moved?"

"I came back here," Mrs. Pratt said. "I run an inn, you know."

"Eddie," Asey nodded toward the car, "thought he saw you walkin' toward the house. So did my cousin Jennie."

"Permit me to assure them both," Mrs. Pratt said, "that they are mistaken."

"Thank you. You won't mind if I keep the pin for the police, I'm sure." Asey turned, took Jennie's arm, and started for the stone steps. "Oh, by the way, Mrs. Pratt. One more thing. You mind explainin' why you burned them gloves?"

"Liz Tyler gave them to me as a present," she said, and Asey found himself wondering why the fire from her eyes didn't melt the screen in the door. "I couldn't refuse the gift, so I accepted it. Because I had no intention of wearing the gloves, ever, I destroyed them. There is, I presume, no law against that?"

"None I know of, ma'am. Good-by!"

The shell-crusted door slammed behind them as they entered the roadster.

"Well!" Jennie said. "Well, I never! Why didn't you harry her more? Why didn't you tell her we *knew?* Why'd you let her off so easy?"

"Why waste time?" Asey returned. "She made her points.

She's goin' to deny ever bein' in the house an' insinuate the pin is a plant—an' can you picture the cops tryin' to faze her with it? I can't. An' she flaunted that knife at us. An' she's goin' to deny walkin' toward the house after it started or bein' anywhere near it."

"But Eddie saw her! So did I!"

"Uh-huh. I'm sure you both did. But a good lawyer'd make hash out of what you claim you saw at that distance— you wasn't wearin' your glasses, was you? An' wasn't Eddie a bad boy skippin' school, an' hadn't he climbed a tree to escape a spankin'? An' as for those gloves she burned, I bet Liz *did* give 'em to her, probably in the presence of witnesses. Like Page an' Bob."

"I know one thing!" Jennie was seething with indignation. "*She'll* never get written up as any jolly innkeeper! I wouldn't stay in that awful shelly place with that old iceberg, not if it was the last hotel on earth! I should think Bob Pratt would thank his stars every night that she's only his stepmother! Think of bein' really related to someone like that! Where you goin' now?"

"To Calvert Hamilton's house," Asey said. "At least," he added with a chuckle, "Hamilton'll have to ask us in. We're potential votes!"

Jennie exclaimed over the broad sweep of green lawns as they turned into the grounds of the Hamilton estate.

"I wonder if it'd do any good to bring the Perkins boy here so's he'd know what a lawn should look like," she said. "The way he mows ours, he's only read about lawns in books. Oh, look at that formal garden! What a cute little boy spoutin' water out of his mouth!"

Eddie peered around interestedly. "Aw, it's only a statue!" he said. "Wonder how it works. Can I go in here with you?"

"I think," Asey said, "you'd best stay in the car an' amuse yourself with my fishin' tackle. I don't want to have to pull you out of lily ponds an' goldfish pools!"

It seemed to Asey that he and Jennie were kept waiting rather a long time in the broad front hall of the vast white house. Fully a quarter of an hour elapsed before a maid led them through a maze of halls to a room at the rear, overlooking more gardens.

"Goodness me!" Jennie said. "I must look close an' remember all this! What would you call it?"

"Search me!" Asey watched her survey the rattan furniture, the batik walls, and the framed water colors, and heard her exclaim at the leopard skin thrown carelessly over the back of one chair. Within two minutes, he knew, she'd memorized every leaf on the man-sized tropic plant in the corner, and he felt sure that the Sewing Circle was going to get an earful about the silver-lacquered wooden bowls sitting on a table made of solid glass, and the marble arms perched in a niche between the bookshelves.

"Ah, Mayo!" As Calvert Hamilton entered, Asey couldn't decide whether he looked more like a senator in the movies or a distinguished man extolling whisky in an advertisement. Certainly if he wore those riding clothes to rallies, he'd get the feminine vote. "How do you do! And— er—Mrs. Mayo. My daughter, Julie."

A sulky smile flitted briefly over Julie Hamilton's sulky mouth, and she tossed back her long blond hair with an impatient gesture. "How d'you do. Father, you're not going to be long, are you, darling? You've simply got to write your speech for tonight."

She spoke in a flat voice, without intonation, like a child reciting poetry, Asey thought.

"Yes, dear," Hamilton said. "I'm sure Mr. Mayo and his —er—cousin won't keep me long. I'm giving a little talk tonight at the war-trophy display," he added explanatorily. "Er—you've come for my comment about this terrible business of Liz Tyler, I assume? I met the doctor's wife in the village, and she told me. Julie and I are deeply moved, of course. I've already written a few lines to send over to Nick Fox for the *News*, expressing my sympathy. Just a short statement for the record."

"We're so sorry," Julie said. "Now, father, do run along back to your study and finish your speech!"

"Really, Julie!" Hamilton sounded embarrassed. "The Mayos will think you're trying to hurry them!"

"I'm sure they understand that you're a very busy person." Julie's eyes were fixed on the batik wall, as if she were concentrating, and Asey began to wonder if considerable rehearsing for this brush-off scene hadn't gone on during the interval in which he and Jennie had waited in the hall. "Run along, dear. We'll excuse you."

"*Will* you forgive my running?" Hamilton said. "Julie, see if perhaps you can't scare them up some tea. Why *not* stay to tea, Mayo? No trouble, I assure you. Delighted to have you, if you're able to stay."

"I'll go in and finish your typing as soon as I'm free." After managing another sulky smile in her father's direction, Julie paused.

Hamilton, in the doorway, also paused. Both were obviously waiting for their guests to take their departure.

But Asey winked at Jennie and strolled over to the windows overlooking the garden.

"Er—good-by," Hamilton said tentatively.

"Was she blackmailin' you?" Asey asked in conversational tones, as he turned from the window.

"I beg your pardon? Oh," Hamilton said, "I thought you were speaking to me! Good-by!"

Jennie took one look at Asey's face as he started for the door through which Hamilton had hurriedly left, and then sat back and smiled expectantly.

A minute later, Asey returned carrying Hamilton in his arms like a baby and dropped him into the chair with the leopard skin.

"Now, Mr. Hamilton," he said briskly, "it was a lovely brush-off you planned, but it isn't workin'. Had Liz been blackmailin' you, or just borrowin' money?"

"Don't tell him, father!" There was plenty of intonation in Julie's voice now. "Don't *tell* him! If the papers find out—"

"So it *was* blackmail," Asey said. "Thanks. Now, where's Nick Fox's Commando knife? At the trophy display, or here?"

He spoke to Hamilton, but Julie answered. "We haven't got it! It's—it's mislaid! It's at the display! It's *not* here!"

"Go get it," Asey said, "an' bring it to me. Bring me the silver box Pete says he let you take from the house this mornin', too. Right away, please!"

"I don't know what box you mean! And we haven't got the knife—"

"Get the box, get that knife! Bring them to me, at once!" Asey's quarter-deck voice didn't disturb Jennie, who had been waiting for it, but it had the effect of sending Julie out of the room as if she'd been shot from a gun.

"Mayo," Hamilton moistened his lips, "this is a very high-handed, I might say inexcusably high-handed—"

"Take off your coat."

"I must ask you to leave—"

"Take off your coat!" Asey said. "I want the police to investigate that smudge on the arm, which looks to me perilously like it come from the Dutch oven over in Page's house!"

Hamilton's face was like chalk. "I will not permit—"

"You can take the coat off," Asey said, "or you can preface your speech this evenin' with a few well-chosen words of explanation, like how you run into some doors, an' that's why you got them shiners!"

Without another murmur of protest, Hamilton took off his riding coat and gave it to Asey.

"Thanks. An'," he took the cigarette box and the Commando knife from Julie as she returned, "thank *you*! Now, go write your speech, Mr. Hamilton!"

"But the police! Really—"

"They'll drop by to see you," Asey said. "An' take my advice. Don't make the mistake of offerin' them tea, will you? Come on, Jennie!"

As he paused in the hall, Jennie clucked her tongue appreciatively. "Tch, tch, that was something *like*, Asey! That's what I call getting down to business—say, do you

know the way out? I don't think we come by this hall
you're turnin' into!"

"It's the way we're leavin'," Asey said.

"Why was Liz blackmailin' him?" Jennie asked. "Or *was*
she?"

"My guess is that she's been borrowin' money from
Hamilton like she did from Page. Casual an' careless an'
often."

"But was it really blackmail?"

"Wa-el," Asey said, "I'm sure Julie thinks it was, but I
gather Hamilton knew Liz well enough to know her borrowin' habits. An' with him so frightened of publicity, he
was probably only too glad to lend her all the money she
wanted—until after election. He wouldn't want to annoy
her into maybe chattin' about their relationship."

"But just his givin' her any money," Jennie said. "Isn't
that sort of politically bad?"

"Uh-huh, but Hamilton's politically new."

"What come over you all of a sudden in that room?"
Jennie inquired. "Did you see somethin' when you looked
out of the window then? Or did you just think of somethin'? What—"

She continued to pelt him with questions as she trotted
along behind him from one hall to another.

"Ah!" Asey said at last, and stopped at an open door.
"Here we are!"

Beyond them, at the back of a garden, stretched a long
white picket fence, freshly painted.

"What in the world," Jennie demanded, "are you ah-in'
at? A picket fence? What's a picket fence—"

She broke off as a thin, elderly man in white overalls

walked past the doorway and hung up a "Wet Paint" sign over one of the fence posts.

"Ah!" Asey said dreamily. "If that ain't a white, claw-like hand, I never seen one!"

Jennie stared at him blankly. "White, clawlike *hand?* But that's only old Enoch Snow, Asey!"

"Snow?" Asey turned quickly and faced her. "*Snow?* One of the old Snow-place Snows?"

"Why, yes," Jennie said. "He's a queer old thing, but harmless as the day is long. He—"

"Asey!" Dr. Cummings's voice rang out behind them. "Asey, are you—oh, I see. I must say," he added as he bustled up to them, "I thank God I'm not rich enough to live in a damned rabbit warren like this! Six music rooms!"

"*Six?*" Jennie said.

"Well, maybe I kept bumping into the same one over and over; I don't know. I've had a terrible day, Asey, and I don't know what I'd have done without Bob Pratt. We haven't even stopped to eat. Wasn't I right about Calvert Hamilton? Don't you think he's mixed up in this? Where have you got?"

"He's got to a picket fence," Jennie said, "that seems to have given him more pleasure than anything he's seen in years. I don't know why!"

"Doc," Asey said, "you know Enoch Snow, the old feller out there?"

"Sure. I meant to have written in my note to you that if you wanted any data about Murder House, ask him. That place is the only thing he's very lucid about or cares a rap for. He was born in it and lived there till his father died and the place was sold. Always hung around there, you know. Mrs. Hamilton let him work for her and sleep in the old barn, and when she died, Calvert took him under his wing. Bit queer," Cummings concluded.

"How queer? What d'you mean?"

"Oh, he just never was very solid mentally, but he's harmless enough. And when it comes to the history of Murder House, he's keen as a button. Nick Fox got all his dope for the paper from Enoch," Cummings said. "Nick told me the old fellow cried when he learned the place was to be moved. Wanted to rush right out and stop Page—"

"Asey!" Jennie interrupted. "I've just thought! Suppose *he*—listen, Enoch is sort of vague. Like sometimes he thought that Liz was Page! Suppose he killed Liz, thinking she was Page, who was movin' his precious house! Suppose—"

But Asey had turned and was making like a homing pigeon for the Hamilton's front door.

"Sounds like a splendid thought to me," Cummings said as he and Jennie followed. "But apparently Asey doesn't care for your Snow, or Old Settler, theory."

"Sometimes," Jennie said irritably, "I think I'll never understand Asey Mayo! He didn't follow up Mrs. Pratt—an' she was there, an' she has a Commando knife, an' she hated Liz, an' she burned up those gloves! An' he didn't follow up Calvert Hamilton just now. An' his ridin' coat's got a smudge on the arm like it came from his stickin' his hand in the Dutch oven. An' he had Nick's Commando knife, an' Julie Hamilton as good as admitted that Liz was blackmailin' 'im!"

"I don't understand a word of it, but it sounds horribly

incriminating," Cummings said. "Julie was pretty jealous of her father and Liz, my wife said."

"An' she was pretty hysterical an' suspicious-actin', if you ask me! But Asey—he's just passed 'em all up!"

"When I went back to Murder House a few minutes ago," Cummings held open the front door for her, "Nick Fox told me that Asey had left him on toast with a wonderful circumstantial case against him. He admitted he'd been in the house when it started from the inlet, and then hopped off."

"Him, *too*? That"— Jennie counted on her fingers— "that makes him, an' the Hamiltons, an' Mrs. Pratt that we all know was in the house, up there by the pond. An' goodness knows who couldn't have got into it while it was parked at the school, before Asey an' I come. Page could have, an'— Asey!" she called to him as he came around the corner of the house. "Where's Eddie gone?"

"I been lookin' about for him." Asey strolled over to them. "I think he must have got into some mischief an', since Bob's not in the car, I guess he's probably gone after him. What're you two discussin' so earnest?"

"Your suspects," Cummings said, "and how you've rejected them. Bob told me he had a feeling you'd have been after him, if I hadn't actually seen him mail his mortgage check at the post office this morning."

"An' did you?"

"Yes. . . . What're you picking up and dropping everyone like hot coals for? If there's any possibility of Enoch Snow's being involved, why not question him? And I do hope someone's pointed out to you that Pete Pulster's the biggest liar in the state! I shouldn't rely much on his word

—why are you entertaining his frightful child, by the way? I noticed him when we drove—oh, here's Bob! Located Eddie?"

Bob Pratt shook his head. "He was sabotaging a fountain and, when I tried to stop him, the little rat soaked me and ran away—look!" He pointed to his windbreaker.

"Are those *blood*stains?" Jennie asked.

"Page punched him in the nose," Cummings said, "and he's bled intermittently. Isn't that jacket a repulsive sight? I do wish, Bob, that you'd take it off or wash it off!"

"I could wash it in the fountain right now!" Jennie offered.

"No matter. I'm equally messy underneath," Bob said as he fumbled for a cigarette, "and I'm not sure I'm not going to bleed again any minute."

"We'll have to organize for Eddie," Asey said impatiently. "Bob, take that side of the house, will you? Doc, come with me this side. Jennie, blow the horn if you catch any sight of him. I want to get on!"

"Now," Cummings said, as he followed Asey, "tell me! What've you found out? And don't tell me you haven't got anywhere? I know that cat-and-canary look in your eye!"

"Why d'you always want me to go off half-cocked, doc?"

"Aha!" Cummings said with triumph. "Then you have *got* somewhere!"

"I only got some crazy ideas that won't jell—where *is* that kid? There's one thing I'm yearnin' to ask him!"

They found him at last, innocently sitting on an ornamental iron bench, playing with a kitten.

"I'm sorry about the fountain," he said. "I didn't *mean* to wet Bob. It just went off!"

"Uh-huh. Hustle along, now," Asey said. "I'm in a hurry. . . . Say, did you help your pop take that log out of the way, back at the pond this mornin'?"

Eddie nodded.

"What kind of a log was it, remember?" Asey asked casually. "Your pop told me, seem's if, but I forgot."

"Maple," Eddie said promptly.

Asey looked down thoughtfully at the child. He knew perfectly well that Pete had also said maple, but he had thought that Pete was merely trying to give an example of how to be detailed and specific.

"You sure, Eddie?"

"Pop an' I both noticed it. On account of there's no maple in them woods."

"Eddie," Asey put his hand on the boy's shoulder, "forget that maple log till tomorrow, will you? Don't speak of it again today. An' d'you like that fishin' tackle of mine? It's all yours." He gave Eddie a little push. "Get to it! Now, doc, listen to me!"

"Asey, what earthly difference does a *maple* log make?" Cummings demanded. "Why do you care if a log was maple or oak or pine?"

" 'On account of there's no maple in them woods,' " Asey quoted Eddie. "So that's where someone *left* a log, an' where someone *meant* to stop the truck. An' there Jennie an' I was, watchin' all the time, an' wrappin' wax paper around the stems of Mayflowers! Now, doc," he looked at his watch, "we got less'n an hour an' a half. You listen careful, because I can't think of another way to do this, an' it's got to work! You take Jennie an' Eddie, an' have Bob drive you to these places for me—"

Cummings stared at him when he concluded. "Some-times," he said in an awed voice, "sometimes you scare me, Asey! It won't work! It *can't*!"

"It's got to! Remember, now, at five minutes to six I'll be waitin'!"

At seven minutes to six, as Bob drove the doctor's car onto the main street of Pochet, Jennie said plaintively that she couldn't understand what Asey thought he was up to. "An' *you* don't care that I'm starved an' Eddie's starved. You just keep goin' to places on that old list of Asey's, an' never lettin' us stop anywhere for a bite! I don't know what you been seein' so many people for! The places don't make sense."

"Look," Cummings retorted, "I've told you a million times, I'm doing what Asey told me to do! I've got what he told me to get! We're supposed to meet him in the drug-store at six, and you can ask him yourself—oh, there's Page, and Nick, and the Hamiltons, and your mother, Bob, all going in. And Pete. Quite a group—*oh*!"

"What's the matter?" Bob asked as he got out of the sedan.

"My bills!" Cummings said. "If I don't remember to mail this batch of bills, my wife'll murder me with a Commando knife! Take 'em over to the post office for me, will you? I'm so tired, I haven't the strength! Come along, Eddie! Come along, Jennie. Meet you at the drugstore, Bob!"

"I don't see Asey! *He* isn't there!" Jennie said.

"Don't stop!" Cummings' voice was sharp. "Come on!

He's in the post office. Keep walking, Jennie! This may not work out even now!"

"What's he in the post office *for?*"

"Hop along to your old man, Eddie," Cummings said. "He's calling you. Asey's in the post office, probably hidden behind a War Bond poster, waiting with cops for Bob Pratt to mail the mortgage-check letter he said he mailed this morning—Don't stop, Jennie! That letter was his alibi, you see, that he left the inlet after the house started, and went about his business. Only he didn't. He killed Liz instead."

"*He* killed her?" Jennie said in a weak voice.

"Yes, and if you must stop and goggle, stop behind this car, and pretend to look into the drugstore window. Then I can watch the reflection and see if anything happens across the street. I wish they'd hurry!" Cummings said impatiently. "I hope nothing's gone wrong. . . . In a nutshell, Jennie, Bob had till six to mail his letter. He had to mail it before six because of the postmark. He knew that was something Asey could check up on. And with our two time changes a day, if he mailed it *after* six, it would be marked 6:00 a.m. tomorrow. Get it?"

"But why didn't he mail the letter during the day?"

"We think he meant to. Only," Cummings said with a grim smile, "Asey and I tied him up doing things for us, the first part of the day. Asey made him stay at the house, and then I put him to work driving for me. He never had a chance to get near the post office. This driving around, now, was deliberate, to keep him away. He's probably been itching to get to the post office, and he couldn't suggest stopping here or let me see him go near the place, because I unwittingly upheld his alibi."

"What d'you mean?"

"He foxed me into saying I saw him mail the letter. Said he saw me in the post office, and I agreeably assumed he did. I was there. Always do go there every morning around ten-thirty. Now," Cummings said, "we've given him every chance, including the excuse of mailing my bills. They're not, by the way. I picked up envelopes wherever I stopped on Asey's wild-goose-chase list and addressed 'em. . . . Jennie Mayo, I shall burst if something doesn't happen *soon*!"

"But the rest, in there!" Jennie pointed inside the drug-store. "What're they here for?"

"Oh, they're local color to soothe Pratt's suspicions, if he had any. Asey always thinks of ev—" Cummings smiled and shook his head as a shot rang out. "I *did* hope they'd take him without shooting! I wanted a soda myself. Well," he patted Jennie on the back, "as I always say to Asey, he and the cops catch, then I patch!"

Later that evening, Page and Nick and Jennie pounced on Asey as he drove up to Murder House, which was still parked on the Weesit line.

"There's still things Page doesn't understand!" Jennie said. "Explain it all to her!"

"Not all," Page said. "I understand how Bob put the maple log in the rut to stop the truck, so he could get on at the far end of the pond, and how he used a back road to circle there. I know he killed Liz with another Commando knife he had and about the letter posting being his alibi. But how'd you suspect him?"

"If someone planned to stop the truck," Asey said, "the

chances were they'd planned an alibi. Bob had the only real one. He'd mailed a letter. But I remembered how he kept fumblin' for cigarettes in one pocket that he kept zipped, an' then he had to reach into another pocket. I wondered why he wouldn't let his jacket be washed or touched. At Hamilton's, he wouldn't even take it off when Eddie soaked him. I decided he had the letter still in his pocket. An' he did."

"Why'd he take Jennie's knife?" Nick asked.

"From what he said, Bob intended to get off the house when Pete stopped to turn on the main road. But Pete stopped for my roadster, an' Bob recognized it an' got a little panicky. He took a chance an' slipped out—an' spotted Jennie's knife, an' grabbed it. Sort of clever of him. He had a spare knife to substitute for his second one, if anyone found out he'd had two. An', more important, he wanted me to follow the house an' find Liz."

"But why?" Page said. "I should think he'd have wanted to keep you away from it!"

"No; the quicker he set me goin', the better for him," Asey said. "The sooner I found Liz, the shorter space of time people would get quizzed about. An' he had his alibi— did Jennie tell you it was Bob who egged Liz on to wantin' to ride in the house durin' the movin'?"

"I guessed he must have," Nick said. "What did you mean when you told that cop that Bob didn't care a hoot about Liz? Wasn't that why he killed her, because she turned him down?"

"His sole interest in Liz," Asey said, "was to work on Page through her. He'd have put a stop to that Calvert

Hamilton affair, you know, if he'd really cared about her."

"Work on me for what?" Page demanded.

"To move your house. Because," Asey said, "once you moved it, Nick would have no further interest in his land and would sell it to Bob. Nick told Bob an' me, an' apparently everyone else that, once the house was moved, he'd sell the land to the first comer. Bob knew that, an' was goin' to be the first comer. That land adjoins the Shell Inn, which no one ever run at a profit or ever will, an' which the Pratts never had any intention of runnin' very long. But their nice level fields plus Nick's nice fields, plus the inlet, all would make a dandy airport, see?"

"Airport?" Page said. "Airport?"

"Uh-huh. Rumors been buzzin' around about an airport here for years. The *Pochet News* mentioned it in the last issue. But Nick was so busy thinkin' of his land in relation to you an' the house an' all, he never stopped to look an' see that he had part of a fine airport right in his hand. An' in about a week the Pratts were goin' to cash in. But—"

"What about Mrs. Pratt?" Nick asked. "Was she an accessory?"

"She was an accessory to the airport plan, but not to the murder. She told the cops that when Bob phoned her that Liz'd been killed, she guessed it was his work, but was frightened stiff that if she let on, Bob would go for her. There wasn't any love lost between that pair. The only reason they were together was poolin' their resources to buy the inn property. At least, that was Mrs. Pratt's story, an' I believe her. But Liz was the fly in the ointment. She found out what was goin' on."

"Why didn't she tell me?" Page said.

"Bob's a handy talker," Asey said. "He talked you from a state of nose-punchin' into comparative amiability in just a few minutes. He talked Liz into keepin' quiet, an' then talked her into wantin' to ride in the house. An' I still think he was pretty bright to pick a movin' house for his murder. . . . Now, Jennie, get in, an' let's get home!"

"The hand—was it really old Enoch Snow?" Jennie asked. "What was he doin' in there?"

Asey smiled. "He crept in early this mornin' to find a gold thimble his great-great-grandmother lost durin' the last movin'. And don't ask me why he expected to find it in *this* movin', or why he even knew it or thought of it! He was hunting around when all the people come, an' they scared him, so he hid under the trap door. He was kind of hazy about details, but he must've left when Page an' Bob were yellin' at each other. An', believe it or not, he found the thimble at the base of the dinin'-room wainscotin'. Happy as a clam with it, he was. . . . Now, Jennie, come on!"

Halfway home, Jennie gave a happy little sigh. "Tomorrow," she said, "we'll go get more."

"More what?"

"Mayflowers. Mine are all dead. Maybe," she added innocently, "we'll see the house goin' back. Isn't it nice to think it all turned out so fine with Page an' Nick, just as Mrs. Hamilton planned. Yes, tomorrow we'll go get *more* Mayflowers!"

"Tomorrow," Asey said, "I'm goin' fishin'! One murder in motion is enough for me!"

MURDER RIDES THE GALE

CAST OF CHARACTERS

ASEY MAYO—*Cape Cod detective*
JENNIE—*His talkative cousin*
MADAME MERTON—*Head of a girls' school*
SAM MERTON—*Her black-sheep son*
WILBUR MERTON—*Who tried to fool Asey*
LYNN CLIFFORD—*Teacher of English and History*
GREG DUDLEY—*Her fiancé*
DEBORAH RICE—*Athletics instructor*
ADELE PAROT—*The mysterious new teacher*
JINX GRANVILLE—*The outrageous student*
DR. CUMMINGS—*Medical examiner*

MURDER RIDES THE GALE

Asey Mayo, speeding in his Porter roadster along the Skaket shore lane, diagnosed the northeast storm coming up as one of Cape Cod's September superdoopers. Appraising the rising wind, the bulbous black clouds streaking overhead, the odd atmospheric light that cast a purple tinge over everything, from the white beach to the scrub pines, he decided he'd miss getting home before things broke by about ten minutes of his cousin Jennie's chatter. For even if she fulfilled her promise to be packed and waiting on the doorstep of the Merton Hall School for Girls, where she'd been helping the housekeeper prepare for opening day, Jennie would still waste time in conversational afterthoughts.

Storm or no storm, Asey thought, as he slowed for the turn into the school grounds, Jennie could be relied on to talk!

His grin faded suddenly, and he braked to a quick stop, at the sight of the bizarre procession hurtling down the driveway toward the gate for which he was heading.

"The crazy fools!" he muttered. "What're they *up* to?"

Shoving his yachting cap back on his head, he stared in bewilderment at the old-fashioned, hearselike carryall drawn by two galloping black horses, and driven by a terrified-looking young woman in red. Behind her a bespectacled young man pedaled furiously at a girl's bike three sizes too small for his long legs. Bringing up the rear was another girl, a white-faced blonde, riding a motor scooter whose backfires made Asey wince.

None of the fleeing trio noticed either him or the roadster as they swooped through the gate in front of him and swerved off down the lane in the opposite direction!

Involuntarily, Asey looked back toward the school to see what could be pursuing them. From the urgency of that headlong flight and the general aura of frenzied escape, he somehow expected at least one or two maniacs armed with shotguns. But no one emerged from the main building or either of its brick wings, no lions prowled around the well-kept tennis courts or the semicircle of Cape Cod cottages that served as dormitories. No school ever looked quieter or more placid.

Asey rubbed his chin. If those three weren't running away from something, they must be rushing *to* something. In that case, he wondered, why hadn't they all rushed off together in the carryall, instead of risking their lives three separate ways?

He turned and watched the procession curiously. Spitting clouds of smoke in its uneven wake, the motor scooter had taken the lead, and now the lurching carryall and the teetering cyclist were fighting it out for second place. All of them still give the impression of animals running hysterically ahead of a forest fire.

"I hope," Asey said aloud, "you all got good, strong collarbones! Because, whatever you may be aimin' for, you're goin' to land in the ditch when the storm breaks!"

With a shrug, he drove on between the stone gates, whose posts were topped with grinning gargoyles, and drew up by the terrace outside the dining-room wing.

His eyes opened wide as he glanced down at the flagstones and found them littered with a miscellaneous assortment of lethal weapons—old muskets, old flintlock pistols, old Indian tomahawks. And he unashamedly blinked as Jennie, wearing an apron over her print dress, bustled through the door brandishing a cavalry saber.

"What in time," Asey demanded as he got out of the car, "are you wavin' that around for? What're you doing with this arsenal out here—repellin' boarders?"

"It's part of the library ornaments I been trying to get dusted and polished, and don't you scold me for not being ready!" Jennie vigorously shook a can of metal polish. "We been having a terrible distractin' afternoon—we've lost twenty-two girls!"

"That's a lot of girls," Asey said. "Er—where'd you see 'em last?"

"That's just it; we've *never* seen 'em! They haven't come! And I can't go home now. I got to stay and get cocoa and sandwiches for the poor things when they do arrive."

"You mean," Asey asked, with a grin, "they're not so much lost as sort of strayed in transit?"

"They're lost, I tell you. . . . Asey," Jennie wailed, "why didn't you dress up to come here? I been bragging about my famous detective cousin they call the Codfish Sherlock, and how you're a Porter director and home on vacation from makin' Porter tanks, and you turn up in dungarees and rubber boots like a fisherman! I promised

Madame Merton you'd find the girls if they didn't come, and I declare I'll be ashamed to introduce you to her. She's the head, you know. Her first husband was the Reverend Merton, the son of old Cap'n Merton—"

"Whoa up!" Asey interrupted. "What's this all about, Jennie? Where *are* those lost girls?"

"As if I wasn't trying to explain. Listen, now! This Boston woman who's supposed to herd this batch of girls onto the Cape train, she phoned, all excited-like, that the girls were lost and somethin' was wrong with the train! Before she calmed down enough to make sense, she was cut off. She's never phoned back, and Madame can't reach her. I tell you"—Jennie lowered her voice confidentially—"fur's been flyin' here! Madame's so mad! Why, the way she sent Mr. Merton and those two girl teachers packin' a few minutes ago—like they'd been shot out of a gun!"

"Oho!" Asey said. "So that's who those three were. What were they rushin' to, anyway?"

"Madame sent 'em to cover the stations. You see, we kept expectin' to hear more from the Boston woman, and first thing we knew it was nearly train time, and Mr. Merton remembered there wasn't a drop in the regular school bus. And did Madame make 'em scurry then, harnessin' the horses and gettin' the scooter goin', and all! And everybody white-hot mad! I had a feelin' they never wanted to go to stations so much in their lives—anywhere to get away from her tongue!"

"You keep sayin' 'stations,'" Asey said. "Why more'n one?"

"Well, even if that woman lost the girls in Boston, each

has her ticket and directions to get here. By rights they'd come to the Skaket station—that's where Miss Clifford was goin' with the carryall. But troop trains've upset the service. Mornin' train was a bus, and no one'd say for sure the afternoon train wouldn't be a bus, too. So Miss Rice went to the Billingsgate bus station, and Mr. Merton to the Tonset one. Mr. Merton's only—" Jennie broke off abruptly. "Here's my cousin Asey, Madame!"

Asey turned and looked interestedly at the white-haired woman in the black dress who had so quietly approached. The purple lace shawl over her shoulders and the touch of white at her throat gave her an air of fragility which was further accented by the carved ivory cane on which she leaned. Her blue eyes reminded Asey of someone he'd recently seen, but he couldn't track down the elusive resemblance.

"Mr. Mayo." There was a note in her voice which made Asey feel his appearance was a disappointment to her. "Since Jennie has said that we may count on your aid, perhaps you'll start by taking me to the old West River railroad station?"

" 'Course he will," Jennie said promptly. "I thought of there, too. It used to be the regular school stop— Hurry, Asey!"

"I'm just thinkin', it's goin' to pour any minute, an' the roadster top is down for the duration—"

But Madame Merton was already seated in the car.

"The short cut," she told him peremptorily as they left the school grounds. "There, to the right."

Asey rather dubiously surveyed the overgrown rutted

lane. As he turned to warn Madame Merton that the passage would be bumpy, he remembered where he'd seen blue eyes like hers before; they belonged to a Tank Corps general who'd inspected the Porter plant!

Without comment, he aimed the car at the ruts.

Back on the tarred road a few minutes later, Asey relaxed his grip on the wheel, darted a look at his companion, and privately decided that the only fragile thing about her was her lace shawl!

"Seems to me," he observed, "you go to—uh—considerable lengths to make sure your girls're met."

"Our catalogue," Madame Merton said tranquilly, "promises that girls will be met on arrival, and they are."

"Isn't abidin' by catalogues sort of hard these days?"

"Sometimes. Last week we encountered some difficulty in locating at short notice a new teacher of French and Spanish who also knew Russian, as the catalogue specified. But we did. Now, you may leave me here"—she indicated the boarded-up station ahead—"and, if you will, I'd like you to go to the main Skaket station and help Miss Clifford with the carryall. I'm quite capable of returning to the school by myself."

Asey was within a mile of Skaket village when the heavens fell in layers of water which the wind picked up, an instant before they touched the ground, and sent swirling back toward the sky.

He was soaked before he could stop to put on his oilskin coat, and as he struggled to set the overwhelmed windshield wiper going again, a yellow coupé passed at tremendous speed—another Porter, he noted professionally, wiping from his face the churned-up mud it had thrown at him. Although his own pace was far more moderate when he started up again, he splashed in a similar manner a sedan stalled by the side of the road. Howls of rage floated after him from the splattered driver.

The Skaket station was closed and empty. There was no sign of a train, of the carryall, nor of the missing girls. Nor could he see, as he drove slowly back, any trace of the motor scooter or the cyclist. Nor of Madame Merton at the West River station, to which he felt it only his humanitarian duty to return.

Back at the school, the driveway was a river, the tennis courts were ponds. He circled around to an old barn he'd noticed in the rear, and drove in. He had just about decided to slosh on up to the main building, where Jennie could no doubt provide him with dry clothes, when he saw the carryall loom out of the deluge and careen toward the open door.

Noticing without surprise that the wildly galloping horses had no driver, he stepped aside and watched them come to a halt, shivering and panting, while the carryall continued to lurch, its rear door banging.

He dismissed as nonsensical his sudden feeling that the vehicle contained passengers, but still he looked inside.

A second later he whipped back to the roadster and grabbed his flashlight.

Instead of twenty-two youngsters, there was only one occupant, a black-haired young woman in a dark red dress, with an orchid pinned on her shoulder and a silver fox scarf dangling around her neck. She was sitting on the long side seat, her arms slung through the side straps, her head bent forward.

Even before he reached her side Asey knew that she was dead. And the wound on the base of her skull had not been caused by any accidental slatting around inside the carryall, for the straps supported her and there was a padded cushion behind her.

Whoever she was, she had been murdered.

As he automatically played his flashlight around the interior of the carryall, Asey found himself wondering what sort of blunt instrument had been employed. Obviously, it had been pointed—but not too pointed—and it had been wielded with force. But the cramped interior precluded the use of a very large object, for the top was too low to permit anyone of even average height to stand erect, and the narrow aisle would cause an uncomfortable knee jam if two tall people chose to sit directly opposite each other.

A tentative swing with his right arm succeeded in barking his knuckles and very nearly smashing the flashlight, but at least he proved to his own satisfaction that no one standing up had much elbow room.

"I wonder," he murmured, "if she *was* killed in here."

He decided that she had been. The matted floor showed no mudstains, or footprints other than his own. Her clothes were dry and unspotted with rain, and her dress looked very much as if she'd sat down and smoothed it out herself, not as if she'd been lifted or dragged onto the seat by someone else. And there were no visible signs of any struggle.

"S'pose," Asey thought aloud, "someone was standin'— or sittin'—sort of sideways to her. Whatever they bashed with, it'd have to be somethin' small an' innocuous-lookin', or this girl'd have got suspicious. You can't cuddle up to someone with a reasonable facsimile of a blackjack in your hand, an' not at least have 'em edge away!"

But, of course, you could almost always trap even the most suspicious person by suggesting excitedly that they look at something, quick! And while his head was conveniently turned, you could bash with ease and to your heart's content.

Asey sighed. As his old friend Dr. Cummings, the medical examiner, always feelingly remarked, while a bash was as easy to diagnose as a common cold, it was just as hard to be specific concerning the cause of the first as the cure of the latter!

He shouldn't waste time surmising, he told himself. All he could be sure of was that the young woman was too old to be a pupil, that she had been killed before the storm struck, before the murderer had got wet enough to leave any dripping footprints. At least, it had all happened within the hour.

He left the carryall, walked to the barn door, and stood hesitantly by the threshold. He wanted to go phone Dr. Cummings and notify the state police, but he didn't want to leave the girl and the carryall alone. He wanted to set out at once in the roadster and find Miss Clifford and question her, but he knew that she might have been spilled off along the wayside of any one of the three roads leading from the village. If she were injured, if the blinding rain kept up, it would take a posse to locate her.

Jennie, splashing into sight under an enormous black umbrella, seemed to be the answer to his problems.

"For goodness' sakes, I never saw *you* come!" she said in

astonishment as she laid the umbrella down on the barn floor. "I saw the carryall, and I came to help Miss Clifford rub down the horses. Poor things, they're all lathered! Where's Madame?"

"If she's not back," Asey said, "it's no fault of mine. I tried—"

"Where's Lynn Clifford? Is that her inside?" Jennie peered into the carryall, and when she spoke again, her voice was a full octave higher: "Asey *May*-o! She— Oh, how awful! Who *is* she?"

"My guess," Asey said, "is that she's most likely the new teacher of French, Spanish, an' Russian."

"But where's Lynn Clifford?" Jennie demanded.

Asey shrugged. "Bounced off, I'd say."

"Tch, tch!" Jennie clucked her tongue. "I been worryin' about her and the horses. Oh, for her sake, I—" She stopped short and bit her lip.

"You what?" Asey inquired.

"Oh, nothin' much, really. I hadn't ought to have thought of it, even, because I must say Lynn Clifford's been real nice to me this week I been here, and Ella—Mrs. Parr, that is— *she* says—"

"Who's she?" Asey interrupted.

"Who's she!" Jennie's indignation knew no bounds. "She's the housekeeper I wrote you all about, and practically your own relation! *Her* great-great-grandfather and *your* great-great-grandmother was—"

"Distantly connected. I remember. What does Ella say?"

"Well, Ella says Lynn Clifford's always nice and accommodatin', and no trouble, ever, and no complaints about the food, which goodness knows Ella does as well with as any-one could these days. Lynn Clifford taught in a very swell New York school before she came here, you know. If she hadn't been sick, and the doctor wanted her to go to the country, she wouldn't've come here to Merton. A fine girl, and nice-lookin', too. Ella says that road engineer, the gov-ernment one that boards in Weesit, is head over heels in love with her. An awful nice girl— What're you grinning about?"

"Go on an' tell me," Asey said. "What about this Lynn Clifford an' the new teacher?"

"I never said a *thing* about her and the new teacher!" Jennie protested quickly. "Not a *thing!* Why, they don't even know each other! They never even seen each other! Ella's just an old gossip sometimes, the way she runs on about things. *I* don't see how anyone that had to teach French and Spanish and Russian would have any time left to teach English and history, besides!"

"I get it," Asey said. "There was some talk that this new teacher might take over Lynn Clifford's job. That right?"

"Ella didn't say that! She just said the new teacher was so much more expensive than old Mademoiselle had been, that most likely Madame Merton'd inveigle her into teach-ing English, too, and make Miss Rice take on history, and then they wouldn't need Lynn, see? Or else Madame'd get someone to do Lynn's job for less than Lynn gets, to even up expenses. . . . Asey, sometimes you make me so mad, the way you *worm* things out of people! I can see it written on your face that you already wonder if Lynn didn't kill this girl so's she wouldn't lose her job! Why," Jennie sniffed, "you aren't even sure this girl is the new teacher! If *I* was a famous detective, I think I'd have enough wit to find her pocketbook and look inside and learn her name!"

"She hasn't got a pocketbook," Asey said gently.

" 'Course she has! All women have!"

Asey shook his head. "If she had one, either someone swiped it, or else it fell on the floor and bounced out."

"Robbery!" Jennie said with triumph. "Someone stole her bag, and then killed her when she tried to stop 'em!"

"If someone had only taken her rings an' watch an' that diamond bracelet on her right wrist," Asey said, "I maybe might be inclined to agree with you."

"Hm. How d'you s'pose she came? By train?"

"Search me. But if it was a Boston train she came on, looks like your twenty-two girls is still lost."

"If she is Miss— Asey, how'd you pronounce P-a-r-o-t?"

"My French's awful rusty," Asey said, with a grin. "Call her Parrot, and I'll understand."

"Well, if it's her, she wasn't comin' from Boston. She was gettin' on at the Junction."

"Oh. I wonder, Jennie, if instead of runnin' the afternoon train straight from Boston, they didn't use a bus from Boston to the Junction, an' a train from there down. In that case, the Parrot girl got the train there all right, but the twenty-two kids probably missed connections. . . . Jennie, d'you mind stayin' here while I go to the house an' phone Doc Cummings an' the cops?"

"What you plannin' to use for a phone?" Jennie returned.

"Golly," Asey said in dismay, "are the phones gone?"

"They went dead almost before the first drop of rain

struck. The electricity's off, too, and the shore lane's flooded. We're marooned here, as far as roads go. Only way to get any place is to do a lot of circlin' on foot."

Asey whistled softly. "I kind of forgot how exposed to the elements we was over here on the shore!"

"And"—Jennie took off her raincoat—"sorry as I am for Miss Parrot, we got to see to these horses before we do anythin' else. If your father knew you let horses stand!"

She continued to find fault with him as they set to work unharnessing:

"All thumbs! Let me undo that buckle— Oh, it's broken. I *told* Lynn not to hammer the clasp. . . . Asey!"

"What's the matter now?"

"Don't make any noise," Jennie said in a whisper, "but glance up into that old mirror over the feedbin. Somethin's just sneaked in the side door of the shed! See, beyond the school bus?"

The cracks and blank spaces in the mirror gave a distorted view of a draped figure which first seemed to be nineteen feet tall, and then not much higher than a mushroom. By craning his neck, Asey finally got a clear reflection of a girl, wrapped to her ears in some involved and mysterious drapery.

"If there was twenty-one more of her," Asey said, "I'd guess that the lost was found."

"Sh! She's comin' in here. Duck back an' let's see what she's up to!"

From behind the stall partition, they watched with interest as the girl, a slip of a thing with short, curly brown hair, unwound herself from a sodden blanket, and then removed from her person two sweaters and a scarf. Rolling them all into an untidy bundle, she popped the whole dripping heap into a lidded chest near the door.

As she wiped her hands dry on the hem of her navy-blue suit, Asey got the impression that, with the hiding away of her castoff coverings, a great weight had been removed from her mind. She was almost dancing as she turned and tiptoed toward the Porter. It seemed to amuse her, for she giggled at it.

But the sight of the horses and the wet carryall had a strangely sobering effect on her. After surveying them thoughtfully for several moments, she made a beeline for the vehicle's rear door.

"Hold on there!" Asey stepped forward.

She jumped at the sound of his voice, stared at him for a split second, and then darted around the roadster, past the school bus, and out the door by which she'd entered.

The slip of a thing, Asey discovered as he raced after her, was not only fleet of foot but also entirely unmoved by the force of the storm. She simply stuck her head down and dived into the rain.

She couldn't keep up that pace very long, Asey thought, as she swerved and headed into the orchard. Neither, he realized almost at once, could he.

His feet suddenly went flying out from under him, and when he picked himself up the girl had completed vanished.

"Shinnied up a tree, I bet," Asey muttered as he wiped his face on his coat sleeve. "An' if you think I'm goin' to scramble around an' pluck you out of boughs— Oho!"

Something was moving behind one of the trees to his

right. Stepping carefully to prevent another tumble, Asey strode across a patch of grass, reached out his hand, and grabbed in an iron grip the blue-clad shoulder that was visible.

A second later he let go and stood back.

This wasn't the same girl he'd been chasing! From the previous glimpse he'd had of her, and from the scarlet jacket tied around her waist, he recognized Lynn Clifford.

She was daubed with mud from head to foot, and one side of her face was swollen and bruised. Although she was looking straight at him, she didn't appear to be aware of his existence.

"Come on, Miss Clifford," he said. "Grab hold of my arm, an' I'll help you— Huh! Guess I'd better carry you! Alley-oop!"

He was halfway to the barn with her before he realized that in her right hand, almost literally under his nose, she was tightly clutching a small triangle of broken brick.

An object, he reflected, that very neatly approximated his general specifications for a blunt instrument that could have been wielded successfully within the confines of the cramped carryall!

Jennie, waiting in the doorway of the shed, clucked over Lynn like a worried mother hen.

"If she managed to get to the orchard from wherever she an' the carryall parted company," Asey said, "she can't be too banged up. Move the stuff off that workbench near the roadster. I'm going to set her down there. I think she's just bruised an' dazed."

"What she went through even before the storm was

dazin' enough," Jennie said, "with Madame on the rampage— What say, dear?"

"Miss Parot!" Lynn pointed toward the carryall. "Did she get here all right?"

She pointed with the hand in which she still clutched the piece of brick, and Asey noted that the sight of it removed from Jennie's manner a sizable chunk of maternal solicitude.

"Did she—?" Lynn paused and looked at Asey as if she were seeing him for the first time as a person and not as part of a bad dream. "You're Asey Mayo, the detective! I've seen pictures of you!"

"Yup," Asey said. "Hold still, please, till I set—"

With a quick movement she wrenched herself out of Asey's arms, ran to the carryall, and jerked open the rear door.

Jennie started to draw her away, but Asey put out a restraining hand. He wanted to see what the girl would do. If her dazed state was a pose, she would probably follow up her act with wild hysterics and a flock of disjointed questions, all of the "I *don't* understand!" "*How* did it happen!" variety.

Instead, she turned to him quietly. "When I recognized you just now, I thought you'd come because there was some trouble. I see there is."

"You know anything about it?" Asey inquired.

"After we left the station, I felt something was wrong. The horses did, too. They acted queerly, and it wasn't just because of the wind or the storm." Her eyes were very bright, but she winked back the tears. "May I sit down in your roadster? Just for a minute?"

"Sure. Help her, Jennie. Thank Heaven!" he added, as he

saw a man approaching the open barn door. "Here comes young Merton. He can take charge of roundin' up his mother an' that other teacher, while I—"

"He isn't—" Jennie began.

"Oh, I see he ain't Merton. Probably someone that got marooned on the shore road. Well, we'll lend him a horse to get to the village with if he'll get hold of Cummings an' the cops."

He started toward the young man who was marching into the barn, but before he could open his mouth to speak, the young man darted outside, scooped up a handful of mud from the nearest puddle, and flung it square at Asey's face!

"There!" The young man spoke so furiously that he drowned out Jennie's indignant splutterings. "I promised myself I'd do that if I ever saw you again! How do *you* like it? How would you like it if there were a few stones in that mud, and you wore glasses, and the stones smashed the frame? It's simply God's will I'm not picking the lenses out of my eyeballs! You rich Willies with Porter cars ought to get a sock in the teeth!"

"D'you mind"—Asey's voice had the purring note which Jennie had learned to treat as a danger signal—"tellin' me what in time this is all about, what you got against people with Porters, an' me in particular?"

"You know! Back on the shore road a while ago—first one Porter tears by and blinds me with mud, then *you* tear by and smash my glasses. And you're going to pay—"

"Greg," Lynn interrupted, "stop acting like a child! Mr. Mayo, this is Greg Dudley, and I apologize for him. He's an engineer, and ordinarily quite sane."

"But he damn' near blinded me!" Greg said defensively. "Uh—Mayo, did you say? *Asey* Mayo?"

"Yes. Now go sit in the corner and cool off. I've got things to tell him."

"But— Well, look here, Lynn; I want you to know I started for the station the minute Mrs. Hopkins gave me your message, but then I got tied up with a call from the boss, and then with the storm, and—uh—" He turned to Asey. "I'm sorry I pasted that mud at you, sir. But I've been so worried about Lynn's getting back safely with the horses."

"Progressive irritation," Asey said. "I understand. Miss Clifford, did Miss Parot come on a Junction train?"

Lynn nodded. "To my surprise. I really didn't expect any train at all. When she said she hadn't seen the girls, I decided they must be on some bus that missed connections with the train. I went into the station to phone the Junction about them, but the line was busy."

"When'd you phone Mr. Dudley?" Asey asked casually.

"When I first got to the station, before I knew the train was coming. I simply couldn't face driving back alone. Then Miss Parot had lost her handbag—left it on the train, she thought—so I tried to phone about that, too. But the lines were all tied up, and I was in *such* a rush to get back before the storm hit. Finally the agent promised he'd take care of everything, so I dashed out, asked Miss Parot if she was all right, and we set off."

"Huh," Asey said. "So you saw her an' talked with her before you left the station, did you?"

"Well," Lynn said, "not exactly. I mean, I called out and said, 'Are you all right? Hang on; we're starting,' or something like that, and she said, 'Yes.' I didn't actually look in at her. I'd wasted so *much* time—certainly ten minutes—in the station. Anyway, I headed for the bridge road, and we got along all right till a buckle broke on Jerry's harness."

"I knew they'd break, with your hammerin' on 'em so!" Jennie interrupted. "I told you as much!"

"I know you did. Well, I got off to try fixing it again, and the storm hit. The horses bolted. From there on, I'm vague. I started to run, and then I just went to pieces." Lynn made a little gesture of despair. "Mr. Mayo, how did it happen?"

"You didn't talk with her, or hear her say anythin' after leavin' the station?"

"It was blowing so," Lynn said. "We couldn't have carried on a conversation even if I hadn't had my hands full, driving."

"Did she," Greg Dudley asked hesitantly, "did she—uh—get back here all right?"

"You'd better go look in the carryall," Lynn told him.

Greg's low "The poor thing!" was the same phrase Jennie had used, Asey recalled. But Greg's words were more personal, almost as if he knew her and felt a sense of loss.

Asey watched him, but put his question to Lynn: "Did you ever see this girl before?"

Lynn shook her head positively as she got out of the roadster. "No. . . . It's all right if I go along now, isn't it? I want a bath and some dry clothes— Oh, I can walk!" she said in answer to Jennie's offer of help. "Greg can give me an arm to lean on. Come on, Greg!"

For a person who'd wanted to sit down a few minutes

before, Asey thought, she was now in a curious rush to leave.

Greg, holding her coat for her, noticed for the first time the triangle of brick still clutched in her hand. "It won't— uh—be much help, but—Mr. Mayo, perhaps I ought to tell you"—he couldn't seem to take his eyes off the brick— "before someone else does. I knew Adele Parot. I was engaged to her when I was in college." He drew a long breath. "Lynn knew I'd been engaged. I told her so. But she didn't know it was Adele!"

"Of course I knew," Lynn said coolly.

"*I* never told you!"

"Plenty of other people did. Mother wrote me about it when I first mentioned your name. She'd known someone who knew Adele— Greg, stop looking so overcome! I'm sure Mr. Mayo isn't going to assume I killed your ex-fiancée because I'm more or less your current one!"

"But look— Oh, for God's sake, Lynn! What's that thing in your hand?"

"In my hand? Oh," Lynn said with a laugh, "how silly of me! I didn't realize I had it. I picked that up to hammer the buckle with before I saw it was broken. Apparently I've been cherishing it like crown jewels ever since. Nervous reaction, I suppose." She paused. "Oh, I *see*. You think— Why, Greg Dudley!"

"I never said so!" Greg couldn't get the words out fast enough. "I never said I thought you hit her with that!"

"But you *thought* it! So that's why you've been floundering around so and bringing up Adele! Putting up a smoke screen because you think I need to be shielded! Mr. Mayo, you don't think that, too, do you? You can't consider *me* a suspect!"

"Wa-el." Asey was still watching Greg. "I don't know as the cops'll label you a suspect exactly, but you can't brush off the fact that you seem to've been the only person around while a murder was committed. If I was you, I wouldn't be surprised when the cops held me for questionin'."

"I won't stand for that!" Greg Dudley rose to the bait, as Asey hoped he would. "I knew Adele was coming here before Lynn knew. Adele wrote me." He pulled a mauve-colored letter out of his breast pocket. "Here, read it! I can recite the opening line to you. It says, 'Probably you'll want to kill me when you know I'm entering your life again.' How she knew I was here, I don't know. But if you and the cops have to collar a suspect, don't pick on Lynn. Take me! No one could have a better motive than wanting to erase his ex-fiancée who's about to bust up his life!"

"What leads you to believe," Asey said, "that she intended doin' anything of the sort?"

"Busting is her specialty!" Greg said bitterly. "Marriages engagements—she couldn't keep out of other people's lives. So I've got motive enough, and I could have killed her during the time Lynn stopped to fix that buckle, and still have got over on the beach road by the time you splashed me. And as for a weapon—" He stopped, smiled, fished in his trench-coat pocket and held out a brass water faucet. "There you are, Sherlock! It's *better* than a brick!"

Ten minutes later Asey stood in the barn door, puffing at his pipe and not more than half listening to Jennie's monologue on the conclusions which she personally had achieved.

" 'Course, Greg Dudley's an awful irascible boy. But he must love Lynn a lot to act like he did to protect her. You see how he put his arm around her when they left? Men are so dumb!"

"So?" Asey said. "Why?"

"Why, it only made him get more soaked," Jennie said practically, "and Lynn wasn't in the mood for it, anyway. But *I* never suspect that excitable, fly-off-the-handle kind in stories. It's the other kind, the broody ones, that always turn out to be guilty."

"Bashin' "—Asey knocked out his pipe—"isn't what you'd sum up as a broody murder. Doc Cummings says brooders poison, an' the jumpy ones bash. Now, the other teacher— What's she *like?*"

"Deborah Rice? Oh, she's a lot different from Lynn. Pleasanter and more friendly, but a whole lot plainer-lookin'. She gets along fine with Madame, and takes just as much pride in the school and doin' things right." Jennie thought a moment. "If she were a man I'd call her sort of self-made. She's a hard worker and awful ambitious. Wants to have a school of her own one day. She helped me a lot, and she didn't have any call to. She has charge of athletics and games, and she teaches the very young girls. . . . Look, Asey; there's one thing I got to tell you before you go, or you'll make an awful break. I know you're usually polite, but when you talk to Madame, remember—"

"I'll be politer than Mr. Post," Asey assured her. "Say, if you'd been in that carryall at the station, an' I yelled out I was startin', an' to hang on, what would you answer?"

"Funny, that struck me, too!" Jennie said. "I don't know as I *wouldn't* say, 'Yes,' but there's so many other things I'd probably say instead. Like, 'I'm all right' or 'Let's go.'"

"Uh-huh, I wouldn't have said it, either. An' I don't think anyone as glittery an' dashin' as Miss Parot would've been content with anything so simple an' restrained. Yup, I think that's a mite fishy!"

"How do you really feel about them two?" Jennie asked.

"Lynn's pretty bland. As for Greg—there's nothin' more disarmin' than to claim you done somethin', in such a way that nobody believes you. . . . I'm goin' to the house now and see if the phones are workin' yet."

The rain had stopped, and there was even a patch of blue sky, Asey noticed as he strolled around the mud puddles toward the main building. He flipped open the iron latch of the dining-room door and walked past the rows of pine tables to a hall.

After a moment's hesitation, he continued toward the opposite wing, where he assumed the school offices would be. He knew that the old, central section of the building had once been the Merton family's home, but he wasn't quite prepared for the splendor of the high-ceilinged, glass-chandeliered parlor.

A sudden feeling of guilt at leaving wet footprints on the high gloss of the parquet floor made him turn back toward the hall.

Madame Merton stood in the doorway, dry and unruffled, leaning on her ivory cane.

Asey decided it must be the white lace shoulder shawl, which had replaced the purple one she'd worn earlier, that made her look so much less regal and so much more motherly. But there was nothing motherly about her manner, nor about her voice.

"Lynn has just told me what happened, Mr. Mayo, and there is one point which I cannot emphasize too strongly." Each word fell like an icicle. "You must see to it that no mention of Merton Hall is made in connection with this affair. No mention whatsoever! It can be called 'The Skaket Murder,' or 'The Carryall Murder,' or 'The Storm Murder,' but under no circumstances are you to permit anyone to refer to it as 'The Merton Hall Murder'! Do you understand?"

"Uh-huh," Asey said. "But I'm not the title department, you know. What the reporters may dream up—"

"May I point out to you," Madame Merton interrupted, "that since you have seen fit to assume considerable responsibility, I shall insist that you also make yourself responsible for the nomenclature of this case!"

Asey, recalling Jennie's injunction to get along well with Madame, choked back the first comment that came to his lips.

"I know you won't mind my pointin' back to you that I found Miss Parot," he said, "an' that I sort of had to assume responsibility, no one else bein' available."

"Furthermore," Madame said, "I wish that carryall and its contents removed at once from the school grounds and returned to the spot where the murder was committed."

Asey decided that even Jennie couldn't expect him to take that graciously.

"Madame Merton," he said, "maybe I assumed responsibility, but I'm goin' to keep on assumin' it till the cops can get here. I got some honorary police badges in the car, an' if it'll make you happy, I'll string 'em across my chest. Just bear in mind that anyone tryin' to move that carryall or disturb its contents will have to figure out first what to do with my dead body. Now. Are the phones workin'? . . . No? Well, then, when Mr. Merton gets back, he'll have to walk to the village an' get word to the cops for me. . . . By the way, how'd you get back from the River station without gettin' drenched?"

"I walked. I was quite wet, but I've had time to change. Mr. Mayo, perhaps I appeared unreasonable in wanting that carryall moved." From her slight hesitancy, Asey gathered that Madame was not accustomed to making concessions. "But certainly you must understand that it would be fatal to have the school's name involved with a murder.

"Consider, Mr. Mayo!" She raised her cane and tapped his arm lightly. "For forty years I've built up the good name of Merton Hall. I've carried it through wars and depressions—" She paused. "Had Miss Parot been killed here, had any of us known her at all, we'd be forced to accept the consequent publicity. But do I deserve to have my work and our reputation ruined, merely because two frightened horses instinctively made for their barn?"

"I think you could suggest to the cops an' reporters," Asey said, "that if two horses brought a body in a carryall to headquarters, or to a newspaper office, it wouldn't be quite fair to sum up the event as 'Murder on the Sergeant's Desk,' or 'Murder in the Copy Room.' Hadn't you ever met the girl?"

"Mr. Merton only interviewed her last week—" She broke off and started up the hall. "I thought I heard a bicycle bell. I've been listening for Mr. Merton— Ah, I was right!"

Asey noticed that her eyes lighted up as the young man, even muddier and more bedraggled than Lynn, wearily entered.

"Leave your shoes by the door, Wilbur, and then go up and change at once!" It was clear that, to Madame, her son was still a small boy, Asey thought. "And perhaps you'd better find some dry clothes for Mr. Mayo."

"Certainly." Merton wiped his glasses and peered near-sightedly around. "I gather the girls didn't come?"

"No, but Adele Parot did." In a few crisp phrases she summed up what had happened. "So," she concluded, "you will help Mr. Mayo in every way. The sooner he gets to the root of this, the better for the school."

"You mean there was an accident with the carryall, don't you?" Wilbur said anxiously. "You can't mean she was *killed*!"

"She was murdered. . . . Wilbur, do hurry and change before you catch cold."

Wilbur obviously did not have his mother's ability to accept a situation, Asey thought as he followed the young fellow up the wide, curving staircase. Wilbur looked shattered to the core.

"What happened to you, Mr. Merton?" Asey inquired as they crossed the upstairs hall. "Fall into a mud hole?"

"Me? Oh." Wilbur had some difficulty controlling his voice. "Oh, I went to the Tonset bus station and waited.

Finally someone said there'd been a washout and no bus could get through, so I started home. I had to push the bike most of the way, and I fell down— I don't understand this, Mr. Mayo! She didn't know anyone here!"

"Madame said you interviewed her. Did she—?"

"In here, Mr. Mayo. These are my quarters."

Wilbur opened the door of a room whose white walls, pale green ceiling, black broadloom carpet, and intricately modern leather-and-chrome furniture made Asey blink and wonder if Madame's tank-commander attitude didn't melt when it came to her son. His impression that the fellow was pampered increased as Wilbur walked over to a large, built-in wardrobe, swung aside the mirrored door, and revealed a larger collection of suits than Asey had ever owned in all his life.

He drew out a plaid tweed coat and a pair of gray flannels. "I think these will do you. . . . Yes, I interviewed Miss Parot at the agency in Boston; Madame was too busy to go."

"She mention havin' any friends in these parts?"

"She told me she'd never been on Cape Cod," Wilbur said. "She wasn't at all keen about coming here, so far from everything, but she had little choice. Most schools have their staffs filled long before now."

"She didn't speak of Greg Dudley?"

Wilbur looked startled. "Why, no! Er— May I ask why you thought of him?"

"Miss Parot was engaged to him once."

"To Greg? Oh, I think you must be mistaken," Wilbur said confidently. "Of course, I told her about us here. Little thumbnail sketches, as you might say, so she'd know the sort of people she would be working with. I mentioned the possibility of Miss Clifford's leaving us to get married, and asked if she would consider taking over the extra work. With extra pay, of course."

Asey nodded. Jennie's gossip about Lynn losing her job, it seemed, had some foundation.

"Miss Parot said—well, in effect, she asked if there were men around. Eligible men. And—er—well, trying to sell her the place, I said that Miss Clifford's fiancée was a road engineer, one of a number here who'd been working on defense projects. I mentioned his name. And so you see that's why I'm sure Miss Parot didn't know Greg, or she would have said so, don't you think? Now, I think you'll find anything else you need in that chest. You use this bath. I'll use the other suite. It'll save time."

Asey, after a quick shower, looked with growing distaste at the tweed jacket Wilbur had picked out for him. Why, he thought with resentment, should he be forced to tog himself out like a college boy in hairy plaids when there were plenty of other suits? He hung up the jacket and picked out a blue serge suit.

As he finished dressing, a pair of pictures in a silver frame on the table caught his attention. One was of Madame, looking as if she were en route to a coronation, and the other was of a soldier, a private in an obviously custom-tailored uniform. Leaning over, Asey read the scrawled signature, "Private Sam Merton." So Madame had another son!

"If you're ready to go," Wilbur said from the doorway, "shall we—? Oh. Oh, you took another suit?"

"You don't mind, do you?" Asey said.

"Oh, certainly not! Of course not! No, not at all!" Wilbur protested, Asey thought, just a little too hard.

" 'Fraid I'm not very plaid-minded. I been lookin' "—Asey indicated the picture—"at your army representative."

"Oh, yes, Sam. We're very proud of Sam. He wrote *Private Pete*, you know."

"That soldier book they made the movie an' radio shows out of?"

Wilbur nodded. "Sam's very clever. He was just getting started as a columnist when he was drafted, and of course we're delighted at his writing success. . . . Aren't those shoulders too tight for you?"

"They're a bit snug," Asey said, "but I'll be careful. Let's go."

He was thoroughly determined not to change the blue serge until he could find out the cause of Wilbur's distress.

They joined Madame in the school's office, a business-like room whose walls were lined with file cases. From one of them Madame extracted a folder.

"I thought you might care to look at this dossier," she said. "You see, we know quite a bit about Miss Adele Parot!"

For her purpose, Asey thought as he rapidly scanned the folder's contents, the information was doubtless very revealing. But it did not tell what he wanted to know about Miss Parot.

The fact that she never overdrew her checking account would not explain why she had said "Yes," and nothing else, to Lynn at the station. The Larrimore School's fervent appreciation of Miss Parot's French accent wouldn't clear up the problem of Miss Parot's lost pocketbook, nor explain why she hadn't noticed her loss before she got off the train. Unless Miss Parot differed greatly from every other woman he knew, she would have located her bag and sat gripping it tightly a good ten minutes before her train rolled into the station. Nor was her ability to toss the conversational ball in three languages at once going to solve the identity of the blunt instrument which had been used to kill her. Or the identity of the killer, either.

"I'm sure," Madame Merton said as Asey closed the folder, "that if she had known anyone in the vicinity, she surely would have told Wilbur so, or mentioned it to me in her letters. It was my first reaction that someone must have followed her on the train, but Lynn has just told me that no one else got off at the station. Now I feel, and I'm sure you'll have to agree with me, that she must have been killed by one of those strange individuals who apparently goes through life placidly enough, and then has one berserk moment when he maniacally kills someone—anyone within reach. There is no other possible explanation!"

She tapped her cane on the floor with finality, and Asey guessed that Madame would cling like a barnacle to her maniac solution until the real murderer confessed and was led away to jail.

"I've sent Miss Clifford and Mr. Dudley out to find Miss Rice and the scooter," she continued. "Wilbur, you go check the emergency electric system. The lights have come on again, but I don't trust them. And look at the main water tank. Mrs. Parr is worried about some leak or other."

"Er—" Wilbur nervously rubbed his hands together as if they were cold. "But—"

"Check up on the storage refrigerator, too. We cannot have that meat spoil. Hurry!"

"I think," Asey said with a smile as Wilbur scurried off, "he's distressed about the snug fit of this suit of his I'm wearin'. Now, Madame, your son tells me—"

"Mr. Merton is not my *son*!" In all his life, Asey had never heard such venomous fury in a woman's voice. "He is my *husband*!"

While Asey fought his face muscles to keep them from relaxing into a silly grin, it dawned on him belatedly that this was what Jennie had been trying to tell him. The possibility that the legal, stony-eyed Madame Merton, well in her sixties, should have such an exceedingly youthful husband somehow had never entered his head!

He managed to control his expression, but the damage was done.

"It was dumb of me to make that mistake," he said with perfect honesty. "But the name bein' the same, an' knowin' the Mertons founded the school—"

"Wilbur's name is Holzwasser," Madame said. "Obviously, it is simpler, for business reasons, to have him referred to as 'Mr. Merton.'"

"Oh, I can see that!" He told himself firmly not to think of how funny "Holzwasser Hall" would sound. "Of course, you know I've been away from the Cape a lot since the war began. I haven't been able to keep up to date on who's married who—"

He saw her lips tighten, and knew that he'd made another break.

"We have been married nearly twenty years," Madame said frigidly. "Since Wilbur graduated from college, at sixteen."

Asey, drawing a long breath to pull himself out of that one, looked on Wilbur's hurried entrance as heaven-sent deliverance.

"Mr. Mayo"—Wilbur had a monkey wrench in either hand, and his face and shirt were streaked with grease—"can you help me, or are you too busy?"

Asey covered the distance to the door in one vast stride.

"Sure—glad to! What," he added as they hastened down the hall, "seems to be the trouble?"

He wiped his forehead with one of Wilbur's linen handkerchiefs, and then suddenly found himself giggling like a schoolgirl.

"Is anything the matter with you?" Wilbur inquired.

"Nothing at all!" Asey assured him. He was doing mental arithmetic, and it kept turning out that this fellow, at sixteen, had married Madame at a good forty-six or so. He thought he began to understand the green-ceilinged elegance and the extensive wardrobe upstairs. Under the circumstances, Madame might have to pamper him. "Uh—what'd you say had gone wrong?"

"Mrs. Parr's been fooling with the water again—thought there was a leak and turned off the water. I need you," Wilbur said glibly as they started to descend the cellar stairs, "to turn on the main shutoff while I adjust the secondary valves."

Asey glanced at him sharply and wondered just what sort of wool this fellow fancied he was pulling over his eyes. An outlander might have been taken in with some such crazy statement, but not someone who had tinkered with every type of water system on Cape Cod!

"Now," Wilbur went on quickly, "if you'll come over to this room here and turn on the valve— Here, I'll show you where it's located."

Warily keeping one eye on the monkey wrenches, Asey permitted himself to be shown the water shutoff and tried to figure out what all this cock-and-bull business was leading to. If the climax was to be a quick biff from a wrench— Asey braced himself, and waited.

Then it came.

"Just give me your coat," Wilbur said casually, "and I'll hang it up with mine."

"Sure." Asey spoke with equal casualness. "I was just thinkin' about dirtyin' up your suit. I wouldn't want to rip the sleeves, either. And—say, get me that flashlight I noticed back at the head of the cellar stairs, will you?"

Wilbur passed over the flashlight a minute later; Asey in turn handed Wilbur the coat, and gravely turned on the shutoff. He didn't even bat an eyelash when Wilbur called in much concern from the main part of the cellar and asked if he'd mind running down to the barn and making sure *that* shutoff was open.

"Well!" Jennie greeted him as he strolled in, grinning from ear to ear. "You sure look better! Where've you been?"

"I," Asey said, "have been aidin' the adjustment of secondary water valves."

"*What?*"

Asey chuckled. "Did they used to have a lot of hired hands here? Handymen an' such?"

"Ella's three boys worked here full time before they joined the navy," Jennie said. "Now there's only her old brother-in-law part time, and everyone has to pitch in and help. Particularly Mr. Merton, and I must say he hardly knows which end of a screwdriver you hold in your hand. I had to show him how to use a monkey wrench— What's so funny?"

"So that's why he had them wrenches! They was the only tools he knew how to handle! Oh!" Asey leaned against the barn door and laughed. "I guessed he was pretty new to work. He ain't got the words straight yet. Speakin' of words, what day did Wilbur go to Boston to interview Miss Parot?"

Jennie thought a moment. "Two days before I come. That'd have been Tuesday, the eighteenth. I know, because Ella told me about having to get up early to cook his breakfast. She said he was so excited, getting away on his own for once, he could hardly eat. . . . Asey, what in the world is he doing with *valves*? What valves? Where?"

"Wa-el," Asey said, "right now Wilbur's probably not so busy with his imaginary valves in the cellar as he is with pawin' through the pockets of the coat that belongs to this suit."

"But why? What *for*?" Jennie demanded.

"For these." Asey reached into his hip pocket and drew out two theater-ticket stubs. "Tuesday the eighteenth, second row orchestra at the Colonial in Boston. He saw the *Monkeyshine Frolics*. I know, because Eb Jordan saw the show, an' gave me a quip-by-quip description of it out fishin' this mornin'. 'N'en there's this match flap from the Club Chico, an' one from the Café Parisienne."

"Asey, I'd never have thought it of him! Of course, Ella did say the girls called him Old Smoothie and—well, she sort of insinuated that Madame had to keep a leash on him. . . . Asey, there isn't *more*!" Jennie said delightedly. "Where else did he go?"

"Your further guesses on Wilbur's night out," Asey said, "are just as good as mine. This next exhibit's a sweet-smellin' handkerchief named Adele in one corner."

"Asey!"

"An' what sort of ties everything together all neat an' pretty," Asey said, "is this piece of paper, torn out of a pocket notebook. It's got a phone number written on it: 'Highlands 1920—Adele.' An' the rest is even more interestin', with what you might call illustrations— Come, come, now, Jennie; don't tear it out of my hand!"

"Look at what he's scrawled underneath— That's his writing, too. I know it! 'Adele,'" Jennie read in fascination. "'Adele Parot. Adele darling. Adele dearest!' Ooh, and look at all these doodles of twined hearts! Ooh!"

"I can understand," said Asey, returning the collection to his pocket, "why my puttin' on this suit bothered him considerable."

"Asey, he was out! He was on that bike! He could've gone to the Skaket station, or to the bridge road!"

"I know. I never realized before," Asey said thoughtfully, "how smart a murderer'd be to kill someone just before the start of a good northeaster. If you knew anythin' about 'em, you could bank on everyone being too busy beforehand— squintin' at the sky, shuttin' windows, gettin' ready for things to break—to pay much attention to what you were doin'. You could almost bank on the first downpour's bein' so heavy that nobody'd hardly see their hand before their face, let alone you sneakin' around. Why, a platoon of murderers could've run around these roads without anyone bein' a whit the wiser! Yessiree, it's a fine, distractin' time!"

"I s'pose you could check up on when Wilbur left the Tonset bus station," Jennie said tentatively. "If you could prove he was there before the train got in at Skaket, say, and for the next half-hour, you'd know he couldn't have been over this way."

"That Tonset bus stop," Asey said, "is a closed gas station. I noticed it when I came. Wilbur claims he left there after someone told him the road was washed out—naturally, that'd be after the storm struck. But if I try to pin him down on who told him, I bet he'll just blink at me through his glasses an' say it was a man with brown hair in a black car, or something just as specific. You see what I mean? There's almost an hour durin' which Wilbur or Greg or Lynn can claim most anythin' they want."

"But you could figure out the distances to the stations, and how fast they went, and such," Jennie said. "You could catch 'em up if they lied!"

"You could figure till doomsday an' make graphs, even," Asey said, "an' it wouldn't get us any forrader. None of 'em was expert on any of the vehicles they was ridin'—probably even Einstein couldn't figure out their rates of speed. Those stations are all about the same distance from here, an' they all had time to get there. What they done afterward is their claim against what we could prove if anyone happened to have seen 'em an' happened to remember the time. An' I'm bettin' no one did—"

"Look!" Jennie interrupted. "There's a basket on the

front of that bike Wilbur used, and in it there's a tool—a sort of cross made of metal, with ends that screw up different sized nuts. 'Course, he didn't know what it was for till I showed him, but most any fool could use that gadget to biff with! *Think* of his going out with her! I wonder, you s'pose he got so involved with her, he got scared at the thought of her living here all the time? Why, if she even breathed a word of such goings-on— Asey!"

She spoke so excitedly, Asey looked questioningly around the barn. "You see somebody?"

"No, no! Madame! S'pose Madame saw those stubs an' all in his pocket! I certainly wouldn't put it beyond her to go through his pockets—how plumb stupid of him to leave 'em there! But then I s'pose he never strayed from the straight and narrow before." Jennie shook her head. "Madame's awful prideful. She might forgive him one break with someone he just picked up, but she couldn't take that girl bein' here all the time, and them carryin' on together. Asey, could she have got to the bridge road from the River station in time to meet that carryall?"

"If she started right after I left her, an' short-cutted around. Only, she couldn't've guessed which road Lynn would take."

"She never had to guess—she knew! She told Lynn to come back the bridge road. I heard her," Jennie said. "I don't think you give Madame enough credit. You don't know how mad she can get. And Ella said she's terrible jealous of Wilbur."

"Ella never mentioned his carryin' on with Lynn or the Rice girl, did she?" Asey asked.

"Oh, Lynn wouldn't look at anyone but Greg, and Deb

Rice has been engaged to a regular army officer for a long time, only they can't get married because he has a sick sister to support. She was readin' a letter from him this afternoon —she looked quite pretty, with her cheeks all bright and her eyes sparklin'. Asey, I think it'd be worse if *she* knew, almost!"

"You mean, if she knew about Wilbur's goin's-on?"

Jennie nodded vigorously. "She's almost firmer with Wilbur than Madame is, and she's just as proud of the school. She'd be mad as hops if she knew Wilbur'd been cuttin' up and makin' scandal— Where are you goin' now?"

"Back to report to Wilbur that the valves is doin' as well as can be expected under the circumstances," Asey said. "Poor Wilbur. He's goin' to be between the fryin' pan an' the fire. He won't know if Madame's got them stubs an' all, or if I have!" He squinted up at the sky. "This breather's just about over; it's goin' to pour cats an' dogs again. I don't like leavin' you here, Jennie. I'll find someone else as soon as I can."

"What about getting the cops?"

Asey shrugged. "If the phone's gone here, the phones'll be gone in the village. An' even if we could contact 'em, I doubt if they could get here very soon. Does Ella's part-time brother-in-law look after the horses? Wa-el, if you could make sure he wasn't one of Miss Parot's intimate friends, you might hire him in my name to relieve you!"

The basket on the bicycle Wilbur had left near the front door was so wet that it hung limply at an angle, like a wet dishtowel. It contained a grayish pulp that had once been the *Skaket News*, and a brown substance that looked like a small serving of chocolate cornstarch pudding into which someone had laced blue and white checked paper. Asey, peering at it, realized that it was a chocolate bar that had been exposed to the storm, and, further, that it was one of the mammoth box of chocolate bars he'd brought home as a present to Jennie, who had written him wistfully about a hankering for candy.

But there was no sign of any tool.

The sound of voices made Asey peer curiously out of the long window by the front door. Madame and Wilbur were there. And—an exclamation of amazement nearly escaped his lips—as Madame passed by the bicycle, she unobtrusively slipped into the basket just such a cross-shaped tool as Jennie had described!

"So!" Asey murmured, and waited for the pair to come in.

But they were delayed on the top step by a gray-haired woman who, Asey guessed, was Mrs. Parr, and three elderly maids in uniform.

While the problems of how many for dinner and if the maids should set the tables when the girls hadn't come were being thrashed out, Asey leaned against the hall table and toyed with the notion of putting on an act—grabbing Wilbur, and making a show of taking him off to the cops. It might make Madame come out with whatever she was holding back. More likely, he decided, she would point out that the flooded roads prohibited the use of his roadster.

He wondered idly why the umbrella stand in the corner, an ugly blue and green pottery affair, should keep catching his attention. Strolling over to it, he found it served as Madame's cane rack, and contained at least a dozen ivory canes, each with a different type of handle.

One, an inverted silver heart, caused him to whistle softly under his breath, and he drew it out for further inspection. It was solid silver, and heavy, and he almost couldn't ask for a better approximation of his mental picture of the weapon used to kill Adele Parot.

Thoughtfully, he slid his hand to the center of the shaft, and swung the cane lightly.

To his astonishment, the head, with about three inches of shaft attached, at once dropped off and fell on the floor!

Asey looked at the piece left in his hand, surveyed the clean break, and then sniffed at the broken end. It had obviously been broken before he touched it, and mended so recently that the smell of glue was fresh.

Closing his eyes, he tried to visualize the cane Madame had carried when he drove her over to the River station, but he could only remember that she had gripped the handle tightly in her hand all the way.

He turned around suddenly, to find Madame standing there watching him. Asey balanced the cane shaft on his finger, and waited for her to speak. It was, he thought, her move. And however she moved, he had her!

Then Wilbur stuck his head in the door. "They're here! The girls! They've come!"

"Remember," Madame told Asey swiftly, "they are not to know anything about Miss Parot. You will be the new hired man."

Asey picked up the heart handle and put it in his pocket. He walked over to the front door and watched the double line of girls, all dressed in sodden navy-blue suits, marching up the side of the driveway toward the main building. At their head, wheeling the mud-covered scooter, was the blond Miss Rice, looking as if she wanted to curl up and drop into an exhausted heap right then and there.

"Twenty-one, twenty-two—all here!" Madame said with satisfaction. "And *met*, too!"

As the girl behind Deb Rice left the column, approached Madame, and bobbed a little curtsy, Asey felt his jaw drop. This slip of a thing was without doubt the very same girl he'd chased from the barn a good hour ago!

He ducked back into the doorway and listened as she began, rather self-righteously, to explain to Madame:

"Of course, we weren't *really* met, but we think Miss Rice was simply trans*cend*ent to find us at all, what with the storm, and we're sure our families will understand." She cleared her throat. "Being the oldest senior, I acted as leader, and, really, we had no trouble getting here from Boston, except for being a bit wet."

"But what happened in Boston, Miss Granville?" Wilbur demanded.

"Oh, we were in the waiting room while Mrs. Hutchins was telephoning you to say that there wasn't any train, but only a bus, and then the man came and said the bus was ready and we had to go right away. But we described Mrs. Hutchins to the train man and asked him to tell her if he could find her. The bus driver didn't know the way at all, and didn't leave us at the regular stop, but we started out, and met Miss Rice. And here we are!"

"I'm so sorry to have missed them, but apparently the

driver simply dumped them on Main Street." Deb Rice sounded as exhausted as she looked, Asey thought.

"I think you did well," Madame said, "and I'm very proud of you, Jinx, for taking charge and showing such self-reliance. As you new girls will find out, we place character—"

Madame's golden words on character were lost to Asey, who was thinking back to the Porter Motors directors' meetings in prewar days, when DeWitt Granville, chairman of the board, livened dull sessions with stories of the outrageous conduct of his hellion daughter, Jinx. The schools from which Jinx had been forcibly ejected, the governesses who'd retired with nervous breakdowns, the cop whose eyes she'd blacked, the ambassador she'd shoved into a lily pond—and here was the little brat pretending she'd shepherded these youngsters every inch of the way from Boston!

"And so I welcome you to Merton Hall," Madame was concluding. "Now, hurry in, all of you. It's beginning to rain again! . . . Mayo," she added, "take Miss Rice's scooter to the barn. We shall not need you again."

"I'll put it up, Madame," Deb said. "It's so muddy, he'll only get covered—"

"Mayo will take it. Good night, Mayo," Madame said. "Come, girls; hurry in!"

"Hold it away from you," Deb Rice cautioned Asey. "It's filthy. I could just as well wheel it down myself. Here, let me—"

"Miss Rice!"

"Yes, Madame, I'm coming!"

The heavens opened again a second after Asey reached the barn and put up the scooter.

"Jennie," he said, "that girl I chased was the Granville brat."

"*Her?*" Jennie clucked her tongue. "Well, from what Ella's told me about her I'm not surprised! Ella says she lies easy as rollin' off a log, and all the time lookin' so righteous! All last fall she chased after Sam Merton, Madame's *real* son, and I guess it drove Madame crazy. Ella says when she stops thinkin' of deviltry to do herself, she teams up with some boy over at that military school in Weesit—Pinky Somebody. Her cousin. The two of 'em raised Cain till they took his car away from him. He had a Porter."

"I wonder," Asey said, "if he's startin' this year with a fresh one. Whoever tore past me in that yellow model drove like a crazy kid. I wonder if she was in that car! I'm dead sure she never come with the rest. . . . Jennie, when's this handyman due? Soon?"

"He should've been here already to feed the horses."

"Then I'll stay and wait till he comes," Asey said. "You run up an' keep an eye on things at the school for me. Try the phones once in a while, an' snoop around all you can in the guise of bein' helpful. I got a feelin' Miss Granville's goin' to sneak back here, an' I want a chat with her."

From the door he watched the girls being herded under umbrellas to their dormitory cottages. About ten minutes later Miss Granville appeared. She wore a blue denim middy blouse and skirt under her drab raincoat, and her hair was tied up with a blue bandanna.

She hurried at once to the chest where she had left her wet draperies, flipped up the lid, and then looked blankly around the barn.

"I took 'em out," Asey said as he stepped in from the shed.

"*You* did? What for?"

"Wa-el," Asey said cheerfully, "call it blackmail. You tell me how you really came down here from Boston, an' a few things like that, an' in return I won't tell Madame how you foxed her into thinkin' you was such a fine, self-reliant leader of lost young things."

"How simply trans*cend*ent!" Jinx said. "I mean, I know who you are, now I've heard you talk! Father quotes you practically every waking moment, you know. I never should have run away if I'd known it was you, Mr. Mayo! I thought it was some new hired man who'd drag me to Madame."

"Who'd you come with? Pinky?"

Her eyes opened wide. "How did you know? How trans*cend*ent you are! Pinky thought it would be fun for me to drive down with him, but I didn't have a chance to skip until that man sent us packing off to the bus. I knew we could beat that down here, easily! I was going to stay here and then join the girls when they came— You know, it was much pleasanter coming with Pinky. Girls are frightfully tiresome on busses."

"An' that's the only reason you chose to be different?"

She nodded. "Anyway, it all worked out. After you chased me from here, I scrammed back toward the village and fell in with the girls just a minute before Deb spotted us. . . . Is that Porter roadster yours? I thought it was Sam Merton's. He's busting out with Porters, now he's so lousy rich from his book. I should have known that only someone like *you* would rate that job."

"I have this feelin'," Asey said, "that I'm bein' soft-soaped."

"But you won't tell on me, will you? . . . Why are you pretending to be the new hired man, Mr. Mayo? Is something wrong?"

"I came here to get my cousin Jennie, who's been helpin' Mrs. Parr," Asey said, "an' I got marooned by the storm. How come you're actually *stayin'* at a school? I thought you just belonged to the transient trade."

"Frankly, we were running out of schools," Jinx said, "and then that efficiency expert of father's showed him that one school tuition, plus upkeep, was much cheaper than lots of tuitions no one would ever refund. So this year father got Madame a new priority electric horse for the gym and a lot of new plumbing, and last year he forked out two tennis courts and a stained-glass window to Womanhood in the chapel. Of course, I'm not saying that's *why* I'm here, but I rather think I'll stay. Anyway, I rather like it here."

"I can see," Asey remarked, "that you are mellowin' with age."

"Languages did it," Jinx said. "I turned out to be a genius for the languages foreign. It simply revolutionized my point of view, finding I was good at something. Besides, it's not a bad school. Madame Merton and Deb are sahibs. Wilbur's a jerk, but he's a good teacher. So's Lynn Clifford, though she doesn't care a cent for us girls. I loved old Mademoiselle. She had a mustache and threw erasers at me, but she was grand. I was really sorry to hear she'd died. . . . I wonder, has the new Mademoiselle turned up yet?"

"I couldn't say," Asey told her truthfully. "Look; where'd you disappear to when I chased you in the orchard? Up an apple tree?"

"Oh, no; I just dodged into the passage. The old smugglers' passage that leads to the windmill. Don't you know about Merton's Mill?" Jinx demanded. "It's the high spot of our social life. We plant corn there every spring, and grind it in the mill every fall—carrying symbolism too far, I think, but it gives us something to drape with bunting and have processions to. Father nearly choked to death when he heard our windmill song."

Asey chuckled.

"Father's priceless on Madame," Jinx added. "He describes her as Whistler's mother with a dagger in her sock— Oh, there's the bell! I've got to dash!"

She got as far as the door, and then turned around. "If it's a murder you're solving," she said casually, "without even knowing who's been killed, I'll bet on Sam Merton, because Madame Merton's Sammy is a bunch of nasty words!"

Asey rubbed his chin thoughtfully as he watched her dash off toward the main building. She knew he wasn't marooned by the storm, she knew there'd been a murder—and how much else did she know? Like her father, she had divulged just exactly what she wanted to, and not a word more.

"I wonder, now," Asey murmured. "If Jinx's so crazy about languages, an' if DeWitt Granville is subsidizin' this school in a refined way, would he be consulted about this new Mademoiselle? Does this youngster know who the new language teacher was, an' know somethin' about her an' this Sam Merton?"

He sat there in the darkness, puffing on his pipe, until Deb Rice appeared with a tray of food some fifteen minutes later.

"Jennie covered it with oilcloth, and I tried to keep it dry," she said. "Madame's told me about everything, and I think it's simply ghastly. Don't you think I'd better walk to the village and see if I can't get in touch with the authorities for you?"

"After your day with the scooter," Asey said, "I don't think you'd better consider any six-mile, round-trip hike in the teeth of a northeaster!"

"But Madame wants—" Deb began peremptorily; then broke off and smiled politely. "It's simply that we feel that the sooner she is removed"—she made a gesture toward the carryall—"the better. Mr. Merton would like to go for you, but Madame thinks he's catching a cold. And Lynn Clifford's not back. I'd be perfectly willing to go. Or, as Jennie suggested, perhaps you'd go yourself, and I could stay here. Jennie said she'd come later and stay with me. . . . But this *must* be removed!" Her jaw was suddenly like granite. "I don't think, Mr. Mayo, that you appreciate what a blow this is to the school."

"While I understand Madame's point of view," Asey said dryly, "I don't think the chances of gettin' through to the cops are worth my plowin' through this storm. An' I wouldn't suggest your tacklin' it, either. You come quite a cropper in that scooter this afternoon, to judge by your looks when you got back."

"I never understood that scooter, but I got to the Billingsgate bus station all right," Deb said. "I waited around, and then I started back in what turned out to be the worst of that first downpour. I skidded into a ditch, and it stunned me a bit. I had to rest quite a while before I could go on—

luckily, it turned out, for I wouldn't have met the girls otherwise."

"I know DeWitt Granville," Asey said matter-of-factly, "an' I noticed his daughter. Does he have an interest in this school?"

Deb's manner changed at once. "Why, yes, he's interested in it," she said guardedly.

"He wouldn't have any say in the choice of teachers?"

"No!" Deb got up quickly from the sawhorse on which she'd been sitting. "None whatever. . . . I really must get back. Someone should start for the village at once."

A firm girl, Asey thought as she hurried out, and just as devoted to Merton Hall as Jennie'd said. . . .

He was finishing the last crumb on his supper tray when Mrs. Parr's tall, lanky brother-in-law appeared. His only comment on Asey's brief recital of what had happened was a laconic grunt, and to Asey's suggestion that he double as watchdog, he merely nodded his willingness.

"Fine," Asey said. "Just don't let anyone bother that carryall, an' though I don't expect anyone'll try to lure you outside, or jump you, keep your ears an' eyes open. Particularly for the girls. There's no sense lettin' them discover about this right now."

Tucking his flashlight into the pocket of his oilskin coat, he started up the driveway, then circled in a wide detour to the wing of the main building which contained the office.

That DeWitt Granville might have had anything to do with the choice of Adele Parot had at first seemed to him a wild idea, but now, after Deb Rice's reaction to his suggestion, he began to feel that he had perhaps guessed right, after all.

He remembered that Madame had Miss Parot's dossier on her desk, waiting for him. There might be much more about the girl which she had not wished him to see. Data, for instance, which might in any way involve her most profitable pupil.

He noted, as he located the office windows, that the blackout shades hadn't been drawn, which would seem to indicate that no one intended to use the room. The first window he tried was locked, but the next gave under his fingers. A moment later he was inside the office, quietly closing the window behind him and starting to grope his way toward the files.

As his hand closed over the steel corner of an open file drawer, he heard someone enter the next room from the hall. A crack of light appeared at the base of the connecting door, and Asey flattened himself against the wall next to it, just a fraction of a second before the door was thrust open and Deb Rice entered.

Asey watched from behind the door as she drew the shades, snapped on the light, and put down on the desk the yellow folder which Asey recognized as Madame's dossier on Miss Parot.

Without any hesitancy, as if her choice had been prearranged, she picked out half a dozen sheets of paper, crumpled them into a ball, and tossed them into the fireplace. She was bending down to touch a match to them when Asey spoke.

"Blow it out, please!"

"These are nothing of any concern—"

"Blow it out!" Asey crossed over to her side and extinguished the little flame.

"But Madame—"

"Madame"—Asey noticed again that determined set to her chin—"is bein' a little hasty, an' displayin' just a bit of panic. Even if you'd burned these up an' tossed the ashes out into the storm, I'd have been phonin' DeWitt Granville just as soon as the phones come back. Even"—he caught her hand as she snatched for the papers—"even if you grab 'em an' run, it won't make any difference. S'pose you just sit down, now, while I peruse them."

While Deb watched him with irritation, he smoothed out the papers, put them in sequence and read them.

Granville had obviously been consulted about the appointment of the new language teacher. His objections were strong and to the point, and the basis for them was a situation which had not occurred to Asey.

"Miss Parot came to us a year ago August as Jinx's tutor and companion. She hated Jinx, Jinx hated her, and on one occasion the services of a chauffeur and a gardener were required to separate them. Miss Parot sustained a broken arm. She was at the Larrimore School during Jinx's stay there, and the upshot was a violent fight during which Miss Parot's arm was broken again. I cannot too emphatically suggest that you find another teacher."

Madame had apparently wired back about the difficulties involved in finding someone else, and suggesting that he talk to Jinx.

His next letter sounded a little exhausted:

"I cannot find out the reason for their flying at each other's throats, nor does Jinx, herself, seem to know why.

But I have explained the problem to Jinx, and she seems to be fond enough of Merton Hall to try to make the arrangement work out. I would, however, suggest that, at least for the time being, a third person always be present whenever they have occasion to meet. Do not leave them alone together. That is when fatalities seem to occur."

Asey looked up, to find that Madame had slipped into the room in her usual catlike fashion.

"I told you"—her blue eyes were shooting sparks—"not to come back here tonight!"

"I wouldn't probably have needed to," Asey said, "if you hadn't tried to fox me on this Granville business. Because, of course, *I* know Jinx didn't come with the rest. I know she was here earlier, and so do you."

He caught her on that one. Madame blinked.

"I shall have the burglar-alarm switch put on!" she said angrily. "It will at least keep you out the rest of the night."

Asey smiled. "You could rig up barbed wire," he said cheerfully, "but I'll wager if you do any more letter burnin' or cane gluin' or tool replacin' you'll find me right at your elbow. When Lynn Clifford comes back, send her down to see me at the barn."

The lanky Mr. Parr was sitting in an old rocker, with a length of broom handle gripped in his fist and a pitchfork on the floor by his side.

"Been thinkin'," he announced.

"That so?" Asey said encouragingly. "Got a good solution up your sleeve for me?"

"Took in my lobster pots this aft'noon, up by the river."

"So?" Asey took Granville's correspondence out of his pocket.

"Seen this." Mr. Parr nodded toward the carryall.

"You mean, you seen it go by?" Asey thought for a moment. "Say, if you was up the river, you'd have seen it near the bridge!"

"Yup. Thought it was funny," Mr. Parr said, "the way she give 'em a wallop an' sent 'em gallopin'."

"*What?*"

"The hosses. They never run away. She walloped 'em. I seen the carryall come careenin' along"—Mr. Parr became practically eloquent—"an' then it stopped, an' the girl got off an' walked back to the rear door."

The Granville correspondence fell out of Asey's hand.

"She went inside," Parr continued, "'n'en, after a few minutes, she come out an' give 'em a wallop, an' they went gallopin' off."

"You mean, you actually seen Lynn Clifford? You recognized her?"

Parr nodded. "You told me the girl said the hosses run as the storm broke. 'Course, I figgered you knew what you was talkin' about. But then I got to thinkin' if she walloped 'em, an' they run, she couldn't've caught up with 'em in time. Because the storm didn't break for—oh, four or five minutes after she hit 'em. Where is she, anyhow?"

"She and her man," Asey said grimly, "are two other places. Madame sent 'em out to hunt Deb Rice, an' they never come back."

"If I was you," Parr said, "I think I'd be inclined to hunt

her up. You could get through in your Porter now. Yessir," he said, fishing a candy bar out of his pocket, "I think Lynn told you a yarn. . . . Have some chocolate?"

"No, thanks. Are you sure that was Lynn, an' not some other girl?"

"Had on her red coat." Parr took the wrapper off the candy in his deliberate fashion. "Seen her in it a million times. Know the way she walks. . . . Sure you won't have some candy? It's a treat I have to thank your cousin Jennie for." Asey, noticing the blue and white checked wrapping for the first time, grinned. "She give this bar to Ella this afternoon, an' Ella saved it for me—"

"Say," Asey interrupted, "was that the flash of car lights, just then? Against the wall?"

"Didn't see 'em, but I shouldn't wonder," Parr said. "I thought I heard a car just after you left. That's why I said you probably could get through the lane now, because it seemed like someone already had. That's why I got me this club an' pitchfork handy, too, in case anyone tried to bother me. Even went an' rigged up a little trap in the shed," he added with pride. "If someone sneaks in an' pushes open the shed door, why then that trowel danglin' on the rope from that rafter yonder—that'll fall down an' hit the floor."

"I'm sure I heard a car." Asey put on his oilskin coat and picked up his flashlight. "I'm goin' to take a look around. Maybe Lynn's got back."

"If I was you," said Parr, finishing the last of the chocolate, "I'd just set an' wait." He painted toward the dangling trowel. "She give a little quiver just now. There—it's droppin'!"

Asey made a dash for the shed, and heard someone run out the door before he was halfway across the barn.

The beam of his flashlight, stabbing through the downpour as he paused for a second in the shed doorway, picked out the hood of a yellow Porter parked near the barn. Beyond it, he caught a glimpse of a figure in a raincoat, heading toward the orchard.

He guessed, by the sound of the footsteps pounding ahead, that he was gaining. But when he threw the beam of his flashlight in that direction, there was no one to be seen.

"Huh!" Asey muttered as he played the light about. "You took that passage to the old windmill, just like Jinx did!"

Clearly, he thought, the windmill would be simpler to locate than any passageway to it. It should be somewhere near the shore, and since he'd never noticed it while driving along the shore road, it probably stood beyond the pines to his right.

He turned and marched toward the beach, and two minutes later spotted the looming structure just in time to keep himself from walking into the picket fence which surrounded it. He located the door, and then waited under a pine tree, while the rain poured down his neck.

Finally he saw the splutter of a match inside, as if someone were trying to find a door latch, and then a figure emerged.

Whoever he was, he strolled jauntily back toward the barn, apparently confident that he'd thrown off his pursuer for good. But Asey noticed that once he was out of the orchard, his cockiness seemed to vanish. He paused a moment by the yellow Porter, then took a few tentative steps toward the shed door, then walked hesitantly back toward the Porter.

The third time that he repeated the maneuver, Asey lost patience. Reaching out, he grabbed the fellow's elbow, twisted his arm back, and propelled him, squirming like an eel and protesting in shrill squeals, toward the open barn door.

"Gettin' worried about you!" Parr advanced with the pitchfork. "Who—? Oh, him!"

"My God, my arm's broken! Parr, tell him who I am!"

"That," Parr said, "is Sammy Merton, the famous writer. Wrote a piece about me once. Want the pitchfork or the club, Asey?"

"Hold 'em in reserve," Asey said, "till we— What's all this you got bulgin' in your bosom, feller? Take it out, Parr."

Parr twisted open Sam Merton's raincoat, and his hand snatched the object buttoned inside Sam's service blouse.

"Bag." Parr gave it to Asey. "Lady's pocketbook."

Even before he opened it, Asey knew by the initials that the bag was Adele Parot's.

"Now, see here!" Sam Merton flung his raincoat on the barn floor and turned belligerently to Asey. "If you'll just stop being so quick on the trigger, and let me see Miss Parot, I can explain everything."

"Always, was a wonder at explainin' everything," Parr observed. "Come to think of it, Sammy, I seen your yellow car on the bridge road, too. Went by just before the carryall did."

"Look, Parr; I know you've always been sore about that

sketch I wrote of you, but be a good guy and get Ella to send Miss Parot, the new teacher, here, will you? I just want to get this bag to her, and I don't want mother to know I'm here."

"Show him the carryall," Asey said. "Look in, Merton."

The last vestige of cockiness drained out of Sam. He could only stand there, wordless.

"Now," Asey said, "start explainin'— My name, by the way, is Asey Mayo. I gather you knew this girl?"

"Only—" Sam hesitated, and then drew a long breath. "Before I went into the army, I wrote a newspaper column. You know, like Winchell, in a small way—"

"Smallest way," Parr observed dryly, "you ever seen!"

Sam ignored his gibe. "And I just happened to mention Adele's name one day. After all," he said, "it was worth mentioning, because she *was* playing around with a very famous man, DeWitt Granville's lawyer—"

"That'd be my friend John Standing," Asey said, "an' far from playin' around with anyone, he's a devoted husband an' the father of six children."

"Well, she was *seen* with him, and I said so, and then other columnists started mentioning her, and calling her the Glamour Governess, and the Symmetrical Schoolma'am, and when the Larrimore School didn't renew her contract this year, she thought all that publicity was the reason why."

"I see. While John was probably patchin' up the second broken-arm incident for Granville," Asey said, "you started some gossip that lost her her job. I see."

"That's what *she* thought! I didn't realize at first that she had it in for me"—Sam sounded very virtuous and blameless

—"but I found out later she did. So when mother wrote me she was coming here, naturally I was very upset. Frankly, I knew she was going to make trouble, and I didn't want the school to suffer."

"You have a financial interest in the school?" Asey interrupted.

"Well, no," Sam said. "Er—no. But naturally I have a family feeling for the place— Anyway, I phoned some of my friends in Boston and asked them to look into things. They found out that Adele was boasting of what she was going to do here at Merton—to spite me. I tell you, she was out for blood!

"I found out when she was coming, and met her at the Junction today. All she wanted was money," Sam said. "It's all they ever want."

Asey opened the pocketbook, picked out a roll of bills, and whistled as he counted them. "An' what *else*," he said suddenly, "were you payin' for?"

Sam made a regal little gesture which reminded Asey of Madame.

"Nothing else. I'm in the money," he said. "I can afford it. That was enough to satisfy her. She said she wouldn't make any trouble—believe it or not, she'd already gone to work on Wilbur! But she promised to lay off him and stay on the beam. I bought her ticket, put her on the train, stuck the ticket in the chair back—and after the train left I found I'd got her pocketbook under my arm. And was I worried!" Sam's voice had the ring of sincerity.

"Thinkin'," Asey said, "that she'd think you give her the cash, an' got her promise, only to snatch back the cash?"

Sam nodded. "I drove down here like crazy! I burned up the roads! I talked myself out of two tickets, but I lost enough time to miss her at the Skaket station. The station agent said she'd left in the carryall, with Lynn, so I tore back here. But I missed the carryall. I waited up beyond the school gates for a while, then I went back to the village, thinking Lynn might've decided to wait there till the storm let up a bit. And I got marooned there—the roads were rivers. If I hadn't been wild to get that pocketbook back to her, I'd never have tried to get through now!"

"Uh-huh, I see." Asey fingered the roll of bills. "Now, what else was you payin' her for? An' don't waste my time, please, with a lot more glib talk! What else?"

"Well," Sam said sullenly, "if you *must* know, Adele happened to find out about me and this girl at Larrimore School. Her name doesn't matter. She was one of the day girls there. And it was all perfectly innocent, only— Well, if Adele had told Miss Larrimore, Miss Larrimore would tell mother—"

"You mean it was cheaper to pay blackmail to Adele than to take the chance of your mother knowin'?"

"Anything," Sam said, "is cheaper than mother in a fury. That's when she calls for her lawyer and starts changing her will—and the money is mine! Wilbur can have the school and welcome to it, but mother promised me the money years ago!" He took a deep breath and quieted down. "Anyway, it wasn't blackmail. Adele and I settled everything today to our satisfaction. I paid her in full."

"What road'd you take from the station?" Parr asked suddenly. "Where'd you go?"

After cross-questioning Sam like a prosecuting attorney,

Parr turned to Asey. "He short-cutted an' got ahead of the carryall on the bridge road, see? Missed it everywhere. Hate to say so, but it could work out like he claims."

"Did you see Jinx Granville?" Asey asked.

"Yes. Near the school. I saw her pal Pinky. I saw Greg Dudley on the shore road. I saw Wilbur in Skaket Square—"

"Whoa up! Don't you mean in Tonset?"

"No. Up in the main square in Skaket, after I left the station. I nearly ran the idiot down. He's a menace on a bike anyway," Sam said, "but today he was in more of a fog than usual. I don't think he even saw me."

"Huh!" Asey said. If, instead of being at the Tonset bus station, Wilbur had actually been in the square near the main Skaket railroad station, he might perhaps have met the train, even seen and spoken with Adele in the carryall while Lynn was talking with the agent.

"Me, I saw everyone," Sam continued, "except Lynn and that carryall and Adele— My God, I never thought of that angle before! You can't think I killed her to get that money back and put a stop to paying her any more!" Sam sounded like a small, anguished child. "I didn't!"

"What was you sneakin' around so for?" Parr demanded, before Asey could speak.

"Look; I couldn't barge into school and risk meeting mother, and I had to find Adele. I thought if you were here, you could give her the bag, or get Ella to. Then Mayo tore at me, and I ran—I didn't know who he was. And I didn't know about Adele's being killed!"

He stopped and ducked behind a horse stall as he saw the

glow of a flashlight coming toward the barn. He emerged again when the newcomer proved to be Deb Rice.

"Sam!" she said in amazement. "What are you doing here?"

"I think by that look on the Codfish Sherlock's face," Sam said, with resignation, "that I'm Temporary Suspect Number One. I had Adele's pocketbook. I'm Mayo's boy."

"But Madame thought he thought—" Deb broke off.

"Are there other suspects?" Sam sounded delighted. "Who? Not Wilbur!"

"We were all of us out," Deb said, and went on to tell about Lynn and Greg. "So you see he knew Miss Parot, and Lynn did, too; in a way. And now they've both disappeared. Jinx—you know about that because Madame wrote you. Wilbur'd met her, too. And Madame and I were out."

"My God!" Sam said. "Well, you and mother are safe. You two are the only ones who never knew Adele!"

"Yes, I did. I met her once at a meeting of private-school teachers. I shared a room with her."

"*What?*"

"Madame knew. I remembered her," Deb went on, "and recommended her. . . . What I came for, Mr. Mayo, was to tell you that the burglar alarm started to go off, and Madame thought you should know."

"You mean," Asey said, with a chuckle, "Madame sent you here because she thought she should know if it was me creepin' in again?"

"No, she was worried because she felt sure it wasn't you!"

"It was me," Sam said. "I started to raise up a window

in the east wing about twenty minutes ago, and then I heard mother's voice. . . . Don't tell her I'm here, Deb!"

"But it wasn't twenty minutes ago; it was just now!"

"I'll take a look around for you. . . . Parr, you feel equal to entertainin' Sam?"

"I'm not going to try to run away," Sam assured him. "I'll even stand on my head and bark like a dog for you if you'll only keep me out of mother's clutches."

A circuit of the school and the dormitory cottages failed to produce any sign of an intruder. But, Asey reflected, there was hardly an inch of the wooded grounds where someone couldn't hide.

He beat a tattoo with the front-door knocker, grinned as the door opened, and saluted. "Mayo reportin', Madame. Nobody— *Doc!* Where'd you come from?"

"Come in," Dr. Cummings said. "I've been here about ten minutes, and I was just going to the barn after you. Lynn and Greg managed to hitchhike over to my office. We drove back as far as we could, and then walked. I've been packing the two of them off to bed—they've got the makings of first-class colds. Incidentally, phones over my way are working again, so I called the cops. They're tied up with flood trouble, but they're coming as soon as they can. Wait'll I get my things on, and I'll take a gander at Miss Parot.

"Why is it," the doctor said plaintively as he struggled to encase his stocky figure in a sodden raincoat, "that every time you come home, you drum up new and unpleasant business for me? As if I hadn't enough to do!"

He was still grumbling half an hour later when they returned to the school.

"It's what I always say—unless a murderer kindly leaves his lethal piano leg or cut-glass vase lying around for you to stumble on, you're licked." Cummings wriggled out of his coat. "But it was something smallish and heavy, with a point. Come into the library and let's draw pictures of what it ought to look like. Might get an idea."

"You seem to know your way around here," Asey commented as he followed the doctor along the hall. "I didn't even know there was a library."

"About four times a year," Cummings said, "someone breaks out in a rash or has a sore throat, and then I come over and sit in the library while the whole school files by with their mouths open for me to peer into. Makes me feel like Mama Robin. . . . Here." He entered the book-lined room, switched on the lights, and pointed to the decorative collection of weapons hung over the fireplace as he sat down at one of the round tables. "Look at those! Tomahawks, sabers—honestly, when you think of all the bona fide weapons in the world, why in God's name do people have to go out of their way to make things hard by bashing? . . . What's that silver heart you're taking out of your pocket?"

"The handle of one of Madame's canes. I can also offer for your consideration a bike tool, a triangle of brick— Hullo!" he greeted Jennie as she bustled in with a tray. "That isn't coffee!"

"It was when I started out to hunt you up! I swiped it from the pantry. And this," she said with pride, "is for you, Doc."

"A chocolate bar!" Cummings started to tear off the blue and white checked wrapper.

"When I think," Asey said, "how I lugged the big box of candy bars over here, holdin' 'em in my hot hand all the way! An' now I find you been passin' 'em out like campaign cigars! What's the matter with 'em? Aren't they a kind you like?"

"I just give everyone here one this afternoon," Jennie said, "as a sort of good-by present because they'd all been real nice to me. That was before the excitement of losing the girls, when I figured I'd be goin' home. . . . Is that cane broken *again*?" She clucked her tongue. "Madame was so provoked with Ella for breaking that heart cane this morning when she cleaned the hall! Ella's had it out in the kitchen all afternoon, trying to mend it and force the glue to set. . . . What are you holding it out to me for?"

"Put it back in the stand," Asey said. "If Ella broke it, I'm not interested."

"Now," Cummings said as Jennie left, "what's the story? I must say," giving Asey no time to answer, "I don't like Sam! He was a shifty, smart-aleck child, and he's never changed. Madame's all right. She had tough sledding after Merton died, when Sam was a baby. I admire her personally. Professionally, just the sight of her and Wilbur together fascinates me. There are more things I yearn to ask! Well, before you begin, *I* must tell you something about Lynn. It —er—seems—"

"Let me guess," Asey said as he paused. "Seems that the second time Lynn stopped to fix the buckle, near the bridge, she looked inside the carryall to see how Adele was, an' found her dead. So she sent the horses gallopin' off, an' then she leaned in some mud, an' come back here with her story of bein' thrown. That right?"

"How the hell do you know that?"

"For a man that's been tied down in a girls' school, I found out quite a lot," Asey told him. "You believe her?"

Cummings nodded. "Yes, and I think if you and the cops don't, you'll have your hands full of Greg howling around with a lot of crazy claims about his ex-fiancé and his faucet. I'm sure he never did it. I'm sure Madame didn't. I think she'd cut off both arms at the elbow before she'd do anything to hurt the good name of the school. Wilbur—hm. I don't really know about Wilbur."

"P'raps," Asey said, "you'd like to see the letter from him to Adele that I found in her pocketbook? I got it here."

After reading it Cummings put it down on the table as if it had burned his fingers. "Wow!" he said. "Now I'll look on Wilbur and Madame with even greater interest. Looks as if he'd got himself in deep water, and with both feet. Why, the man's gaga about the girl! Think he got frightened when he thought of her being here all the time?"

"That was Jennie's theory. If Adele blackmailed Sam," Asey said thoughtfully, "she might've decided to widen her field of operations an' blackmail Wilbur, too. I wonder if Wilbur maybe might've suspected her!"

Dr. Cummings shook his head. "That letter of his is not the letter of a suspicious man! Now, tell me everything again."

At the conclusion of Asey's recital, he said, "I'll still take Sam. I don't trust him. And he's admitted she blackmailed him. But this business of Jinx and Adele flying at each other without apparent reason—I've seen that kind of murder. People tag it with high-sounding names, but it's just something chemical."

He puffed at his cigar, while Asey got up and paced around the library. "Why'd Deb tell you she knew her? I suppose," the doctor answered his own question, "she was just trying to confuse you. She and Madame seem to be taking this murder as a personal affront to the school. Asey, what do *you* think?"

"I'm thinkin' about several things that's bothered me." Asey paused in front of a display case and peered at the collection of old-fashioned toys and dolls and miniatures of old household implements. "Like why someone said 'Yes' to Lynn at the station."

"D'you think she was killed there?" Cummings suggested, "and that someone else—the murderer—spoke to Lynn? . . . Asey, that's the burglar-alarm bell again! Hustle, man —don't just stand there!"

"I wonder, now," Asey said, "if—"

"Oh, get out!" Cummings threw his oilskin coat at him. "I'll stay here and let you know if anyone did get in. Hurry!"

Asey grinned as he put on the coat and left. But he went on down toward the barn without even glancing at the school.

For after all, he told himself, *there was nothing in Merton Hall itself that anyone needed to break in for.*

He heard voices ahead of him, flashed on his light, and found Deb Rice and Jinx engaged in a heated argument.

"I tell you I never went near the school! . . . Mr. Mayo, is that you? Come here. I want to hire you," Jinx said hotly, "to find out who really was trying to get in! Because I'm tired of being blamed for everything! Let *go* of me!"

In the widening beam of his approaching flashlight Asey saw Deb's hand drop from Jinx's shoulder, and gathered from her expression that she was even angrier than Jinx.

"I shall tell Madame!" she said. "Go back to bed at once. . . . Did you see anyone, Mr. Mayo?"

"I've concluded it's a short circuit," Asey said. "Tell Madame so, will you? I'll see Jinx back to her quarters."

"Sometimes," Jinx said as she trotted off beside him, "I get so mad! I get blamed—"

"Uh-huh. *Did* you go up to the school?"

"No! I wasn't asleep, and I heard the alarm and popped out the window—it's right over there! Then I ran into Deb."

"Tell me," Asey said as they stopped outside the cottage. "Why'd you and Adele Parot come to blows?"

"I'd guessed it was her," Jinx said. "Will it matter if I tell you the truth?"

"Considerable," Asey said.

"Well, the truth is, I wouldn't be blackmailed by her! Both times, at the Larrimore School and at home, she found out things about me and tried to make me pay blackmail. Perfectly innocent things, Mr. Mayo, but they just always involved my being somewhere with a boy when I was supposed to be somewhere else with Aunty.

"I wouldn't stand for it! I told Adele if she tried to blackmail me, I'd blackmail her right back for trying, and I followed up," Jinx said with satisfaction, "with a right to her jaw! I broke her arm the next time, and she knew I meant business! That's why I finally told father to let her come here. She was really a good teacher, and I knew I could take care of her if she tried her tricks here!"

"Her tricks— You mean she made a practice of black-mailin' you kids?"

Jinx nodded. "I couldn't prove it in court, but I heard things at Larrimore. I think she taught in expensive schools to get near rich girls, and I think she took on governess jobs to get into rich homes. You can scare some girls so easily! And a lot have enormous allowances!"

"Huh!" Asey said. "That's very enlightenin', an' it sort of puts a finishin' touch on a picture of Miss Parot that ain't very pretty. Thank you, Jinx. If I see the need of more of your help, I'll let you know. . . . Which window?"

"Asey, you transcendent thing, will you? Just boost me, please. I can get out in a flash if you want me!"

Asey walked thoughtfully back to the barn, where Parr was still sitting in the rocker and Sam Merton was sleeping soundly in the roadster's seat.

"Trowel wiggled once," Parr said laconically.

"So? I thought it would have." Asey went over to the carryall, surveyed it, peered at the scooter, and then looked for a long time at Sam.

"What you think?" Parr asked. "Or ain't you thinkin'?"

"I'm thinkin' candy bars," Asey said briefly. "Parr, no matter what happens, you stay put. I'll be back soon."

Cummings looked at him sharply as he entered the library. "Found out something, haven't you? I can always tell. You look like a cat that's swallowed a canary, and you pace around like a tiger. Well, *I* can't make head nor tail of it!"

"Wasn't there anyone out there at all?" Jennie bustled in. "Was it really only a short?"

"If anyone tryin' to get in a while ago heard that alarm, I hardly think they'd try again," Asey said, "an' I don't think there's two prowlers. . . . Jennie, think back to this afternoon before everyone went larrupin' off to meet the girls. Can you remember what people here were doin'?"

"Sure! Lynn was in the office; Deb'd got the mail—"

"Not what they was doin' in general," Asey said. "I mean exactly what they did, an' said, an' where they was."

"Lynn was wearin' what she had on when you seen her, and she was fixin' up new files for the new girls. Wilbur was bumblin' about with grass clippers—got a thorn in his thumb, and Madame took it out for him. In between that and her checkin' up on the sheets, she and Ella talked menus. Deb had got the mail—it was late—and she was readin' a letter from—well, I don't know what her beau's name is, but the army one I told you about. She had on a lavender smock that just matched the envelope, and I said as I passed by that it looked like mail from a foreign land, and she said yes, it was. There! I certainly can't see *that* butters any parsnips!" Jennie concluded.

"Go on," Asey said. "Then what?"

"Well, the woman phoned that the girls was lost. The gas-man hadn't filled the big tank, and there wasn't any gas in the school bus or Wilbur's car. We got out the carryall and had an awful time harnessin' up, the buckles was all so old. The bike seat was too low for Wilbur, but he wouldn't take the scooter 'cause the fumes make him feel sick. The scooter seat was too high for Deb. All of us were outside on the terrace, hurryin' and hammerin'. I tried to help all I could, and still keep 'em from messin' up the stuff I'd been cleanin'. I'd got all those blessed toys out on the flagstones. I couldn't see to dust 'em good in here, and the linoleum wax was wet, anyway. They finally got off, and then you come."

"An' you give 'em all a bar of candy?" Asey asked as he strolled over and looked at the toy collection.

"I wish you'd stop harpin' on that!" Jennie said with asperity. "No harm tryin' to be generous! Well, what're you going to do? Where you goin' now?"

Asey smiled. "I'm goin' to wait for the storm to provide me with another breather, I think. You stayin', doc?"

"When you're in this mood," Cummings said, "I know from experience you'll shortly have someone for me to patch up. Can't I come with you?"

"What I got to do is a bit out of your line, doc. Stay here an' create a soothin' influence. So long!"

"What was he lookin' at?" Jennie demanded the instant Asey left.

"Toys." Cummings walked over and pointed at the collection in the case. "Now, what in hell did he ever find there? Small churn, toy mortar and pestle, china doll, toy spinning wheel— What is there *there*?"

"He was lookin' more down here." Jennie got down on

her hands and knees. "Here's toy banks, a cradle, a tiny washtub—"

Twenty minutes later they gave up.

When dawn broke, Cummings went to the window and watched the first purple streaks spread up from the leaden sea.

"The rain stopped half an hour ago," he said impatiently. "I wish Asey'd get going! I've got my work. . . . Jennie, there's a fire down by the mill! Quick! Go tell Madame!"

He started to rush after her; then he stopped, smiling broadly.

He heard Jennie's voice ringing out, and saw her running toward the barn. Shortly Parr appeared, followed by Asey and Sam Merton. Jinx arrived on the scene with what, he thought, amounted to magical speed!

Madame, wearing a purple boudoir cap and purple dressing gown, stood on the flagstones and apparently issued orders, for Wilbur, Mrs. Parr, Deb, Lynn, and Greg all bore hand fire extinguishers as they raced away from the school.

Cummings, with his cigar at a jaunty angle, followed them leisurely through the orchard.

He looked for Asey among the figures milling around in the billowing smoke.

But Asey had doubled back to the barn, and was grabbing Deb Rice's hand a second after she'd reached into the basket on the front of the motor scooter and started to draw out a toy iron!

"Next time you camouflage with mud," Asey said, "remember the insides of baskets! Wilbur's basket was a mess, you know, but your scooter basket was awful nice an' dry, for all the downpour you was s'posed to be out in. An' that bone-dry candy bar—I'm afraid you'll break your arm if you wriggle so. *Drop that iron!*"

"She's only dislocated that shoulder," Cummings informed Asey as he joined him on the terrace later. "Hefty girl. I suppose she hoped to grab your roadster if she could break away from you. How'd you know it was Deb who said 'Yes' to Lynn in the carryall?"

"Pretty much had to be Deb or Madame, an' Madame's no yes-girl," Asey said. "She was smart, doc. Told me to keep away from the scooter when I took it to the barn, so's I wouldn't get all muddy. I did sort of hold it away from me, but I must've glanced inside the basket, because every time I seen one of those candy bars, I kept wonderin' where I'd seen another. When I really looked in the basket, after that alarm she'd set goin', an' found the bar all fresh an' dry, I knew she'd been lyin' from the start. . . . Where's Jennie —talkin'? I want to get home before it rains some more."

"Let her talk," Cummings said. "*I* want to get things straight. How'd you guess that toy iron was the weapon?"

"Wa-el, I looked in that toy case, an' there was a toy iron stand, but no iron sittin' on it. It occurred to me that a toy iron was just about what we'd been describin'. Nothin' better to hammer with than a little iron!" He chuckled. "You know how women are—they hammer with a shoe heel, or anything as long's it's not a regular hammer. In all the bustle, Deb put the iron into the scooter's basket—I don't think she took it as a weapon, but a tool. But you got to remember that the lavender letter she'd been readin' *wasn't* from her fake fiancé."

"How'd you know he was a fake?" Cummings interrupted.

"I noticed when I flashed my light on her hand—she'd been grabbin' Jinx—that she didn't wear any engagement ring," Asey said. "An' she's the kind of gal that likes to flash a diamond, real proper. Besides, Jennie didn't know the fiancé's name. If she'd had one, you know Jennie'd have found it out in a week! Nope, that lavender letter was to Wilbur from Adele. Greg's letter he showed me was on the same color stationery! It'd come in the morning mail for Wilbur, an' Deb recognized the writin' and the paper from havin' seen Adele's letters to Madame. She stole it, an' opened it an' read it. It wasn't love, like Jennie thought, that made her cheeks flush when she read it. It was jealousy."

"Look here, man, you can't mean that Deb and Wilbur—" Cummings sounded as if he were gargling. "That Wilbur and Deb—"

"Uh-huh. All these years," Asey said. "She found the stubs in Wilbur's blue serge coat pocket, goin' through 'em like a good—er—fiancée. She asked him about 'em, but he stalled by sayin' that he'd been taken to the theater an' the night clubs by the teachers' agency man an' his wife. She didn't swallow it whole, but she tried to believe him, because she wanted to. But when she seen that letter from Adele to Wilbur she burned up. Only, before she could do anythin', Madame sent 'em all scurryin' off to the stations."

"I can only say," Cummings said, "that I always wondered about Wilbur! Go on!"

"Wa-el, Deb was still burnin' up when she went off with the iron. When she fell behind in the procession to fix the scooter's seat, she seen Wilbur followin' the carryall toward the Skaket station—so she followed *him!* She seen him sneak inside the carryall after Lynn'd gone into the station. After he left, all chirky an' beamin', Deb slipped into the carryall, herself. She told Adele to lay off Wilbur, an' Adele said sure—she'd just seen Sam an' had been royally paid to lay off, an' it's my guess she'd decided Sam was her best black-mailin' bet at Merton Hall, even if he thought he'd paid her up in full. But Adele agreed so easy, Deb didn't believe her. So she ducked out to the scooter, got the iron, an' before Adele realized she'd come back—*bang!*"

"So Deb was in the carryall when Lynn came out?"

Asey nodded. " 'Yes' was the only word she could man-age, I guess. She hopped out as the carryall started off. No-body seen her because nobody expected a train, an' nobody was around. Just for the record, she went over to Billings-gate. On the way back it began to rain, an' she went into a cranberry-bog shack an' waited till the breather came. Then she did a mud-smearin' job on herself an' the scooter, an' started home. An' met the girls, by luck."

"But how'd you catch on about her and Wilbur? No one else did!"

"Wa-el, I wondered why Deb let Madame boss her around so, an' why she worked so hard, an' took such a per-sonal interest. 'N'en I remembered Jennie sayin' Deb's great ambition was to have a school of her own some day, like this. I wondered if the personal interest wasn't Wilbur, an' if she didn't hope, by way of him, to get this school! The fake fiancé made a nice smoke screen."

"I wonder if Madame guessed. . . . To think of them—

sitting and waiting for the school to drop into their laps! A little sinister!"

"It was worth waitin' for," Asey said. "An' after the years she'd waited to have her own school, Deb wasn't goin' to have Adele botch it up. Anyway, she was bright about that iron. No one'd guess it was a weapon if she didn't leave it behind. But she didn't want to take the chance that the iron's not bein' in the case would be noticed—someone might start speculatin' about it. So she put it in the scooter basket, intendin' to put it right back in the case where it belonged. Only Madame sent me an' the scooter off to the barn, to get me out of the way—"

"And Deb couldn't get a chance to get it, and put it back!"

"She tried, all right," Asey said. "You realize she was the only one kept tryin' to do anythin'? She kept tryin' to get me away from the barn—Madame kept wantin' me to stay there. She fooled with the burglar alarm, hopin' that might snare us into runnin' out to hunt burglars so's she could slip in an' get the iron. But on the whole, I thought it was easier to trick *her* into slippin' in. You'll never know how hard Sam an' Parr and I worked to set up that bonfire! Jinx kept watch for us. . . . I wish Jennie would hurry!" He stepped over to the roadster and put his finger on the horn.

Cummings laughed suddenly. "Madame wants me to sell this to the cops when they get here as the Station Murder. I said I would, but I'll always think of it as the Sweet Tooth Murder. If Jennie hadn't one, you wouldn't have brought her those candy bars."

"Might's well call it the Generous Mystery," Asey returned. "If she hadn't given 'em away, I wouldn't have had any clue. An'— Hurry up, Jennie! Get in! Because if your best hat gets soaked on the way home, I know there's going to be a sequel named Murder in a Porter Sixteen! . . . So long, doc!"

THE STARS SPELL DEATH

CAST OF CHARACTERS

ASEY MAYO—*Cape Cod detective*
GEORGE DRUM—*owner of an observatory*
EVELYN DRUM—*George's brother*
DR. OLIVER HEASLIP—*prominent astronomer*
SARAH HEASLIP—*his penniless sister*
JACK THACKERAY—*his young assistant*
PERRY LOWE—*his blond secretary*
JABE CULLIS—*local policeman*

THE STARS SPELL DEATH

Asey MAYO, peering vainly around in the dusk for some trace of the Drum Observatory, found his thoughts turning with uncharacteristic bitterness to two men. One was the Starlington ticket agent, who had genially assured him, some three miles and thirty minutes back, that the observatory was not only a mere stone's throw from the station, but also a building no child could miss, even in the coastal blackout. The other man was his boss, young Bill Porter of Porter Motors, now Porter Tanks, who had so casually tacked this letter-delivering detour onto Asey's five-day vacation.

"Starlington's only two hundred miles out of your way, Asey." Bill had made it sound like two inches. "Just give this letter to Dr. Oliver Heaslip and tell him who you are. If he isn't impressed by having a Porter director act as messenger, then drag out your other accomplishments. Tell him you're Cape Cod's gift to the detective world, the Codfish Sherlock or Homespun Sleuth. Tell him you invented the Porter carburetor and ironed out the bugs in the Mark XV tank. Spin him salty yarns of your early life at sea. In short, charm him, and sell him on leaving his stars long enough to solve our lens problem on the experimental model the Signal Corps's howling for. Major Bragg suggested him. Says he's a queer fish, but our boy. Unquestioned integrity, ex-head of the Amateur Telescope Makers, and had lots of desert experience. Shouldn't take you two seconds to sew him up for us."

So far, Asey reflected wearily, it had taken a day and a half, involved two grounded planes, innumerable train changes, and a washed-out bridge. His bag was in the Tulsa airport, his overcoat had disappeared in Boston. His wrinkled, slept-in suit would probably convince Dr. Heaslip that Porter Tanks was a tramp outfit he should shun at all costs. Provided Asey could ever manage to locate him and the Drum Observatory!

In all fairness to the ticket agent, possibly every Starlington child could find the spot blindfolded, but for a stranger in the blackout it was haystack-needle-hunting. Ahead, Asey could see only the blur of pine woods stretching over rolling hills, and behind him, only the silhouette of two church spires and the tall elms and Colonial houses that framed Starlington's village green. Nowhere did a crack of light show. He'd not heard the sound of a person, or a car, or even a barking dog. Everything seemed hushed and withdrawn and slightly unreal. This was more like a stage setting than a flesh-and-blood town. It was unlike any blackout Asey had ever before encountered, and as he peered around, he instinctively turned up his coat collar without being quite aware of his gesture.

He strode on along the dirt sidewalk, focused his pocket flashlight briefly at a corner sign, and followed Main Street around a tortuous reverse curve.

"Oho!" Asey stopped short at the sight of a low, white building looming in the pines to his right. "*That's* it—nope, it's a fancy de luxe gas station—nosir, there's the telescope cupola! What a setup, an' me with my eyes peeled for some dumpy old shed!"

He stood and studied what he could see of the sleek, streamlined structure. The central part, flanked by glass brick wings, apparently bulged off in a circle to the rear to form the working portion which housed the telescope. A graveled driveway curved up to the front steps, and the outlines of cropped evergreens were visible against the glinting glass brick.

The place was dark, but Asey had seen enough of Starlington to know that lack of light couldn't be construed as lack of occupancy. Besides, he reminded himself, as he turned up the drive, the astronomer's working day was only just starting.

His foot was on the bottom step when the wide door above him suddenly jerked open, then as suddenly jerked shut.

Asey looked up quizzically. Did the spot have electric-eye doors besides its other fancy trimmings, or was someone inside just trying to make up his mind about coming out?

As if in answer, the door opened again, and the figure of a woman in slacks—a short, slight woman—showed for the fraction of a second against the lighted interior. While Asey opened his mouth to ask if she knew whether or not Dr. Heaslip was there, she slammed the door and darted down the steps past him, apparently entirely unaware of his presence.

"I beg your pardon"—Asey swung around and spoke to her—"but is Dr. Heas—"

His question was drowned out by the scrunch of gravel under her feet and the sound of a bicycle stand being kicked up.

"Is Doc—" Asey broke off as the bicycle and its rider whizzed out of sight. Then he shrugged, remounted the steps, only to pause with his hand on the doorknob. "Golly, I'm slow on the uptake this evenin'!" he muttered. "Why, she was cryin'! That's why she never noticed me; she was cryin' her eyes out! Huh, I wonder what they meant by callin' Heaslip a queer fish!"

He was disappointed, on entering a large, semicircular room, to find no one there. The hooded lights gave ample illumination, but so distorted his shadow that his hat looked like an erupting volcano on the three closed doors of the curved wall opposite him. The two narrow side doors led to offices, Asey guessed, and the wide door in between them, a chromium-striped affair that would have done credit to a movie house, obviously led into the observatory proper.

The wings to his left and right contained modernistic bookcases and display cases lavishly trimmed with shining chrome. Even the "Do Not Touch" warnings on the latter were chrome cutout letters, a good foot high.

Some young architect had gone to town on the Drum Observatory, Asey decided, as he walked across the white linoleum floor, on which the signs of the zodiac were inlaid in bright yellow. The lucite desk in front of him had clusters of stars for legs, and the lucite telephone was so streamlined that he wouldn't have recognized it except for the cord. And the fact that it started to ring.

He looked expectantly toward the closed doors for some-

one to come and answer—someone must be around, somewhere! After all, that weeping woman could hardly have
been goaded to tears by the zodiac signs!

But no one came, and when the ringing finally subsided,
there was no sound to indicate that anyone might have taken
the call on some possible extension.

In deference to the impression he must make for the sake
of Porter Tanks, Asey stifled his natural impulse to thrust
open the closed doors and bellow for Heaslip in his loudest
quarterdeck voice. Instead, he picked up a lucite chair,
thumped it on the floor, then waited a moment, and
thumped again, harder.

But no one was sufficiently curious to investigate.

How in time, Asey asked himself, as he stalked impatiently around, did you arouse an astronomer politely?
People who ignored phones probably ignored door-knock-
ings— He stopped and looked down at a lunch box on the
floor beside the desk. Would he have to wait till the man
knocked off stargazing for a midnight snack?

After five minutes of pacing round the zodiac signs, he
read, out of sheer boredom, the chromium-lettered text that
formed part of the curved wall's decorations:

"Light travels at the rate of 186,000 miles per SECOND. If
you rode a light beam, a trip to the sun would last 8 minutes."

Skimming through the other informative tidbits about the
universe, the solar system, the planets, and the sun, he read
his way around to two small bronze plaques on the side wall
of the right wing. One, under the name "Oliver Heaslip,"
bore a bas-relief profile of a vigorous-looking man with the

bluntest, squarest jaw Asey ever recalled seeing, and announced that Dr. Heaslip, astronomer in charge, had been honored by some learned society for his research on the rings and moons of Saturn. The other plaque said that the observatory had been built three years before by George and Evelyn Drum, and added:

"Possibly the most paradoxical thing about modern astronomy is that our knowledge of the overwhelmingly great is acquired from the study of the ultimately small."

Asey looked again at the granite-like jaw of Dr. Heaslip and congratulated himself for not having succumbed to the temptation of shouting for him or otherwise taking any steps that might have caused that jaw to jut out any more. It wasn't wise, he thought, as he strolled back and sat down in the lucite chair, to irritate anyone with a jaw like that. After all, the man would come for his lunch box sooner or later, and for him to find a Porter director meekly and patiently waiting might prove best. And there was a three o'clock train, the ticket agent had told him, as well as the midnight he'd hoped to get.

He leaned back, and then, as if ice water had been poured down his spine, he sat up rigidly straight, his eyes glued to the knob of the office door across from him. There was no sound of any person in the room on the other side, there was no sound of the knob turning, but turning it certainly was!

Half fascinated by the soundless, infinitely slow movement, Asey watched till he couldn't contain himself any longer. Springing up, he bounded across and grabbed at the knob, twisted it, and shoved. Then, with an exclamation of bewilderment, he stood back and put his hands on his hips.

The door was locked!

Slowly, with several furtive backward looks at the door, Asey returned to the lucite chair.

He was positive he'd seen that knob turn. It *had* turned. But why? Why should anyone be so surreptitious, particularly about a *locked* door? Asey shook his head. Possibly it was all an optical illusion, a mirage resulting from his thirty-six hours of grounded planes and crowded day coaches.

"But it *did* turn!" he said softly to himself, and looked speculatively at the center door. Odd and mysterious things which occurred in the Drum Observatory were no concern of his, but this silent knob-turning on a locked door was either the work of pixies, or gremlins, or of a two-legged human whose attempted progress from one room to another certainly bordered on the sinister. A prowler? Perhaps, Asey decided, he'd better slip in through that center door and take a look around.

As he stood up, the lights went out.

Simultaneously there was a sound of scrambling footsteps from the office with the locked door, and more noises from behind the wide door—a thudding sound, more scrambling, the thump of someone colliding with something solid. All the noises were inextricably mixed up, and of such brief duration that they were over before Asey snapped on his flashlight and shoved open the center door. He stopped so abruptly in his headlong dash through the doorway that he grabbed at the door handle to keep from falling.

On the floor directly ahead of him was the body of Dr.

Heaslip—there was absolutely no mistaking that jutting jaw, or that profile!

Half a glance, Asey thought, would convince even the most optimistic First Aider that Dr. Heaslip's horrible, recently inflicted head wound had been fatal and that the man was beyond human help.

Asey played the thin, pencil-like beam of his little flashlight quickly around the white linoleum floor near Heaslip, picked up the yellow inserts of the solar system, the base of the telescope, a maze of electric wires. Then he flicked the beam rapidly around the walls of the circular room. Whoever had been the cause of those scrambling noises, and in all probability also the cause of Heaslip's murder, had without doubt rushed out the open French door visible beyond the telescope. By now the fellow had probably melted into the black blur of the pine woods outside, and tracking him down was a job for the local police, whom Asey intended to summon at once by telephone.

As he swung the tiny spot of light back on the body again, an object near Heaslip's foot caught Asey's eye. Bending over, he looked closely at the pint-sized piece of jagged meteorite, and slowly nodded. Here was one blunt-instrument killing where no one would have to waste time hunting for the specific blunt instrument employed. This jagged meteorite was it, complete with bloodstains!

He straightened up as his ears caught the faint metallic slap of a car door shutting, and then the more audible angry grinding of a car starter being kicked at by someone in a desperate frenzy of haste.

"So!" Asey muttered. "Parked out back in the woods,

did you? Huh, if your battery'll only keep on thwartin' you a few seconds more . . ." Sidestepping the telescope base and the assortment of wires, he dashed out the French door and raced toward the noise of the still madly grinding starter.

After sprinting across an open field, he spotted the outlines of a coupé just an instant before the engine caught and the parking lights were switched on. With a superhuman lunge, Asey flung himself at the back of the coupé as it started to move. His feet, groping for the bumper, mercifully slipped down onto the braces where a bumper had once been, and his hands reached up, as the car jerked off, for where the handle of the closed rumble seat ought to have been—and was not.

In second gear, the car shot forward, bumped over a succession of ruts and then tore off, lickety-split, down a wood road.

Asey, hanging on by his fingernails, knew it was a question of seconds before he got jolted off. The slanting surface of the closed rumble seat, damp and slippery with evening mist, was nothing he could long hope to cling to. Any gymnastic, Dick Tracy-ish gesture of hurling himself over onto a running board was out. This coupé had no running boards.

What annoyed him most was that the misted rear window prevented him from catching even a glimpse of the driver. Once he was bounced off, he would have no way of recognizing this particular coupé among all the other streamlined coupés in the world. The lack of the bumper and rumble-seat handle meant nothing nowadays for identification purposes. Hardly a car in the Porter plant parking space hadn't been patriotically stripped of all its hardware for the salvage pile.

But in his right-hand coat pocket were his kit-bag keys. If he could only get at them! Holding his breath, he groped, fished them out, and scratched at the paint in wide, claw-like swoops.

Then the car, taking a curve on two wheels, swerved off on a tarred road, and Asey landed so heavily on its sand shoulder that he saw a batch of brand-new and strangely shaped stars group themselves for a full minute around the new crescent moon.

Asey shook his head to clear it, and ruefully rubbed his hip. Anyway, he'd made some mark on that car, he thought, as he sat and surveyed what by now was the familiar scenery of rolling hills above and the silhouetted town below. And, this time, he should find the observatory in less than forty minutes. His wild ride had taken him cross-lots. A left turn should take him back in no time.

He brushed the sand from his clothes and set off, and then slowed down as he became aware of the tap of footsteps on the pavement behind him. After his earlier experiences with the zigzags of Main Street, he decided he might as well be on the safe side and ask if he were headed in the right direction.

The wide beam of a powerful flashlight suddenly focused on him and continued to spotlight his face, despite his movements to avoid it, while the footsteps approached. Somewhat annoyed by the glare, Asey snapped on his own little light, and picked up the figure of a tall, thin, elegant young man in a dinner jacket, with a white silk scarf tied carelessly around his neck. To Asey, accustomed to husky tank workers, this hatless, black-haired young man seemed almost incredibly fragile.

"Good evenin'," Asey said. "Am I on the road to the Drum Observatory?"

"The observatory? Oh." The fellow sounded vaguely relieved. "Yes. Straight ahead." He snapped off his light, and Asey followed suit. "For a moment back there," he added in his rather high-piched voice, "I though you were a tramp. Visiting fireman, I presume?"

"Wa-el," Asey drawled, "I'm visitin', in a sort of way. Fact is—"

"As the years roll on"—the young man fell into step beside him—"I can spot an astronomer at twenty paces. It's your—er—chins. Very firmly chinned, all of you. After Heaslip, I dare say?"

"In a manner of speakin'. You happen to know him?" Asey doubted if this sleek youth had anything in common with the square-jawed Heaslip, but under the circumstances any information about the man had its use.

"Oh, yes, intimately— What did you say?"

"I just choked." Asey was glad that the darkness concealed the expression which had accompanied his exclamation of surprise. "Known him long?"

· "Years. Able man, but stubborn as the devil. Don't cross him. I say, you seem a bit different from the usual run of astronomers—have you ever noticed the effect astronomy has on people?"

"What?" Asey inquired. His own impression, based on

what had just happened at the observatory, was that a touch of medieval black magic still clung to modern astronomers and their chromium-trimmed environs.

"Well, you take Jack Thackeray!" The young man spoke with such vigor that Asey almost expected someone named Jack Thackeray to be thrust into his hand. "Heaslip's assistant—ever meet him? . . . No? Well, he's able, too, and stubborn as the devil. Why I think of him as an example is that he damn' near made a hit-and-run victim out of me just now! He distinctly saw me hail him—couldn't have missed seeing me! And he absolutely would *not* stop! What I mean to say—"

"Was he," Asey interrupted, "drivin' a coupé?"

"Yes. Had his mind fixed on something else, you see, and absolutely would not be deterred—get my point? One-minded. That's the trouble with you astronomers. You—"

"A streamlined coupé?" Asey tried to make his question sound casual. "With a rear bumper missin'?"

"Aha! You're one-minded, too!" the young man said with triumph. "You probably saw the car pass a few minutes ago, and your one idea is to identify it beyond any doubt! One-minded, and full of whims, all of you. Dallying with such infinite things, you lose sight of the rest of the world. Take Heaslip and his onion sandwiches."

"His *what*?"

"Hideous thick sandwiches filled with raw onions. He insists on having 'em every night. That's, frankly, why I gave up going to the observatory. I bore with his whims, but I simply could not take those things. All a man could smell was onions, onions, all over the place!"

"Let me get this straight," Asey said. "You mean that *you* was a buddin' astronomer? *You?*"

"Not budding; full-blown," the young man returned. "I really enjoyed it, out West—that's where sister and I first ran into Heaslip. My lungs were shot, and there wasn't much to do in the desert. The stars whiled away my time very nicely. I shouldn't have minded continuing my work here, if Heaslip hadn't conceived this absurd whim for onion sandwiches. It's not a bad little observatory. Better-looking than most, don't you think?"

"By any chance," Asey said, "are you George Drum?"

"George's my sister. I'm Evelyn." He gave it the English pronunciation. "Father intended George to be a George, you see, and didn't let her being a girl distract him. Conversely, mother insisted on naming me. . . . You know, Jack Thackeray has no business driving seventy-five miles an hour while I patriotically walk! Probably he's had another row with Heaslip."

"Another row? Don't they get on?" Asey asked.

"Virtually their only point of agreement is onion sandwiches," Evelyn returned. "They loathe each other. Jack can barely wait for Heaslip to be drafted so he can take charge of the observatory and make enough to get married. Why, he—"

"I beg your pardon," Asey interrupted, "but would you say that again?"

"I said"—Evelyn raised his voice, as if Asey were hard of hearing—"Jack can barely wait for Heaslip to be drafted so he can take charge, and make enough to get married. Heaslip's furious that he'll be taken, at thirty-seven, while Jack was rejected, at twenty-five, because of his one eye. So—"

"*One* eye?" Asey said.

"Yes, he lost the other in a football accident. He wears a very picturesque black patch. Gives him an aura of Robin Hood. I can't imagine why he was in such a terrific rush!"

"You're sure it was him?" Asey asked.

"Definitely. I say—" Evelyn Drum stopped. "You're going to the observatory; be a good fellow and take this box, will you? You'd save me no end of time and trouble. Give it to Heaslip with my compliments. Tell him, 'At long last.'"

"I'd be glad to take it," Asey said, "but I think, Mr. Drum, maybe you'd better come along with me. If you've got anything to do with the place—"

"I haven't. Not a thing. Don't go near it any oftener than I can help. It's frightfully nice of you to take this box— Got it? Don't let it drop. And I've enjoyed our chat, and all that sort of thing."

"Wait, Mr. Drum! I think you ought to come back with me and see Heaslip! Because—"

"I've not spoken to him for six montns, and, frankly," Drum said, "I've no intention of going to see him, now or at any other time. I was only going to chuck that box in the door. Never would have bothered tramping over with it if Sister hadn't raised such a stink. Don't say I didn't warn you about those sandwiches, by the way! Good night!"

"But something's happened over there! Heaslip—"

"Not my department. Good night!"

"Listen, Mr. Drum! You—"

"Good night!"

The sound of young Mr. Drum's footsteps receded and finally died away in the night.

Asey shrugged, tucked under his arm the large candy box that the fellow had thrust at him, and continued on his way. Perhaps it was just as well that Drum had departed and given him a chance to sort out his thoughts. The odds and ends of information he'd picked up in the last ten minutes had given his mind a crowded feeling. Things didn't make sense.

Drum had identified the coupé that raced away from the observatory as belonging to and being driven by Heaslip's assistant, who fought with his boss and coveted his job. Drum ought to know, and he certainly had no reason to tell other than the truth. That left you, Asey thought, with an apparent murderer and an obvious motive. That part was all right.

Only, where had this Jack Thackeray been, back there at the observatory? Could he have been the person who, for some fantastic reason Asey couldn't begin to fathom, had turned the knob on that locked door? If he'd been there in that office, why hadn't the fellow answered the phone when it rang, or investigated Asey's chair-thumping? What had prompted the putting out of lights? Was it a short circuit, a blown fuse, or had someone deliberately pulled a switch? It must have been the latter, Asey decided, for ordinarily people made considerable noise and to-do over accidental blackouts.

He paused to shift the candy box, which apparently contained a lump of lead and seemed to get heavier all the time.

Why, he wondered, hadn't Heaslip called out at once, if Thackeray had pulled a switch? The answer probably was that the working part of the observatory had been dark, anyway, and consequently Heaslip wouldn't have been aware of the situation. Or had Heaslip himself turned out the lights? Whatever the case, why should Thackeray, who must surely have known that a third person was out there in the reception room, have picked that particular time to bash his boss?

"It's crazy!" Asey thought out loud. "First the lights go. Then, the way it sounded to me, Thackeray scrambled from his office, bashed Heaslip as he ran through the observatory —huh, must be a connectin' door there! Then he popped out that French door an' sprinted to his car. But, golly, it sure took some genius to locate Heaslip in the dark, an' do such an all-fired efficient job on him in those few seconds there before I came on the scene!"

Of course, it was possible that Heaslip had been killed before the lights went out, perhaps even before Asey reached the observatory. That thudding sound might not have been caused by Heaslip's body falling to the floor, but by Thackeray colliding with something. But if that were so, why had Thackeray stayed, and why had he chosen to make such a spectacular and noisy exit? The knob-turning, the light-dousing, the rushing around, all seemed downright silly when you stopped to figure that the fellow might easily have slipped out like a mouse if he'd wanted to.

"An' left me sittin' there," Asey murmured, "coolin' my heels an' reading' instructive items comparin' the energy of the sun's rays with the energy generated by the wings of a mosquito in flight! Huh, the local cops sure got some jim-dandy detectin' ahead of 'em!"

He shifted the box again and reflected that the actual sequence of events at the observatory was no stranger than the Drum family's apparent relation to their handiwork. That, after building such an expensive outfit—or, at least, being the co-builder, according to that bronze plaque—young Drum should reject the place because of a few onions seemed to Asey to be carrying things too far. It stood to reason that if you built an observatory, you owned it, and if you owned it, you ran it. And you very probably chose and paid the staff you wanted to work there. It should have been a simple matter for Drum to have solved the onion-sandwich problem by prohibiting the eating of them during working hours, or else by spraying the place with perfume as a counterirritant. Instead, the co-builder didn't speak to his astronomer in charge.

"Plumb crazy!" Asey said, and stepped to the side of the road as he caught sight of a bicycle's blue headlight coming toward him. It whizzed past, and he found himself staring with mouth agape into the darkness that had swallowed up the vehicle.

Then he shrugged, and strode on toward the observatory, which loomed ahead. He told himself not to jump to conclusions. True, the rider of that bicycle *had* been crying. Sobbing bitterly, in fact. But that was no reason for him to assume that it was therefore a woman crying, or even the same crying woman who'd rushed away on her bicycle earlier, and whom he'd almost entirely forgotten in the events which followed. He greatly doubted if she could have played any part in Heaslip's murder, but if she had, it was the job of the local police to fit her into the picture.

Turning up the gravel driveway, he discovered five cars parked in front of the observatory. Apparently, during his absence, someone else had found Heaslip's body and had already notified the cops.

And that, Asey thought as he ran lightly up the front steps, was good. Now he could leave Drum's confounded candy box, tell what he knew, and catch that midnight train home!

But in the reception room there was none of the hubbub which, experience had taught him, usually could be associated with a visit from the police. The place was stark empty. And quiet. There wasn't even a whiff of cigar smoke.

Asey set the candy box on the lucite desk and looked around in astonishment. Cops couldn't be *this* quiet!

Then, dimly, he heard one voice. Tiptoeing over to the center door, he leaned against the crack and listened. Maybe they had scientific cops in this hamlet—nothing in Starlington could really surprise him now.

He pushed the door open a little and peeked through the crack at the side. Standing with their backs to him was a group of men and women, men in mackinaws or zipper jackets, women in tweed coats or polo coats. At home, Asey thought, they might have been a group coming home from a church supper or a Grange meeting.

But what were they doing here, now?

And where was Heaslip's body?

Craning his neck, Asey pushed the door open a little wider, and then he nearly let go the door entirely. The voice he'd heard belonged to one of the most beautiful blond girls he'd ever seen. She was wearing an elaborate evening dress and her hair was done high.

Her words came to him in snatches: "Yes, this is a Schmitt parabolic camera . . . pictures. Yes, plates . . . get details not visible to the naked eye. . . . Yes, of course we look through the telescopes, too, but science does a better job."

Where—Asey had a hard time to keep from screaming the question out loud—*where* was that body?

That group, listening so intently to that beautiful blonde, couldn't be standing on it, heaven knew! And yet they were clustered around the exact spot on the floor where Heaslip's body had been, not much more than twenty minutes ago!

"Notice the floor inserts in here," the girl was saying. "Rings of the solar system. . . . I'm sorry you can't see the seventh ring properly. That's Dr. Heaslip's own particular field. And I can't tell you how sorry I am that he's not here. He's *so* absent-minded, as you know, and if it makes you feel any better, he also forgot a particularly important meeting in Boston only the day before yesterday. He was supposed to have been given a gold medal, and they waited simply ages for him to turn up."

Faint giggles from the group indicated that Dr. Heaslip's absent-mindedness came as no shock to anyone.

But Heaslip's absent body, Asey thought grimly, was not only a shock to him, it was soon going to drive him quite mad.

"Yes," the girl answered someone's inquiry. "The seventh ring . . . Saturn. I'm sorry it's covered. . . . I wish I knew more. I feel so inadequate! Now, if you'll come here, I'll show you the teles—"

The group moved away, and Asey's eyes narrowed as he stared at the spot where they'd been standing. The body was there, all right. But it was covered with a tarpaulin. And resting on the tarpaulin was one of the signs Asey had noticed earlier, out on the display cases in the wings.

"Do Not Touch," it said, in chrome cutout letters a foot high.

And nobody was making the slightest effort to disobey the sign!

Drawing a long breath, Asey let the door slip to. Then he returned to the lucite chair and sat down. While he'd been away chasing Thackeray and chatting with young Drum, someone had come, covered up the body, and stuck that sign on it.

Who'd done it? Thackeray? If the fellow'd returned to the observatory as quickly as he'd left, he'd have had ample time to cover up a dozen bodies and strew them with assorted signs. And who was this self-possessed young blond creature, dressed for a ball, who was lecturing to the local boys and girls? Where had she sprung from?

The whole business had gone too far, Asey thought, as he reached out for the lucite phone. Then he slowly drew his hand back.

"Golly," he said softly to himself, "I'm in kind of an awkward position! If the cops ask whyn't I phone 'em at once when I found the body, an' I say I rushed out to chase this Thackeray, an' then he chooses to deny it, I'm sure goin' to look silly!"

To be sure, Drum had seen the coupé and could identify it, but Thackeray could claim he was merely driving and had never been near the observatory at all.

"An' I can't swear I seen 'im here"—Asey rubbed his chin reflectively—"because I never did. Huh, Starlington folks will know Thackeray, an' they'll believe him sooner than a stranger—a trampy-lookin' stranger, at that!"

Although he didn't doubt that Heaslip's body really was under the tarpaulin, he couldn't phone now, at once, without making sure. If the cops, summoned to investigate a murder, were to find under that tarpaulin a bag of golf clubs or a couple of old ironing boards instead of a body, they'd probably rush him to the nearest psychopathic ward.

To burst in now and shout out that it was Heaslip's own body which obliterated the seventh ring—Asey shook his head. At least two women would faint, and at least six of those sturdy citizens would collar him, demand fuller explanations, and he'd never even get the three-o'clock train out of the place.

He glanced at Drum's candy box on the desk, and suddenly noticed beyond it an empty telegram envelope.

"For Pete's sake, *does* this place have gremlins?" he muttered.

The contents of that room were engraved on his mind from his previous visit, and he knew no envelope had been on the desk then! Gremlins were his answer, Asey decided, and the cops could try and find a more tangible solution to who turned doorknobs and covered bodies and left telegram envelopes around!

He reached over curiously and lifted the top off the candy box. Probably he'd find that gremlins had removed its leaden contents.

He peered into the box, and whistled noiselessly. In it was a meteorite, a jagged, pint-sized meteorite, a twin of the one he'd seen near Heaslip's foot!

Replacing the box cover, Asey leaned back in the chair. The sooner people went, the sooner he could check on that body, call the cops, and get out, the better he'd like it. Never again would anyone inveigle him into playing delivery boy to an astronomer!

But, on the other hand, he honestly had to admit to a growing and gnawing desire to get to the root of all these goings-on, himself. Walk out on a thing like this now, and it would haunt you, Asey thought, to the end of your days!

The covering of Heaslip's body was a stop-gap job, he decided. Something hurriedly and cleverly done to keep the murder from being immediately discovered. When the person responsible thought the observatory was empty again, wouldn't he return—either to remove the body, or take some further action? If Jack Thackeray had sped back and covered the body, mightn't he even now be lurking around outside, waiting for the chance to take the remains of his former boss to some far corner of the surrounding woods, or to the near-by coast, where the Atlantic offered a vast and handy means for the disposal of a body? Asey told himself he had nothing to lose by lying low and playing possum for a while after this group left. It was a hunch worth following.

Not ten minutes passed before he heard the restless feet

scraping and polite murmurings that indicated the group's impending departure. With a quick motion, he slipped out of the chair into the nearer wing, and ducked down behind a display case while the girl shepherded her flock out and slammed the door behind her with an air of finality.

But there was no click to indicate she'd snapped the lock, nor did she bother to turn off the lights.

"I wonder!" Asey murmured, and continued to crouch behind the chrome-trimmed case. Did her rapid shunting of these people mean that *she* intended to return, perhaps?

One by one the cars outside departed, and then, from the office directly in back of him, the same office whose door handle had turned, came a faint scraping sound.

So the girl had sneaked around to the rear of the observatory, and was creeping in the back way, was she?

As Asey started to his feet, the front door opened, and the girl herself made a beeline dash for the observatory!

With a muttered exclamation of bewilderment, Asey followed her.

When he swung open the center door, she was already kneeling beside Heaslip's body, from which she'd lifted back the covering, and on her face was a look of abject, wide-eyed horror. She glanced up at Asey without seeming actually to see him, and then her hand groped out and tremblingly replaced the tarpaulin. Her lips moved, but no words came.

Obviously, Asey thought, she was looking for the first time at the body. That reaction time, a combination of utter shock and horrified surprise, was nothing the average person could assume at the drop of a hat. That was genuine.

"I guessed you'd be back," he said. "Now, let's see what goes on in here!"

Striding across the floor, he pulled open the connecting office door and snapped on the light.

The room was empty. But a door to Asey's right, leading directly outdoors, was ajar. He swung it open, peered out into the gloom, then closed the door, locked it, and looked thoughtfully at the master light switch on the wall. This was Thackeray's own office, and from it he could have cut all the lights with a flick of his finger.

Turning, Asey walked slowly back into the observatory. Someone had been in that office, and skipped when he heard the girl re-enter. Someone was probably waiting outside right now for another opportunity to sneak back. And as soon as he found out a few things from this girl, Asey thought, he'd give the person every chance to return. However much he yearned to go after the bird in the bush, though, he shouldn't lose sight of the bird in hand.

"You're Asey Mayo!" The girl was white-faced and wide-eyed, and she kept nervously fingering a bracelet on her left wrist. "I know you from pictures—my little sister has a bedroom wall covered with you and Superman. How did this happen? When? Who did it? That's Dr. Heaslip, you know."

"I know," Asey said. "An' who are you?"

"I'm Perry Lowe. The secretary here. I'd just finished dinner at the Vinings', and I opened my purse to get a handkerchief before the musicale started, and found this memorandum about Dr. Heaslip's having asked guests here tonight. They were his First Aid group. So I rushed over just as they were arriving, and the place was pitch-black, and—"

"Did you put on the lights?" Asey interrupted.

"Yes. The switch in Jack's office was off. Anyway, no one was here, so I did the honors. I kept feeling something was awfully wrong all the while. I didn't think anything of this"—she indicated the covered body—"because Heaslip's always leaving things around with signs on 'em not to touch. But then the shape of it began to unnerve me. I rushed the group out and came back to see— Have you called Jabe Cullis, the cop? You haven't?" she added as Asey shook his head. "Shouldn't you?"

"Presently. But first—"

"Oh, it *must* have been a tramp!" The girl sat down on a low stool and gripped the sides tightly, as if she were afraid of falling off. "We've had a wave of tramps lately, all taking this place for a roadhouse in the blackout. Were you here when this happened? Why'd you march into Jack Thackeray's office like that? Where *is* Jack? How'd you know who Heaslip was? Has—has anyone *else* been here? I—" She paused and bit her lip. "I hate to keep asking questions like a fuzz-wit, but I've never seen anything like this before, and I feel as if I'd been hit over the head, myself! How did you happen to be here?"

Without answering, Asey crossed the observatory and made a rapid survey of the office opposite Thackeray's. Except for the arrangement of the furniture, it was an exact duplicate, including an outside door. Any number of people, Asey thought with irritation, might have been hiding in either office.

"That's Heaslip's office," Perry Lowe said. "Miss Drum works there, too. . . . How d'you happen to be here?"

No light switch in Heaslip's office—Asey made mental notes as he closed the door. But there was another master switch in the corner of the observatory.

"Why two?" he asked. "Two switches, I mean."

"Oh, this was the original," she said. "The one in Jack's office was put in so we could blackout quickly during the period before we were permanently dimmed. . . . Mr. Mayo, *will* you tell me how it happens you're here?"

There were half a dozen tall metal file cases under the switch. Movable file cases, on wheels. Dandy things, Asey thought, for anyone to hide behind.

"For Pete's sakes!" He stooped down suddenly and picked up from behind one of the cases a white silk evening scarf. Not only was it was like the one Evelyn Drum had been wearing, but it bore his initials!

"That's Evelyn Drum's!" Perry said. "How'd *that* get here? Why, that's incredible! It's—look; before I go mad, will you tell me how you happen to be here, anyway?"

"I came on an errand." Asey dropped the scarf on top of a file case. After all, Evelyn couldn't have been at the observatory before Heaslip was killed unless he possessed wings. Besides, he'd been wearing a scarf, back there on the road. "Who's here nights, besides Heaslip an' Thackeray?"

"Usually Miss George Drum, who owns the place. But she loathes explaining things to people and answering all their silly questions about the North Star, so she never comes if she knows groups are expected. I understand why she's not here, but I don't understand where Jack Thackeray can be!"

"Neither," Asey said, "do I. But wherever he is, he sure rushed off there in a powerful hurry!"

"Rushed off? From here? You mean"—her eyes were like two blue saucers—"that Jack ran away after—after Heaslip was killed? Oh, I don't *believe* it! You can't think Jack had had anything to do with this?"

"Wa-el." Asey was apparently scrutinizing the telescope, but actually he was watching the reflection of the girl's face. "I'm told that Thackeray fought with Heaslip, an' could hardly wait for Heaslip to get drafted so's he could be head man here, with enough salary to get married on."

The girl's cheeks flamed, and she bit, just as Asey hoped she would: "Money hasn't a *thing* to do with our not getting married! It's mother's worrying about the war! And Jack didn't really fight with Heaslip; he only bickered! And, anyway, Jack couldn't have killed him—not *this* way! He'd have used his *own* murder device!"

"His own what?" Asey said gently.

"I know it sounds frightful, but Jack has a murder device, and if he'd been going to kill anyone, he'd have used it! . . . Mr. Mayo, you're just baiting me to find things out! I don't believe you ever saw Jack run away from here, at all! You're simply making deductions like a book detective— someone bickered with his boss and wanted his job, therefore someone has a motive for murder! Why, Jack hasn't half the reason to kill Heaslip that I have!"

"So," Asey said.

"Yes, it's so!" Perry told him furiously. "Heaslip's carped

and fussed and complained to Miss Drum about my work —not because it wasn't really perfectly satisfactory, but because I wouldn't go out with him! He's pestered me—" She hesitated and bit her lip. "Well, there's no use going into *that* angle! But I'll tell you frankly if Jack hadn't intervened on several disagreeable occasions, I'd have hit Heaslip with the nearest heavy object, myself! If you're so bent on finding a suspect, you've more reason to pick me than Jack!"

"Uh-huh? How many people," Asey said, "was at this dinner party you was attendin'?"

"Eighteen or twenty. . . . Why? What difference does it make?"

"The difference between eighteen or twenty people knowin' that you was somewheres else this evenin'," Asey said, "an' two people knowin' Thackeray was here, an' that he beat it after Heaslip was killed."

"Look; Jack has just two interests in life: astronomy and the perfect murder story he intends to write some day. It's for that story that he's built this murder device. I don't know the technical words to describe it, but everyone who knows Jack knows about the thing, and knows he'd certainly use it if he had any intention of murdering anyone. . . . Have you called Miss Drum? . . . No? Well, *I* will, then—right now! She'll uphold everything I've said about Jack! *She'll* tell you Jack wouldn't have *hit* anyone!"

Her skirts swirled angrily around her ankles as she flounced out to the phone on the lucite desk.

Asey strolled after her thoughtfully. It wasn't his desire to have the place cluttered up with people, not until he'd had another chance to discover who was lurking around outside. But Miss Drum should be informed. And he should find it no harder to maneuver two women out of the way than one.

"The Drums' house, please!" Perry said crisply.

Her voice was different as she talked to Miss Drum, Asey noticed. She was more formal than she'd been with him, and there was a note of deference in her manner.

"Is Miss Drum elderly?" he asked curiously when she finished.

"Well, she's getting along. She's over thirty-five!"

"An' how old are you?" Asey asked with a grin.

"Twenty-one. Listen, Mr. Mayo; you asked me if I turned on the lights when I came here—did the lights go when Jack ran away? Were they switched off?"

Asey nodded. "An' I'm not kiddin' you about his rushin' off, either. Evelyn Drum spotted him, too."

"Oh."

The reception room seemed suddenly very quiet, Asey thought, with only the monotonous tap-tap-tap of the girl's sandaled foot against the linoleum floor. He couldn't even guess, from the masklike expression that had settled on her face, what she might be thinking. But something was going on inside that blond head, something that had apparently been inspired by his mention of Evelyn's having seen Thackeray leave.

"You know," she said at last, "that this place was built for Evelyn? He got interested in astronomy at the Minter desert observatory while he was West for his lungs. He wouldn't leave, even after he was cured, till Miss Drum agreed to build him this. The instant it was done, Evelyn became passionately interested in Ming vases, or Roman coins, or interior decorating—I don't know which. I wasn't here then."

"I thought Heaslip's onion sandwiches drove Evelyn away," Asey said.

"That's just his excuse. Evelyn has an excuse for all his spent passions. He's been sickly and spoiled all his life, and he loves to draw warped pictures of everyone and everything— Oh, I can't be fair about him!" She stamped her foot. "Devoted as I am to George Drum, I can *not* be fair about that boy!"

"What d'you mean?" Asey asked.

"Oh, I meant to be dispassionate and objective, and point out that if Evelyn's been your informant about the observatory and Jack, and all, you should take what he says with a couple of grains of salt. But I can't do it. Mr. Mayo, Evelyn's forbidden to come here, to set foot in the place, yet his scarf's on that file! Evelyn hasn't spoken to Heaslip in months. He hates the man! And he has a fiendish temper —I've seen him pitch a vase of flowers through a closed window! I never thought it was a tramp; I felt this was Evelyn's work, all along! . . . There, I've said it! Now come, and I'll show you the first thing!"

"First thing?" Asey asked as she pushed open the observatory door.

"About Jack's device. I want you to understand. I'd show it to you, but he keeps it locked in his desk. Come over to the telescope! . . . Now, Jack has this unit all built and put together, and he puts it into the small, movable rear section of a telescope. Into the eyepiece part. It's made basically out of a rifle barrel, and it has braces that make it fit into a tube. Jack unscrews the regular part of the telescope and substitutes this gadget in about two seconds. Usually he puts it into the finder here, and—"

"Whoa up!" Asey interrupted. "Is the finder this small telescope thing here that you use to focus the big fellow with?"

"Yes. Jack unscrews something here"—she pointed—"and puts his gadget in its place." Her foot began to tap impatiently as Asey stood and silently surveyed the finder. "Well, d'you understand?" she demanded at last.

"I sort of think"—Asey spoke slowly and in a soft, purring voice that would have put the whole Porter plant on guard—"I get it, in a general way. Tell me, how does this thing work, after you get it set in place?"

Perry drew a long breath. "Well, a thing hovers over the end of a cartridge that's in the rifle barrel, and it's connected with a lot of things—it's like a Rube Goldberg cartoon, as far as I'm concerned. The theory is that someone will look through the eyepiece, see nothing, and then push in the tube to focus. At that point, things press against other things—I'm sorry I don't know the proper names of 'em—and the thing that hovers over the end of the cartridge strikes it, and then—"

"Then, *bang!*" Asey finished the sentence for her. "You get a bullet through your eye."

"You mean"—she looked at him with awe—"you *really* understand how it *works*?"

"Sure," Asey said easily. "The striker's held back from the primer of a cartridge till a trigger's pulled by some sort of simple device. Probably the trip's pivoted inside the tube, with one end comin' through a slot. When you push the tube into focus, you cause the trip to be pressed in, an' that in turn would press down an' back on the trigger. *Bang!*"

He turned as if to leave, but Perry remained beside the telescope. Asey, looking at her out of the corner of his eye, found that she was strangely pensive.

"Some of sister's clippings call you 'The Uncanny Mayo,' " she said. "I agree with 'em."

"Figurin' out that gadget isn't uncanny," Asey said. "I've seen variations on the same principle before. . . . Comin'?"

She ignored his question. "If you've seen things like it before"—she reached out her hand and almost absently touched the finder—"I wonder if you haven't spotted the flaw in this. Don't you think the use of it assumes that your intended victim's somewhat of a fool?"

"Because he's got to be lured into standin' with his eye glued to the eyepiece, an' then coaxed into fiddlin' with the tube?" Asey strolled back to her side. "I wouldn't say so. An astronomer like Heaslip would come in here an' automatically start to work. When he didn't see anythin', he'd just push in the tube. After all, you don't stop to investigate things you use a lot."

"But it limits your victims to astronomers," Perry said, "while you might want to kill—oh, your milkman, or your senator!"

"You only got to ask 'em here," Asey said, "an' give their native curiosity free rein. There's nothin' folks like much better than lookin' through things an' playin' with 'em. Ever watch anyone with binoculars?"

"Yes, I suppose you're right. I can see where a telescope would fascinate a layman so that he'd be tempted to fool around and regulate it, but I don't think anyone like *you* would! Not with your self-control and will power. You'd have to be enticed into toying with it."

Asey grinned. "I been itchin' to fiddle with that telescope ever since I first seen it."

"Then, for goodness' sake, go on and fiddle!" Perry moved out of his way, and Asey leaned over and peered through the finder. "Then I want to show you something else. . . . Can you focus, all right? D'you know how?"

"Sure I know; just push it in," Asey said, and did so.

The sudden report of a shot reverberated through the observatory, and Asey went down like a log on the white linoleum floor.

With a swish of her flowing skirts, Perry darted across the room and disappeared out the French door.

Almost before she was through the doorway Asey was up on his feet and starting after her. Once outside, he paused for a second to listen to the sound of her footsteps. She was racing around the wing toward the front.

Asey raced after her, cut the distance between them down to a space where her billowing skirt was nearly within his grasp, and then his foot caught on a wire wicket of a flower bed, and he tripped headlong.

By the time he picked himself up and reached the graveled driveway, Perry was well on her way to parts unknown in a car whose dimmed headlights were just visible on the road.

Asey shook his head. She must have been very sure of the

results of Thackeray's gadget to rush off without even waiting to see whether the bullet landed in him or in the wall
behind him! From the moment when a casual wave of
Perry's hand had directed his glance toward the telescope's
framework, where he'd spotted the ocular lens and mount of
the finder neatly tucked away, he'd been on his guard. For
it stood to reason if the lens was out, Thackeray's device
might well be in place. That was why he'd ducked before
focusing the finder—and lucky for him that he had!

And yet, until that bullet had whizzed over his head into
the wall, he hadn't really believed that Perry knew the
gadget was in the finder. While he'd given her every chance
to lure him into position, and while she'd done it, he still
found himself wondering if she'd meant to kill him. Had she
known the device was there? Was she in cahoots with
Thackeray?

Anyway, after that brisk chase, she knew he was alive.
And her driving off didn't matter. In these days, she couldn't
go far.

He started back around the wing. Then, after considering
the area of light by the open French door, he detoured some
fifty yards to the edge of the woods and sat down. Anyone
lurking about would have heard the girl depart in her car.
Anyone wanting to peek inside the observatory would be
thwarted by the blackout shades. Thackeray's office door,
on the other side of the building, was locked. This open
French door, therefore, offered a fine peephole as well as an
easy entrance. And if someone chose to sneak in by the
front door, his first gesture on entering the observatory
proper would be to close this door.

Fixing his eyes on the wedge of light, Asey leaned back against a maple tree and thought of the new complications arising from the presence of that infernal gadget.

Had Thackeray been sitting in his office waiting for Heaslip to stick his head, so to speak, into the lion's mouth? With visitors coming, Heaslip might be expected to fuss around the telescope more than usual and have it ready to show his guests. Had Thackeray planned on that? If so, what'd gone sour, and why had Heaslip been bashed?

"Say Thackeray's waitin' in his office," Asey murmured, "but Heaslip won't bite. They're both used to workin' in the dark of the observatory. Thackeray knows his way around. S'pose he turns off his office lights, waits a bit, then pulls the master switch, rushes in, an' bashes Heaslip. Figurin' it that way, his one eye'd see more than Heaslip's two. I wonder, did Heaslip guess that thing was in the finder?"

While it was possible someone might be sneaking back to remove the gadget, it didn't fit in with the rest of what had happened. If it took only seconds to put the thing in place, as Perry said, it shouldn't take more than seconds to remove it. Less time, in fact, than someone had spent covering Heaslip's body.

Asey leaned forward suddenly, and then quietly got up. A woman, wheeling a bicycle, had just passed through the shaft of light by the door!

Stealthily Asey started to circle back toward the observatory. The woman, having propped her bike against the side of the building, was now creeping nearer to the door. Her short, slight figure was outlined against the light, and Asey, recognizing it, could hardly contain a whoop. It was the same weeping woman whom he'd seen leaving when he first arrived!

Jumbled thoughts raced through his mind as he drew nearer. Supposing Heaslip had been killed before he came? But then why had Thackeray rushed out, and why had the lights been switched off? While Thackeray waited for Heaslip to get a bullet through his eye, had this woman beat him to it by bashing Heaslip with that meteorite?

He stood stock-still by a tree as the woman turned and glanced nervously over her shoulder. Once again, at the sight of her profile, Asey could hardly keep from whooping aloud. He had a good, long look, too, for she was listening intently.

Someone *else* was coming around the wing!

Asey stood like a statue, his eyes boring into the darkness. But before he could make out the figure of the approaching person, the woman slipped away from the doorway, grabbed her bicycle, and scurried off.

Asey almost didn't waste a look in her direction. No one with that characteristically jutting Heaslip jaw would be too hard to track down later, but this far more furtive newcomer was an unknown quantity.

It was another woman!

She passed so near Asey that he could have reached out and touched her. But her gaze was riveted on the open doorway and never once did she turn her head from it.

As she paused a moment in the shaft of light, he saw that she was tall and slim. Over her shoulders, cape-fashion, hung a coat whose dangling sleeves not only accentuated her height, but somehow added to the illusion of secrecy. And for all that her hair was snow-white, she was young. In her thirties, Asey decided. Unlike her predecessor with the Heaslip jaw, she was neither jittery nor nervous, merely very noiseless. She walked into the observatory as if she owned the place.

And unless he was very much mistaken, Asey thought, as he moved up to one side of the doorway, she probably did. But why Miss George Drum chose to enter her property in this fashion, he couldn't begin to imagine.

Watching her as she crossed over to Heaslip's body, Asey suddenly understood the reason for Perry's deferential attitude while speaking to her over the phone. She had the same intangible quality that caused young Bill Porter, grease-smeared and in dungarees, to be addressed as "sir" at the plant, even by visiting generals.

Her composure never wavered as she lifted the tarpaulin, but after a brief glance she let it drop and made straight for the file cases in the corner. Catching up Evelyn's white scarf, she stuffed it into the pocket of her coat. Then she returned to the body, and without a change of expression, picked up the meteorite that had been left under the tarpaulin and started for the door.

Asey flattened himself against the wall, let her pass by him, and waited until her arm was raised to pitch the meteorite into the bushes before he spoke. "I wouldn't, Miss Drum. That's evidence, you know."

She swung around. "Who are *you*?" she asked coldly. "What are you doing here?"

"I'm Asey Mayo." When a woman, caught in the act of

pitching out Exhibit A in a murder case, could make you feel like an illegal intruder, he thought, you had to hand it to her!

"Oh." She lowered her arm. "Perry said you were here. Where's Perry?"

"She left. Er—you're goin' back inside, aren't you, Miss Drum?" He politely indicated the doorway, and stood his ground until she turned and entered the observatory. "Yes, Perry was provin' Thackeray's innocence by showin' me—in theory, of course—how his murder device worked, an' it seems, by the purest chance, the device was in the telescope finder all the time." He pointed to the bullet hole in the opposite wall. "But she didn't wait to see that. She beat it when I flopped on the floor."

"I don't understand any of it," Miss Drum said flatly. "You mean *Perry* tried to kill you? But you're not hurt!"

"Havin' some slight suspicion of the situation," Asey said, "I ducked. Now, Miss Drum, why—"

"Why are you here?" she interrupted.

Asey explained his errand. "An' now, just what was your idea in swipin' that scarf an' tryin' to throw away that meteorite? Shieldin' your brother?"

"Not my brother. Myself."

Her answer was so unexpected that Asey's first impulse was to think he hadn't heard her correctly. "You mean your brother, don't you?"

"Myself, I said!" George Drum's face was as white as her hair, but her voice never faltered. "If anyone left that scarf here, *I* did!"

"So?" Asey said. "An' what about that meteorite?"

"That belongs to me. If I wished to throw it out, I had every right to do so."

"It's my impression," Asey returned, "that the average judge would rather you put it back where you found it. D'you mind doin' just that?"

Miss Drum obviously minded very much. But she replaced the meteorite and then imperiously asked where Jabe Cullis was.

"Who? Oh, the cop," Asey said. "Perry mentioned him. But I haven't got around to callin' him yet."

"But *I* called him, and he said he'd come at once!"

Asey sat down on a stool. "Miss Drum," he said quietly, "you an' I can spar an' fence the rest of the night, or you can save time an' tell me right now why you swiped that scarf an' why you tried to throw away that meteorite. Why don't you break down an' say you're coverin' up for your brother! Because you know I seen him comin' here this evenin'."

"Evelyn does not come here," George Drum said with dignity. "We have an agreement about that. *I* left that scarf here, and that meteorite belongs to *me*. I use it for a paper weight."

"I see. Although you called the cop yourself, you're tryin' to make me believe *you* killed Heaslip." Asey sighed. "Perry Lowe's just gone through that phase. Where did you spend the evenin'. Miss Drum?"

"I was home. But," she added quickly, "it can't be proved. The maids saw me only at intervals up in my workroom."

"I s'pose you got a good motive for killin' your astronomer in charge?" Asey inquired.

"While Oliver—Dr. Heaslip—and I were not formally engaged, and while the fact wasn't known, we were to be married as soon as he learned whether or not he was going into the army."

"That," Asey said, "is no motive at all."

"But he changed his mind about marrying me. He jilted me," George Drum said breathlessly.

"Uh-huh, an' this is revenge. I see," Asey said. "I might even believe you if you could look me in the eye an' say it. Miss Drum, when I seen your brother comin' here, Heaslip'd already been killed. Your brother was wearin' a scarf then—he probably has several? . . . I thought so. An' he was carryin' a meteorite in a box. One like that you picked up, but not the same one."

George Drum sat down suddenly on a bench, and the coat slipped from her shoulders. Her dress was like the ones Bill Porter's wife wore, plain and simple. But Asey had heard Bill's angry comments as he signed the checks for those deceptively simple dresses!

"I can't say anything." For the first time, she smiled. "I— may I explain to you why— Oh, I feel very foolish!"

"You're not the first person who's tried to shield one of their family," Asey said. "But there's a few things I'd like you to explain. By the way, are you one of the Drums of the old Drum Silk Company in Boston?"

"Yes, I ran it after my father died, until I sold out three years ago. I started all this"—she made a gesture which included the entire observatory—"for Evelyn. But while his interest in astronomy waned, mine grew. Ordinarily I'd be working here tonight, but Oliver told me weeks ago that a group was coming, so I stayed home. My knowledge," she added a little ruefully, "is rather specialized. It irritates me not to be able to answer laymen's questions. Anyway, Mr. Mayo, Evelyn got along famously with Oliver out West, and back here too, until he was told about our plans a few months ago—"

"You mean, you did intend to marry Heaslip?" Asey interrupted.

She nodded. "But it wasn't generally known. The news infuriated Evelyn. He has nothing against Oliver. He only violently resented the idea of a third person in the house. He's made things very difficult. It's easy to spoil a boy who's sickly, and I spoiled Evelyn; you see, mother and father died when he was very small. I have now a bitter realization of what I unwittingly did, but it's too late to try to repair the damage. Evelyn and Oliver had some ugly scenes. I finally had to forbid his coming here."

"So that's why he was so eager to thrust that box on me!" Asey said. "But he told me you made him come tonight!"

"I did." She drew a long breath. "Evelyn had a little meteorite of Oliver's that Oliver wanted to give this group he'd invited. A prize they could draw for. I've asked Evelyn for it repeatedly. This morning I reminded him again, and told him to leave it here before he went to the club tonight. After he left, I found the meteorite at home, which made me very angry. I phoned him, told him to return and get it, which made *him* very angry. He said he hadn't enough gas, and I told him to walk, or do without next month's allowance. Oh, I shouldn't have let the thing become an issue or made him come here! I should have brought it myself! Since

Perry phoned, I've been almost sick with worry about Evelyn!"

She broke off, drew a cigarette from a case in her pocket, and lighted it. Asey noticed suddenly that the knuckles of her tanned hands were white with tension, and it occurred to him that after her first brief glance she had never turned her head in the direction of the covered figure on the floor.

"I called the club," she went on, "but no one knew where Evelyn was. He hadn't returned. I could only think he might have been angry enough about the meteorite to have had words with Oliver, and to have done this. That's why, when the place seemed so deserted, I crept in the back way. I had this awful feeling Evelyn might be involved. That he might even be here. And please believe me," she added with a flash of her imperious manner, "I'd have admitted to this before I'd have permitted anyone to implicate him in any way! I still will, if there's any chance of his being suspected!"

"Unless your brother can fly like Superman," Asey said, "I don't think you got any cause for worry."

"Still, if it's possible, I'd like to hire you to prove he's innocent," George Drum said, "and to get to the core of this. Tell me—what happened? Were you here? What about that terrible device of Jack Thackeray's?"

Briefly, Asey summed up what had taken place. "That's the story," he concluded. "Now, is it true, Miss Drum, that Thackeray sort of had his eye on Heaslip's job?"

"I wondered, myself," she said thoughtfully, "when he asked me for the fourth time who'd take over if Oliver were drafted. To be honest, he and Oliver didn't get along.

Things had reached a state where I decided to tell Jack to hunt another post. I didn't, because he felt so bad about not being in the army, it seemed cruel to fire him now."

"What about him an' Perry?" Asey shifted his position slightly on the stool. There was a crack in the blackout shade on the window next to the door, and something had flitted past it!

"She's a nice child. Very fond of Jack. I can't imagine what's come over her. Or him, either! If that device was in the finder, Jack must have put it in. Perry couldn't. It's all she can do to change a typewriter ribbon. But they're both nice youngsters, Mr. Mayo! I can't bring myself to believe that either of them, particularly Perry, could have anything to do with this!"

"Did Heaslip have any enemies?" Asey spoke casually, but he shifted his position again and leaned forward. Someone was outside, all right!

"No," George Drum said hesitantly. "He was impatient, and he wasn't tactful. I don't mean to make him sound cantankerous, but he never troubled to endear himself to people just in order to be liked. He lived for his work. I wouldn't say he had many friends. Neither did he have any enemies."

"I s'pose he has relations— By the way," he added, "have you told 'em about this?"

"He has a sister." She might have been admitting to Heaslip's owning a bath mat, Asey thought, for all the feeling in her voice. "I didn't phone her. I think you'll find that the less Sarah Heaslip enters into things, the better for all concerned!"

"Why so?" Asey asked, and privately wondered why the

woman with the Heaslip jaw, if she didn't know about ner
brother's murder, had been sneaking around the observatory, and just what she might be up to now.

Because two seconds after her name was spoken, she had
crept past the doorway, and was standing there listening!

"It's a trying situation." George Drum dropped her cigarette stub on the floor and ground it out with the toe of her
black pump. "When the college where Sarah taught San-
skrit was taken over by the government, she was thrown
out of work. Instead of taking a war job, or any job at all,
she begged Oliver to let her live with him."

Asey thought he heard an indignant rustle in the doorway.

"Naturally," George continued, "I can't pay my staff
very princely salaries. While Oliver was more free to follow
his own interests here, he worked for less than he might have
received elsewhere. But he paid Sarah's bills and debts,
agreed to support her, and only asked in return that she keep
house for him, which she agreed to do. But apparently she
finds housework excessively tiresome, and she's been very
trying and unreasonable about it, and everything else.
There's been constant friction between them."

So far, Asey thought, everyone in any way involved with
Heaslip seemed to be in a constant state of friction with him
except George Drum, herself!

"She's fallen into such a melancholy state," George went
on, "that I've urged Oliver to send her to a psychiatrist."

"You mean"—Asey eyed the door—"that she's melancholy in the sense that she cries?"

George nodded as she lighted another cigarette. "Even

Oliver's onion sandwiches upset her! Oliver merely asked her to bring them here in the evening, but she's provoked such scenes, night after night, that he's had to tell her to put the sandwiches in the reception room and leave at once. She was distracting him to such an extent that his work suffered. She's been a nuisance to all of us, but it's absurd to think of her in connection with this. She was utterly dependent on Oliver for everything; it wouldn't be to *her* advantage to kill him! Besides, she'd never *dare* come in here!"

"Wouldn't she, Miss Drum!"

The slight figure of Sarah Heaslip precipitated itself through the doorway. She was trembling with anger. "I've been listening to your lies!" Sarah cried. "Lies, all of it!"

"Sarah"—George got up and drew her coat back on her shoulders—"you're obviously overwrought. You'd better let me take you home at once!"

"I understand all this! I saw Evelyn coming here! He told me once he'd kill Oliver before he'd ever let you marry him —and that's just what happened! Evelyn killed Oliver, and you think you can get him out of this with lies, and the Drum money!"

"Tell me," Asey said before George could speak, "how'd you know your brother'd been killed, Miss Heaslip?"

She stopped trembling and her face drained of color as she turned and looked at him. She was younger, he realized suddenly, than her unkempt gray-streaked hair and lined forehead had led him to believe. A few licks of a hairbrush and clothes like George Drum's, and Sarah Heaslip wouldn't be half bad-looking.

"How'd you know about your brother?" he asked again,

and tried not to stare at the two black-and-blue marks on her left cheek. Those weren't the kind of marks you got from falling off a bicycle or running into a doorjamb. Someone had slapped her!

"Yes, Sarah, how did you find out?" George inquired.

"I heard about it!"

"How?" George asked coldly.

"Jabe Cullis phoned his wife, and she phoned her sister—"

"Ah, yes, the party line!" George gave an ironic little laugh. "Oliver said you listened to the party line. Come along, Sarah. I'll drive you home!"

Sarah never moved. "But I didn't hear about your precious brother on the party line! I *saw* him leaving here this evening!"

Asey thought back rapidly. So it had been Sarah who whizzed by him when he was carrying Evelyn's candy box to the observatory! After passing him, she would have overtaken Evelyn in a minute or two. Was there, he asked himself, a chance that not Thackeray but Evelyn might have rushed off in Thackeray's car? It was possible. He could have stopped the car up the road, after Asey had been bounced off, and then purposely have overtaken him on foot.

"I tell you I *saw* him!" Sarah said. "Not when I came with the sandwiches, but later! He was walking away from here!"

"Oh, so you came twice, did you?" George said. "That's very interesting, Sarah, and perhaps I was wrong when I told Mr. Mayo that he shouldn't waste his time considering you! Perhaps he ought to consider you rather seriously!

Heaven knows Oliver had little enough, but I suppose you inherit what he had. Probably in your present financial state that little savings account loomed like a fortune!"

"If it's the last thing I do on earth, I'll prove that Evelyn killed Oliver!" Sarah sounded as if she meant it. "I'll go tell Jabe I saw Evelyn—"

"You don't have to *go* tell him," George interrupted. "Jabe will be here any minute. By all means tell him you saw Evelyn, Sarah. And we can tell Jabe you came here twice—I think I hear his car, now!"

It was a car whose engine spluttered and coughed, and finally subsided altogether after a series of backfires.

"Without doubt, that's Jabe," George said. "Tell him, Sarah. Tell him—"

But Sarah burst into a violent flood of tears and fled out the open door.

"Get her!" George said to Asey. "Go get her. You're certainly not going to let her get away, are you?"

"I don't think there's much use tryin' to talk with her," Asey said, "in the condition she's in now—which, if you don't mind my sayin' so, you didn't improve much!"

"But she accused Evelyn! She says she saw him. Mr. Mayo, you've got to let me hire you to clear him and solve this! I can't let Sarah accuse Evelyn. . . . We're here, Jabe!" She raised her voice as someone called out from the reception room.

Asey looked expectantly toward the door. After these last few hours in Starlington, he was prepared for almost anything or anybody—except the genial ticket agent who breezed in, grinned at him, tipped his cap to George Drum, and launched at once into a wordy explanation of his delayed arrival:

"It was sixty of the airfield boys wanted to go to Blairville to see a movie star sell bonds in the square, and the only way they could make it was for me to flag the express. That meant getting permission, and then selling sixty tick—"

"I suppose," George Drum interrupted, "you'll call the state police at once, Jabe?"

"Why, ma'am?"

"Surely you don't expect to solve this by yourself!"

"I already got a good theory, ma'am."

Asey looked suspiciously at the ticket agent's bland, round face, and then decided no one would probably dare kid George Drum in any such casual fashion.

"Indeed? And what is your theory?" she demanded.

"Well, ma'am, this fellow"—Jabe pointed to Asey—"he comes rushing in asking for Heaslip, and how can he get to the observatory quick, and how soon can he get a train back to Boston. Well, ma'am, he finds Heaslip, and then you phone me Heaslip's been killed. Looks to me this fellow might be what they call a material witness, if not maybe—"

"This is Asey Mayo, the famous detective!" George Drum's scorn would have withered most men, but it didn't faze Cullis.

"If he was governor, ma'am, I still think he could be asked a lot of questions. When I finish grilling him"—Asey was sure he caught a twinkle in the man's eye—"I'll turn him over to the state cops, and if they want to make any charges—"

"Come, Mr. Mayo!" George took Asey's arm. "Jabe, when you want him, he'll be at my house!"

"But I want him, here and now, Miss Drum!"

"Out of the way, please!" Her eyes were blazing. "If the state police wish Mr. Mayo, he'll be at my house. One side!"

She forcibly propelled Asey past the astonished Cullis, out through the reception room, down the front steps and the driveway to an open roadster parked on the tarred road. "Get in!" She opened the door and gave him a little push. "Hurry, before that idiot starts after you!"

"But see here, Miss Drum, there's a lot I should tell—"

"He means to arrest you!" She got in behind the wheel. "Hurry! He thinks you came here to kill Oliver."

"I don't think he'll keep that impression long," Asey said soothingly. "Matter of fact, it occured to me a while back that someone'd have a lot of fun makin' out a case against me. . . . No, Miss Drum, I can't go off. I got to stay—"

He had to sit down abruptly and grab at the door to keep from falling out as the car shot off.

"You're going to clear Evelyn and find out who killed Oliver, and you're not going to be impeded by that idiot!" George said furiously, and jammed her foot down on the accelerator.

Asey looked from the speedometer needle to the small patch of road made visible by the dimmed headlights, and then he looked at Miss Drum's chin, and decided against trying to stop her or to interfere in any way with this slightly mad expedition. This wasn't the time to cross the head woman of the Drum Observatory, not with all these rock-bound reverse curves! After she calmed down he'd induce her to turn back.

At least, he reflected as the roadster raced on, Evelyn's flippant estimate of astronomers had been right as far as it went. They were certainly firm-chinned and full of whims. From his own personal experience, he could add that they were obsessed with an overwhelming impulse to rush off at top speed into the night. First Thackeray, then Perry, now George Drum!

The car slowed, turned into a tarred driveway, and coasted to a stop before a vast fieldstone house.

"I shouldn't have done this. I'm sorry," George said slowly. "I'm not excusing myself, but I *had* to do something! I *had* to get away from there. I'm all right now. I hope you're not too annoyed with me."

"It was a very refreshin' outin'," Asey said, "but I do honestly think we better go right back."

"First, will you go in and find out from Evelyn if he went to the observatory, and if he can explain how his scarf happened to be there? He's home. His car's yonder. I'll go apologize to Jabe, and then return for you. Don't you think he really meant to arrest you?"

"I doubt it," Asey said, with a grin. "Besides, I don't think the state cops'd let him. Most of 'em are friends of mine."

"Jabe loves having his picture in the papers," she said dubiously. "I'm not at all convinced he won't jump at the chance to publicize himself by arresting you, even if it's only a brief and nominal arrest. . . . Will you see Evelyn? It would take so little time. I'll be back for you within fifteen minutes!"

"Wa-el," Asey said tentatively. He thought privately it might be a good thing to check up on Evelyn. If he could find any clue to indicate that Evelyn and not Thackeray had been driving that coupé, the situation would be considerably altered. At any rate, Evelyn could tell him more about Sarah Heaslip, and Evelyn's slant might be interesting to hear. He opened the roadster's door. "I'll see him."

"Bang on the knocker—can you find it? Bang hard. . . . Helen," she said to the maid who opened the door, "take Mr. Mayo to see Mr. Evelyn. I'll be back very soon."

The maid, a frightened-looking, middle-aged woman, let him in and hurried ahead of him down a long hall. The tall mirror at the end was smashed, Asey noticed, and flowers from a broken cut-glass vase littered the floor. He looked questioningly at the maid, who stoically averted her eyes from the damage.

"You'll find him in there, sir." She pointed to a doorway hung with heavy, green-tasseled portieres, and scuttled away before Asey could ask her if the damage was, as he rather suspected, the result of Evelyn's temper.

He pushed aside the green tassels, then paused and whistled softly at the sight of the large rectangular room before him.

The carpet was thick red plush, the huge, elaborate pieces of furniture were covered with blue plush, and there seemed to be acres of carved black walnut. Enormous pictures of cows and castles and clouds in wide gilt frames all but obliterated the blue wallpaper. There were Rogers groups, pink marble statues, whatnots stuffed with bric-a-brac, towering rubber plants, marble-topped tables, painted seashell ornaments. Asey hadn't seen anything like it in years, and the contrast with the chromium and lucite of the observatory made the room appear more crowded and cluttered and plushy than it probably was.

What he'd seen of the rest of the house, as he passed along the hall, looked normal enough.

"I wonder," Asey thought to himself, "if this isn't maybe some of Evelyn's decoratin'—and where *is* the fellow?"

For the second time that night he restrained his impulse to bellow out someone's name. You couldn't summon Evelyn Drum like a deck hand, and then expect him to answer questions like an obedient little lamb. Not if he was in a mirror-smashing mood!

Making no attempt to conceal his annoyance, Asey sat down in a plush chair and impatiently drummed his finger tips against the arm. He wanted to see Evelyn, but he wanted to see Sarah Heaslip, too. And to find Perry. And Jack Thackeray.

On the surface, it looked as if Thackeray was the man he wanted. Thackeray's device had been set up, waiting for Heaslip. Thackeray would get Heaslip's job. Thackeray'd rushed off after the murder. Or *had* it been Evelyn? It might have been. And Evelyn didn't want his sister to marry Heaslip.

But it had been the women who returned to the observatory. Perry'd egged him on to play with Thackeray's gadget. Perry disliked Heaslip, admitted he'd annoyed her, and insinuated that he'd been something more than a simple nuisance. As for Sarah—Asey shook his head. She'd been at the observatory delivering those sandwiches. She'd at least been in the vicinity during the time when the body must have been covered. She must have been the cause of the noise he'd heard in Thackeray's office. She'd come back again, and still again, later.

Stripping George Drum's story of Heaslip and Sarah down to the bone, Heaslip appeared less of a Good Samaritan than a selfish man who forced his college-professor sister to work like a hired girl in payment for what couldn't have been too much of an outlay on her bills, not if his salary was as small as George had suggested. If Heaslip was responsible for Sarah's black-and-blue mark, it was possible that Sarah might prefer to be entirely destitute and alone in the world rather than to depend on her brother any longer.

Of course, Asey thought, as he got up and returned to the hall, there was always the possibility that George Drum might have been telling the truth when she said that Heaslip had jilted her! This episode of rushing away from the observatory just now proved that she had considerable of a temper herself.

He peered into the deserted rooms that led off the hall, listened vainly for some sound of Evelyn, and finally, after deciding to give the fellow five minutes more before setting off to the observatory on foot, he started back through the green tassels into the living room.

But a brief, fluttering movement of one of the long, red plush curtains at the far end of the room caught his eye, and he quickly ducked back behind the tassels. The curtain blew out stiffly, as if it were propelled by a sudden jet of air, and then everything was still.

Asey remembered seeing the outlines of a terrace at the

side of the house as George drove up to the front door. Was someone slipping in from out there? It looked that way, and certainly it wouldn't be Evelyn, sneaking like a burglar into his own home!

The curtain rippled again, this time from the definite movement of someone behind it. Then a hand groped for the parting, finally found it, and the curtains were pushed apart.

A broad-shouldered young man stood there, a young man wearing a green Alpine hat, a green coat, and a black patch over his right eye. All he lacked of Robin Hood, Asey thought, was a bow and a quiver of arrows. He crossed the room—and Asey spotted the bulge of a gun in his coat pocket—and rapidly moved to one side a picture of cows and chickens that hung next to the black marble fireplace.

Asey's eyes opened wide.

It would seem as if Jack Thackeray intended to add a charge of safe-breaking to Heaslip's murder!

Thackeray's hands were poised over the dial of the wall safe, when a door slamming in some distant part of the house caused him to look up, nervously move the picture into place again, and dart across the room to the red plush curtains. Without even a backward look, he slipped out as noiselessly as he'd entered.

Asey, darting after him, made sure that the curtains were drawn behind him before he opened a French window to the terrace. While he was sure Thackeray didn't suspect his presence, still there was no sense in advertising his silhouette.

This was one of those times, Asey thought, as he sidled along against the cold fieldstones of the house, where you had your choice of yelling at someone and scaring them away, or where you could follow, and then pounce on them and discuss the situation with an overpowering amount of evidence on your side!

He could dimly see Thackeray's figure moving off down a garden path, and when it disappeared behind a clump of bushes, Asey swung over the low terrace wall and followed. The path wound past an empty swimming pool, past tool sheds and an old stable, and finally through an apple orchard.

It was clear, as the fellow strode boldly across an open meadow without making any attempt to conceal himself, that he had no sense of being trailed. The only problem, Asey thought, was to keep him in sight, and to step carefully enough so his own movements didn't become audible. That wouldn't be hard. A regiment of Commandos could cover the ground with a fraction of the noise Thackeray was making. To jump him would be a cinch, Asey decided —only, where was the fellow headed? Why had he broken off his safe-opening project to hike through the countryside like a Boy Scout?

Asey followed on through pine woods and rocky pastures, and finally to a tarred road, where Thackeray paused, and then walked toward his streamlined coupé, parked in the bushes. If he had that car now, he'd had it all evening, Asey thought, as he started to creep up on him. This time he had no intention of pulling any human-fly act on the rear of that coupé.

He slowed down when it became apparent that Thackeray was only pausing long enough to take something from inside the car, probably either cigarettes or matches, for he was lighting a cigarette now. Then he plunged into the woods again, and Asey wearily followed. Did the fellow have a rendezvous with someone? Perry, perhaps? Were the two of them in cahoots?

They covered almost another mile before Thackeray's footsteps halted. Asey, flattened against a tree trunk, could just make out Thackeray's figure standing by a large boulder. From behind him came the sound of water and lapping waves. No wonder that had seemed like some hike, Asey thought; it had taken them to the coast!

Thackeray leaned against the boulder and started to whistle softly in a minor key. Without doubt he was waiting for someone, and Asey guessed it was Perry. And while it might be entertaining to wait and see, he'd wasted enough time in this cross-country event! Quietly he circled around and approached the boulder from the rear.

A minute later he had Thackeray's gun tucked away in his own pocket, and Thackeray was still wriggling to work the upper part of his coat and his coat sleeves, with which Asey had strait-jacketed him in a quick jerk, back into place.

"You don't read the comic strips," Asey said. "Any Junior Commando could tell you the defense against that one! Now, just what was you after, back there at the Drum house?"

"You're Asey Mayo!"

"Uh-huh. What was you after?"

"How d'you know I—? Oh, God," Thackeray said with resignation. "If you've followed me all the way from there, I might as well tell the truth! I wanted to see if George's master keys to the observatory were in the safe. There are two—one for the outside doors, and one for the lockers and files. Perry and I decided if Evelyn had taken those keys, he could've swiped that gadget out of my desk. But I lost my nerve. Even with the combination, I couldn't bring myself to open that safe!"

"So Perry knew where you was all the time, did she?" Asey said. "I'll give her credit. She put on a corkin' good act!"

"Perry *didn't* know!" Thackeray retorted. "And she didn't know my gadget was in the finder, either!"

"So she didn't know it was loaded!" Asey said. "Well, well, think of that!"

"She didn't! Neither did I! Listen; I jumped when the lights went, and raced for my car. I never saw Heaslip or gave him a thought. I came straight here! And—"

"Of all the forsaken places in this forsaken town," Asey interrupted, "why *here*?"

"We can't hear the town's air-raid siren at the observatory," Thackeray said. "So we arranged with a man at the power plant to black us out for a minute or so at night, if the siren goes. It's a signal for me to come to my post here. Half a dozen of us cover the inlet. We've already picked up two saboteurs off subs. That's why I had that gun, incidentally. Anyway, you told Perry the lights went off when I left, and she guessed I'd assumed the switch-off was Harry's signal for me to go. Now, d'you understand?"

"I know she suffered a sort of sea change," Asey said, "but if she guessed you'd come here, why in time didn't she say so?"

"Her idea was first to show you how my gadget worked, to prove to you I'd have used it and not bashed anyone," Thackeray said, "and then she intended to bring you here and display me, triumphantly. But that damned thing went off. Honestly, she didn't know it was there, nor did I! I know it sounds crazy, but it's all the truth!"

"So you *was* there at the observatory," Asey said. "Huh! Didn't you hear me thumpin' around in the reception room?"

"Of course I did, but I thought it was Sarah Heaslip with Oliver's sandwiches! I couldn't listen to her troubles again. She'd collared me last night, and three times last week, and Heaslip'd given me hell for talking with her. He said he'd fire me if I bothered with her again."

"I see," Asey said.

"That's why I let the phone ring and ring," Thackeray went on. "To avoid going out and facing Sarah. When I heard that thumping I decided she was still hanging around, and ignored it. Later—look; I know you think I'm a fool, but I forgot I'd locked my office door against her, and I turned the knob to open the door quietly. Perry'd forgotten about Heaslip's visitors, and I intended to phone her at Vinings'. I went at it quietly, because Heaslip was sore about her not coming, and I didn't want him to know I was tipping her off. *You* grabbed the knob, didn't you? Well, I thought it was Sarah! That's why I jumped so quickly when the lights went. I'd rather guard this inlet from saboteurs than listen to Sarah and get in wrong with Heaslip for it!"

"I don't get this," Asey said. "What's Heaslip's idea in keepin' Sarah out, and all?"

"Perry and I think he's jealous of her. She's got more college degrees than he has, and half a column in *Who's Who*. She's no dope about astronomy, either. She taught it once. We always thought Heaslip was afraid Sarah might get to working around the observatory, and maybe cut him out. You know, you can't take someone like Sarah and bully her and stick her in your kitchen, and never give her two cents, or even let her think! Perry and I hate the situation, but we've had to take it. Things at the observatory run the way Heaslip wants 'em, the old goat! I've beat him up twice for chasing Perry—if only you'd believe she didn't know that gadget was in the finder! She said you'd never believe she didn't lure you into working it!"

"You got to admit it seemed that way," Asey said.

"She thought you *wanted* to play with the telescope! I think," Jack said earnestly, "she was so anxious to put me in a good light, and you in a good mood, she'd have let you tear the telescope apart if you'd shown any indication of wanting to! Mr. Mayo, when I drove away I saw Evelyn Drum. He was on foot, but his car was parked up the road. I think *he's* mixed up in this! Think he got George's master keys. Someone *must've* had keys to get at my gadget! You can't pry open those metal drawers!"

"When'd you last see the gadget in the drawer?" Asey asked.

"This afternoon. Perry and I figure it was taken after she left and before I came. That would be between five-thirty and six-thirty. Someone *had* to have the key!"

"Why'd Evelyn dislike Heaslip so?"

"I don't think he disliked him as an astronomer, or even as an acquaintance," Thackeray said. "I think he simply didn't want such a damned disagreeable person for a brother-in-law. I can't say I blame him! George has control of Evelyn's money till he's thirty-five, and I think Evelyn saw breakers ahead if Oliver had a voice in the family affairs. Oliver's probably the stingiest man you ever met."

"But George Drum loves him?"

"Sixty per cent of her heart is named Evelyn," Thackeray said, "and the rest Oliver Heaslip. She never cared a hoot for his faults and weaknesses—his chasing Perry, and bullying Sarah, and fighting with Evelyn, and fuming with me. Listen; I don't care about my being framed in this mess, but you won't get Perry wrong, will you? She didn't know!"

"Where is she now?" Asey asked.

"While I went to look into the safe, she was going to Heaslip's house to see if Sarah knew where his extra keys were. You *do* believe Perry's got nothing to do with this, don't you?"

"As you tell it," Asey said, "it sounds fine an' convincin', but I don't—"

"Hey, look!" Thackeray said suddenly. "A signal light!"

"Where?"

"Just beyond the flash of the inlet buoy, off the point! See? Look out; I've got to get my night glasses!"

Asey, automatically watching the flashing buoy, was totally unprepared for the fist that smacked to his jaw and drove him flat on his back on the pine needles. His last conscious impression, as his jaw took it again, was of Thackeray's dim words:

"That'll hold you, Sherlock, till I find—"

Asey felt the sand under his fingers before his eyes opened and he saw the stars twinkling above him. His first vague reaction that he must be back home on a Cape Cod beach gave way to the firm realization that he was in Starlington, where anything could happen, and usually promptly did.

He sat up, rubbed his aching chin, and peered around. It was sand, all right. Sand and beach grass, and beyond him loomed the outlines of a sand dune. "Huh!" he muttered. "When I left, it was pine woods, an' bushes an' maple trees, an' boulders!"

He stood up, slowly walked the dozen-odd feet to the water's edge. He was beginning to understand what had caused this startling change in terrain. The small flash of the bobbing inlet buoy had been to his right, back there by the boulder. Now it appeared to his left. "Huh!" he said aloud. "Jumped an' taken for a ferry ride at your age!"

What must have happened was clear enough. He was now on the side of the inlet opposite where he'd previously been. Thackeray must have rowed him across.

Why? Asey shrugged. Probably Thackeray figured that he suspected Perry, and decided that the best hope of saving her from suspicion lay in getting him out of the way and solving things by himself. Probably the fellow'd rush around trying to find master keys, probably he'd storm in on Evelyn Drum, perhaps even take a few cracks at him in order to find out the truth.

If it weren't for the clue supplied by that flashing buoy, Asey thought, Thackeray would have succeeded in mixing him up completely. He had no foolhardy notion of swimming the inlet, whose swiftly eddying current he could hear from where he stood. But he still had two feet. It shouldn't take him long to walk around the inlet's shore.

But after more than an hour of picking his way along the beach, he began to realize that Thackeray's scheme for immobilizing him was a lot more successful than he'd at first suspected. While the row across the inlet was probably a matter of a few minutes, the inlet itself seemed to extend inland indefinitely.

As he plodded along, Asey considered, and dismissed as of not much importance, the key situation which had so concerned Thackeray. Only honest people worried about an extra key, as if there could be only one, or at the most two. If two master keys existed, there might be a dozen kicking around. Or a hundred. In fact, all you had to do to get a duplicate key was to borrow or swipe the one you had your eye on, spend ten minutes in a hardware store, and then return the original.

The problem of the light switch, which had bothered him earlier, he also dismissed. Whoever'd covered Heaslip's body had only to leave the switches as he wanted them found. It didn't matter what switch Perry put on to restore the lights. They could have been reversed before she came.

He wished he knew more about that empty telegram envelope that had appeared on the desk in the reception room. For whom had the telegram been intended? Who'd read it? Was it freshly delivered, or was it an old envelope someone had just left there? It'd looked new to him. It had none of the smears or wrinkles that envelopes acquired after a stay in people's pockets. That envelope was an item he intended to look into.

He paused long enough to wipe his forehead and shake some of the wet sand out of his sodden shoes.

Evelyn was the fellow who kept plaguing his mind, he reflected as he tramped along. Who'd angered him to the point of mirror-smashing—the maid who'd scuttled away, or his sister, or who? Probably if he'd hurled the mirror itself at George Drum, she'd have accepted the incident with tight-lipped control. In passing, Asey recalled George's statement that while she'd spent the evening working at her house, the fact couldn't be proved.

Most particularly, he thought about Sarah Heaslip. He would have to see Sarah.

Only one more thing really bothered him, and that was so silly he couldn't think whom to ask about it.

It was nearly dawn before he reached a tarred road at the foot of the inlet. Although he figured that a left turn should ultimately take him back somewhere near the Drum house, he found himself hesitating. If he'd covered one mile since he was ferried across that inlet, he'd covered a dozen, and he'd no desire to fritter around and cover any more without knowing exactly where he was.

A car engine coughed and spluttered in the distance. It was a reminiscent sound, and Asey planted himself firmly in the path of the approaching vehicle.

"Well, say!" Jabe Cullis's genial voice was music to Asey's ears. "I been hunting you all over. So's Miss Drum.

We been awful worried. . . . I hope you ain't mad with me!"

"Far's I'm concerned, you're an angel with wings," Asey said. "Move that basket off the seat. I want to sit down!"

"*I* never meant to arrest you!" Jabe said. "I was only having a little joke, like. You see, when you first come to the ticket office, I felt I knew you, but I couldn't place you. Honest, I'm sorry I told you the observatory was only a stone's throw! I didn't mean to send you off on a snipe hunt, but I don't like Heaslip. If you'd asked for Miss Drum, I'd have driven you up myself. I kept wondering—"

"Look," Asey interrupted; "I want to see the telegraph agent in town, Jabe. Can you drive me to him?"

"Why, I'm the agent!" Jabe said. "That's what I was telling you. I kept wondering where I'd seen you, and when that telegram came for you—"

"What telegram came for me?" Asey demanded. "When?"

"Wasn't long after you left the station. Three quarters of an hour, maybe. 'Mayo, care of Heaslip.' I phoned the observatory, but nobody answered, so I decided to take it up myself. . . . Why, say, Asey, I used to know you! I was cook on Tobey's 'Lady Ann' when you was cap'n of Porter's yacht. Remember them days? . . . So, anyway, I drove up to the observatory with the telegram. I meant to tell you then how I remembered you, and—"

"Whoa up!" Asey said. "You mean to say you delivered a telegram addressed to *me* to the observatory tonight?"

"Well, of course, it was last evening," Jabe said. "The place was pitch-black, but the front door wasn't locked, so

I guessed you was busy with Heaslip out back where the telescope is. So I yelled, 'Telegram,' and left it on the desk. Believe me, I know better than to barge in and bother Heaslip if he's busy! I did that once, and he near took my head off. I had to get back to flag that express for the airfield boys, but I figured I'd get a chance to talk over old times with you when you come back for the Boston train. Remember when—"

"Did you take that telegram down when it came?" Asey broke in. "Do you know what it said?"

"Sure. Say, didn't you ever get that message? . . . You didn't? Why, it was from young Bill Porter. Said to call him without fail at ten this morning at the Evanston plant."

"Oh." Asey felt slightly disappointed, although he didn't know why he should have expected the message to be anything spectacular. "Oh, so that's all—huh!" His voice brightened suddenly. "So! I wonder, now!"

"I'm wondering, too," Jabe said. "I don't know what to make of all this. No clues, no nothing! The state cops come, but they can't find any clues either."

"Why—" Asey started mentally to collect Evelyn's scarf, Thackeray's gadget, his own telegram.

"No motives, neither," Jabe went on. "The cops are awful worried about motives."

"Why—" Asey started another mental line-up, and then the question he'd been wanting to ask someone flashed suddenly through his mind: "Tell me, Jabe; you're a good person to ask this of. Why'd you forget a medal?"

"*What?*"

Asey repeated his question.

"Oh, a medal," Jabe said. "Thought you said 'metal,' at first. I know why you ask me that, but there's no wonder Heaslip forgot; he was so busy all day with those telegrams about it. Terrible thing."

"What?" Asey sat up straight. "What was a terrible thing?"

"Why, those two cousins of his that was killed in that plane crash. Pursuit ship landed right on their house and killed 'em both, day before yesterday. Must've been a dozen telegrams about it. Then come this long telegram from some man in Boston all about Heaslip's forgetting to go get a medal. I hope," Jabe said anxiously, "you won't think I snooped, but when things pass through your hands, you can't help knowing about 'em. But I haven't even told my wife how much Heaslip inherited by that accident."

George Drum's angry words to Sarah echoed in Asey's ears: "Oliver had little enough, but I suppose you inherit what he had!"

"Yessir," Jabe said, "Heaslip was going to be a mighty rich feller!"

"What about his sister?" Asey asked.

"Sarah? Me and my wife feel awful sorry for her," Jabe said. "A dog's life, that's what she leads! Why, do you know? My cousin who lives near 'em says she's seen Heaslip strike her. You never seen such a change in anyone as Sarah Heaslip since she come here. I thought to myself, if Heaslip's got that money coming to him, I hope he gives Sarah a break! But look, Asey, how'd you know about that medal?"

"Perry Lowe mentioned it," Asey said, "an' it stuck in my mind. I wondered why even an absent-minded man'd forget a medal, if at the same time he had bronze plaques stuck up sayin' how good he was. I want to see Sarah, but first, where's this road go? Anywhere near the Drums'?"

"Right past it. You know," Jabe said hesitantly, "I been sort of wondering about Evelyn Drum. He's got an awful temper, and he hates Heaslip like poison. Everyone in town knows it. 'Course, I couldn't say anything with George Drum around, but I did tell one of the cops about him. Then when he asked her about Evelyn, why she flew right off the handle! Said if anyone suspected him, they'd better check up on *her*, first! What d'you know about that? And the cop did, too. He'd had many's the run-in with George Drum for speeding, in days gone by. But she was home all the time, working in this place she's got rigged up like a little observatory, with a little telescope and all. But don't you think maybe you ought to look into Evelyn, Asey?"

"It's a peculiar time to go callin', but s'pose," Asey said, "we drop by an' see him right now!"

A protracted knocking at the front door finally brought the same maid who'd let Asey in before. Her hair was in curlpapers and she gripped her striped wrapper about her as if it were a shield.

"Miss Drum's still out hunting you, sir," she said in response to Asey's question. "Mr. Evelyn? I haven't seen him since Mr. Thackeray called. I suppose he's in bed. Shall I," she added without enthusiasm, "call him?"

"Will you, please?" Asey said. "We'll wait in the livin' room."

"You know," Jabe said as they walked through the doorway with the green-tasseled portieres, "I always liked this room. It's homey, kind of— Gee whiz, Asey, look!"

He pointed a shaking finger toward Evelyn Drum, lying on the red carpet in front of the fireplace. The long fringe of red, plush-covered ottoman hung over his outstretched hand. And just out of his reach, Asey noticed as he bent over the still figure, were two keys.

"Gee, Asey, he's dead! Gee, what hit him?"

"Offhand"—Asey looked from Evelyn's head up to the black marble mantelpiece—"I'd guess someone had taken him by the shoulders an' shaken him hard, an' that durin' the process his head banged against that marble. Yup, I'm sure of it. See that stain?"

"Look, keys!" Jabe pointed. "What you suppose he was doing with *them?*"

"Nothin' "—Asey rose to his feet—"at all."

"Then what're they there for?"

"Someone," Asey said, "thought it was a nice gesture to leave 'em there, I think."

"But why? Asey, who killed him? What'd anyone want to kill *him* for?"

"I don't think anyone really meant to kill him," Asey said. "I think someone shook him, an' banged harder than they meant to."

"Gee, as if we didn't have trouble enough, with Heaslip —Asey! Hey, Asey! Where you going?"

"To find out," Asey said, "when Thackeray was here,

an' if it was Evelyn that broke the hall mirror, after
all!"

It was exactly ten o'clock that morning when Asey
piloted Jabe's car to a wheezing stop in front of the observatory, jumped out, and beckoned to Jabe, standing on
the steps.

"You ready? Everything all right?"

"Yup. Thackeray and Miss Drum and Perry're all in
there. I only told 'em what you said. Asey, this don't make
sense to me!"

"It will in time," Asey said, "if you'll do just as I told
you. Hurry, now, an' come back when you're through."

He waited till Jabe's car left the driveway, and then
briskly mounted the front steps. In the bright sunlight,
the observatory looked clean and scientific, like a laboratory.
There was none of the sinister atmosphere that had hung
over it in the blackout the night before.

Thackeray, Perry, and George Drum hurried toward
him as he entered the reception room.

"Jabe says you understand about me and the gadget—"
Perry began.

"Jabe says you're not sore about that crack on the jaw,"
Thackeray chimed in.

"Jabe says you've taken Sarah!" George Drum said.

"Jabe says he told you I went straight to him when I
heard about Evelyn," Thackeray said. "Because I *did* go
to see him. But I never laid hand on him. I just asked if
there were master keys, and he opened the safe, and they
were there. Evelyn had thought about that key angle, too."

"What about Sarah?" George Drum's voice was like a

violin string, and Asey noticed that she almost winced when Evelyn's name was mentioned.

"Sarah claims"—Asey sat down in one of the lucite chairs—"that she left Heaslip's sandwiches, an' then rode to the village. Says although she started to come here again, she didn't because she saw cars out front. Says she was cryin' when she first left because her brother'd been nasty to her. Says she cried later because she found out her brother'd lied to her when he said that group wasn't comin' last night."

Thackeray and Perry looked quickly at George, and then busily studied the zodiac signs in the linoleum.

"Seems to me," Asey went on, "it wasn't awful wise to keep kickin' Sarah out of everything. I don't blame her for gettin' sore. Well, Sarah rode past Evelyn on her way home. She told the truth about that part. Then she heard about Heaslip's bein' killed from party-line gossip. She claims she came back here, an' then after Miss Drum an' I had words with her, she spent the night with a friend. Claims her brother never told her about the money he inherited, which she'll get now. That's her story."

"But of course she's lying!" George Drum said.

"Wa-el," Asey drawled, "seems like she was tellin' the truth, but then things aren't always what they seem. I was thinkin' about that last night while I waited here, an' read these sentences on the wall. Somehow, you take a lot for granted in this universe. You see the sun rise, an' the heavens movin' overhead, an' the stars seemingly fixed in place, an' the moon changin' shape each month. Seems like you're restin' on a flat, solid, stationary earth. Seems so, but none of it's true. I got to thinkin' of the days when I sailed Porter's yacht. Old Cap'n Porter liked to fish at night—" He broke off as the telephone started to ring.

George Drum, sitting at the lucite desk, picked up the receiver. "Mayo? Yes, he's here. . . . Long distance? Who's calling? Mr. Porter? . . . Oh. . . . A state police captain wants you, Mr Mayo."

Asey answered with monosyllables half a dozen questions, and then replaced the telephone.

"Like I was sayin', things aren't what they seem. Now, last night, after I fell off Thackeray's car, I—"

"*Off* my car? I never knew you were on it!" Thackeray said.

"You took me," Asey told him with a grin, "from here to a tarred road, an' if you doubt me, look at the scratches on your rumble-seat back. I landed with an awful thud, an' I seen clusters of imaginary stars all around the new moon. Looked real as could be. When my head cleared, I saw a real star sittin' in the horns of the moon. I hadn't happened to notice anythin' like that since the days when I used to fish with old Cap'n Porter. He was a great hand for spottin' a star in the horns of the moon. You happen to notice that one where you was, Miss Drum?"

"Yes."

"Did you, now!" Asey said. "Did you indeed, Miss Drum!" He watched her hand, which had been toying with the meteorite from Evelyn's candy box, as it suddenly gripped the jagged little rock. "So you really saw that star! Now, I wonder, how'd you guess that might be Bill Porter phonin' me?"

"Why, I guessed!" Her knuckles were white from the force with which she was gripping the meteorite. "I guessed!"

"So? An' now, I s'pose"—Asey's voice had a purring note—"you got some notion of jumpin' up an' bashin' me with that thing in your hand? Well, why not?" He leaned back in his chair and made no effort to seize her upraised arm. "Don't stop her, Thackeray. She's only got to bash, an' rush out to her car, where the cops are waitin'. They know about the telegram, Miss Drum. Perry an' Jack heard your slip of the tongue about it. An' anybody who was really lookin' at the sky last evenin' knows there *wasn't* any star in the horns of the moon, at all. But if you want to bash, go on!"

The meteorite dropped from her hand, and George Drum, the imperious George Drum, burst into tears. . . .

An hour later, Thackeray and Perry cornered Asey in the former's office.

"*Why*," Perry demanded, "did you let us think it was *Sarah?*"

"I only told the truth as if it wasn't," Asey said, "hopin' George'd feel safe, an' fall for that phone call."

"I understand how you tricked her about the star," Thackeray said. "You made her agree with you that there was one in the horns of the moon when there wasn't, and if she'd really been working home last evening, she'd have known it and contradicted you. Instead, she lied, which proved she wasn't where she claimed. But what *about* that phone call?"

"She read a telegram Jabe brought here for me last eve-

ning," Asey said. "She knew I ought to phone Bill Porter
at ten this mornin'. I timed it so's I came here just at ten.
When that call came for me about ten minutes later, she
figured it was Bill phonin' me to find out where I was. She
asked if it was him."

"But who *was* it?" Perry asked.

"Jabe, by arrangement. George had my telegram on her
mind, an' I made her think of the Porter name by inventin'
that fish story about the cap'n. She made the slip, proved
she'd read the telegram, an' so was here. I didn't pick her
up then, because I wanted to prove it the other way
too."

"How'd you guess it was George, though?" Perry asked.
"And how'd you know she meant to hit you, just now?"

"Seemed a habit of hers to grab things an' either throw
'em, like vases of flowers at mirrors in her house—"

"But Evelyn told me *he* smashed that!" Thackeray interrupted.

"He was coverin' up for George," Asey said. "Anyway,
she either threw things, or bashed with 'em, like she bashed
Heaslip. When she lost her temper at Jabe an' rushed me
out of here last night, she begun to give herself away. I
wondered if she was honestly removin' me from harm, or if
she was tryin' to keep me from talkin' with the cops. Now,
I'd been tryin' to find out who'd come back to the observatory. George did. An' after dumpin' me at her house,
she come back again an' cleaned fingerprints off the finder's
lens. She got Jabe out of the way by askin' him to go an'
look for the cops."

"And it was she who set up Jack's gadget?" Perry asked.

Asey nodded. "You can't use that for offhand murderin'. You got to plan. An' the time someone planned it to be used was when that group was expected. I tried to think what might've happened quite recent between her an' Heaslip that'd make her decide to kill him. An' it stuck in my mind that Perry said he'd forgotten to get a medal—"

"I never did!" Perry protested.

"You told that group so. I asked myself, did what happened to make him forget that medal also affect George so she decided to kill him? I asked Jabe, an' it was simple. Heaslip's rich cousins got killed in an accident. As of a couple of days ago, Heaslip's rich, see?"

"No," Perry said promptly.

"After your sayin' he chased you," Asey said, "an' George's sayin' they planned to get married when his draft status got settled—which wouldn't matter much, if you stop to think—I wondered if Heaslip cared so much for her. If maybe he didn't play up to her because he liked a job where he was cock of the roost. I wondered if George hadn't told me the truth when she said he jilted her. An' she did, an' he had. He jilted her yesterday."

"You mean, once Heaslip saw himself independent of his livelihood here," Thackeray said, "he ditched her?"

"Just so. It was pretty bright of her to tell me the truth," Asey said. "I thought she was shieldin' Evelyn, an' she found out how safe she was. Probably she always suspected Heaslip didn't care as much for her as she cared for him, but to be told so, an' realize she'd been played for a sucker, was somethin' else again. She decided if she couldn't have him, no one else would."

"Hell hath no fury, and all that," Perry said. "I finally get it. Revenge."

"Revenge on Thackeray, too," Asey said, "because he liked you an' you liked him, an' you took Heaslip's eye. Usin' a master key, she got that gadget yesterday evenin' an' stuck it in the finder, an' waited for Heaslip to use it."

"Wasn't it dangerous, her staying here?" Thackeray asked.

"Usin' the gadget implicated you, not her. She kept out of sight."

"But why didn't Heaslip get shot?" Perry asked. "Why'd she bash him?"

"When she told the cops about that part," Asey said, "she really crumbled to pieces. Seems the lights was out in the observatory except for a small bulb near the finder. She was waitin' behind the files, Heaslip was fiddlin' around, but he never touched the finder! At last he turned an' laughed at her. Said she might's well give up, because he wasn't bitin'. Seems he saw her put it in!"

"Was she in a spot!" Thackeray said.

"Uh-huh, an' she thought quick. If she pulled the light switch, chances were you'd rush out, thinkin' it was that signal. She wasn't sure Sarah wasn't outside, but Sarah didn't count, an' probably wouldn't dare come inside the observatory, no matter what happened. So she pulled the switch, an' bashed him with the meteorite that was on top of the files. It worked fine. She got him, you dashed out. Only problem was me bustin' in."

"Wow!" Perry said softly.

"But I went after Thackeray. I never guessed she was

there. She must've lived through an awful thirty seconds, crouched behind the files, while I flicked my light around. But after I went, she was safe. She covered the body an' put on that sign, hopin' it'd delay discovery. Then she changed the position of the switches, makin' it seem the lights'd been cut from here. She left the gadget to incriminate Thackeray. When Jabe came with my telegram, she was ready to go, but she couldn't resist findin' out who it was for."

"She has a weakness for opening telegrams and answering phones," Perry said. "Must have been a blow to see your name!"

"She admitted it was. Anyway, then Perry an' that group started to come, so George left."

"Where was her car?" Perry interrupted. "I never saw it or heard it. Was she parked out back?"

"She used a bicycle. After goin' a little way, she got panicky about Evelyn's scarf that she'd worn an' forgot. She came back to watch her chance to get it. It was she I heard in here. Then she hustled home, slipped up to her workroom, an' rang for the maid, who assumed she'd been there all the time. After Perry phoned her, she called Jabe, which made her seem innocent an' honest. Findin' the place deserted when she came back, she had another go at the scarf, an' made a fine recovery, when I confronted her. Made a fine false clue, that scarf. 'Course, she knew Evelyn was innocent, so she could insinuate what she wanted to about him."

"Did she mean to kill Evelyn, really?" Thackeray asked.

"No. After you left him last night, she came in from

huntin' me, an' found Evelyn waitin' for her. He'd learned a lot from you, an' he suspected her anyway. He waved them keys at her, started talkin', an' they both lost their tempers. In the ensuin' scuffle, his head hit the marble mantel. What was left of George's heart broke right then, I think."

"I still," Perry said, "don't see how you found it all out!"

"Wa-el, all of it couldn't have been done by any one of the rest of you, an' all of it could've been done by George, except she said she was home. But that telegram business an' the fake star proved she was lyin'. Like that line on the reception-room wall," Asey said. "You learn about big things from studyin' little ones."

"I wonder," Thackeray said, "what becomes of us now. Anyway, Sarah's got a break—" He paused as the phone rang, and Perry answered it out in the reception room.

"It's Bill Porter!" she called in. "He wants Asey!"

She and Thackeray listened unashamedly to the conversation.

"No, Bill, he can't. He got murdered. . . . No! I won't get you another astronomer! . . . Who? . . . All right, I will. Right away." He hung up and turned around. "Come, Thackeray! Your name was next on Bill's list. Hustle. We're makin' the noon train—"

"You can't!" Perry said. "You couldn't catch that train even if it stopped here! You'd never make the station!"

"Jabe can flag it, an' the station," Asey said with a grin, "is only a stone's throw. Come on, Thackeray!"

A Phoebe Atwood Taylor Rediscovery

Murder at the New York World's Fair

By Phoebe Atwood Taylor

writing as Freeman Dana

Few of Phoebe Atwood Taylor's many fans are aware that, as "Freeman Dana," she was also the author of this delightful period mystery. First published in 1938, *Murder at the New York World's Fair* offered a preview of the gala 1939 event while introducing a heroine, Mrs. Daisy Tower, that could hold her own against even the likes of Asey Mayo and Leonidas Witherall.

"It is a merry melange of mirth, murder and mystification." *- New York Herald Tribune*

This large-format paperback includes an introduction and an afterword presenting a behind-the-scenes look at the book and its author.

Trade Paper 256 pages **$8.95**

Available from bookshops, or by mail from the publisher: The Countryman Press, Box 175, Woodstock, Vermont 05091-0175. Please include $2.50 for shipping your order. Visa or Mastercard orders ($20.00 minimum), call 802-457-1049, 9-5 EST, Monday through Friday.

Prices and availability subject to change.

Available from Foul Play Press

The perennially popular Phoebe Atwood Taylor whose droll "Codfish Sherlock," Asey Mayo, and "Shakespeare look-alike," Leonidas Witherall, have been eliciting guffaws from proper Bostonian Brahmins for over half a century.

"Headed for a lazy week at the shore? Pull up a sand dune and tuck into one of Phoebe Atwood Taylor's charming Cape Cod mysteries. These period how-dunnits recall simpler, more carefree times, and sparkle with the Yankee wit and salty idiom of Asey Mayo, a local handyman who knows something about police work and everything about everybody's business."

– Marilyn Stasio, *Mystery Alley*

Asey Mayo Cape Cod Mysteries

The Annulet of Gilt	*288 pages*	*$5.95*
The Asey Mayo Trio	*256 pages*	*$5.95*
Banbury Bog	*176 pages*	*$5.95*
The Cape Cod Mystery	*192 pages*	*$5.95*
The Criminal C.O.D.	*288 pages*	*$5.95*
The Crimson Patch	*240 pages*	*$5.95*
The Deadly Sunshade	*297 pages*	*$5.95*
Death Lights a Candle	*304 pages*	*$5.95*
Diplomatic corpse	*256 pages*	*$5.95*
Going, Going, Gone	*218 pages*	*$5.95*
The Mystery of the Cape Cod Players	*272 pages*	*$5.95*
The Mystery of the Cape Cod Tavern	*283 pages*	*$5.95*
Out of Order	*280 pages*	*$5.95*
The Perennial Boarder	*288 pages*	*$5.95*
Sandbar Sinister	*296 pages*	*$5.95*
Spring Harrowing	*288 pages*	*$5.95*

"Surely, under whichever pseudonym, Mrs. Taylor is the mystery equivalent of Buster Keaton." – Dilys Winn

Leonidas Witherall Mysteries (by "Alice Tilton")

Beginning with a Bash	*284 pages*	*$5.95*
File For Record	*287 pages*	*$5.95*
Hollow Chest	*284 pages*	*$5.95*
The Left Leg	*275 pages*	*$5.95*

Available from bookshops, or by mail from the publisher: The Countryman Press, Box 175, Woodstock, Vermont 05091-0175. Please include $2.50 for shipping your order. Visa or Mastercard orders ($20.00 minimum), call 802-457-1049, 9-5 EST, Monday – Friday.

Prices and availability subject to change.

Now Back in Print

Margot Arnold

The first four adventures of Margot Arnold's beloved pair of peripatetic sleuths, Penny Spring and Sir Toby Glendower:

The Cape Cod Caper	*192 pages*	*$ 4.95*
Death of A Voodoo Doll	*220 pages*	*$ 4.95*
Death on the Dragon's Tongue	*224 pages*	*$ 4.95*
Exit Actors, Dying	*176 pages*	*$ 4.95*
Lament for A Lady Laird	*221 pages*	*$ 4.95*
The Menehune Murders (cloth)	*240 pages*	*$17.95*
Toby's Folly (cloth)	*256 pages*	*$18.95*
Zadock's Treasure	*192 pages*	*$ 4.95*

"The British archaeologist and American anthropologist are cut in the classic mold of Christie's Poirot...."
> – *Sunday Cape Cod Times*

"A new Margot Arnold mystery is always a pleasure...She should be better known, particularly since her mysteries are often compared to those of the late Ngaio March."
> – *Chicago Sun Times*

Joyce Porter

American readers, having faced several lean years deprived of the company of Chief Inspector Wilfred Dover, will rejoice (so to speak) in the reappearance of "the most idle and avaricious policeman in the United Kingdom (and, possibly, the world)." Here is the series that introduced the bane of Scotland Yard and his hapless assistant, Sgt. MacGregor, to international acclaim.

Dover One	*192 pages*	*$ 4.95*
Dover Two	*222 pages*	*$ 4.95*
Dover Three	*192 pages*	*$ 4.95*
Dover and the Unkindest Cut of All	*188 pages*	*$ 4.95*
Dover Goes to Pott	*192 pages*	*$ 4.95*

"Meet Detective Chief Inspector Wilfred Dover. He's fat, lazy, a scrounger and the worst detective at Scotland Yard. But you will love him." — *Manchester Evening News*

Available from bookshops, or by mail from the publisher: The Countryman Press, Box 175, Woodstock, Vermont 05091-0175. Please include $2.50 for shipping your order. Visa or Mastercard orders ($20.00 minimum), call 802-457-1049, 9-5 EST, Monday – Friday.

Prices and availability subject to change.